D1488559

A Room with
a View

By E. M. Forster

Novels

Where Angels Fear to Tread (1905)
The Longest Journey (1907)
Howards End (1910)
A Passage to India (1924)
Maurice (1971)

Short Stories

The Collected Short Stories (1948)
The Life to Come and other stories (1972)

Other Works

Alexandria (1922)
Pharos and Pharillon (1923)
Aspects of the Novel (1927)
Goldsworthy Lowes Dickinson (1934)
Abinger Harvest (1936)
Two Cheers for Democracy (1951)
The Hill of Devi (1953)
Marianne Thornton (1956)

A Room with a View

E. M. Forster

Hodder & Stoughton
in association with Edward Arnold
LONDON SYDNEY AUCKLAND

British Library Cataloguing in Publication Data

Forster, E. M.
  A Room with a View.
  I. Title
  823 [F]

  ISBN 0-340-51213-X

First published by Edward Arnold in 1908
Edward Arnold Abinger edition, edited Oliver Stallybrass, first published in 1977
Hodder and Stoughton/Edward Arnold edition first published in 1992

Published by Hodder and Stoughton, in association with Edward Arnold.

Hodder and Stoughton Ltd,
Mill Road, Dunton Green, Sevenoaks, Kent TN13 2YA.
Editorial Office: 47 Bedford Square, London WC1B 3DP.

Printed in Great Britain by Biddles Ltd, Guildford and King's Lynn

E. M. Forster dedicated
A Room with a View
To
H. O. M.

Contents

Part 1

1 The Bertolini   2
2 In Santa Croce with no Baedeker   14
3 Music, Violets and the Letter S   29
4 Fourth Chapter   39
5 Possibilities of a Pleasant Outing   46
6 The Reverend Arthur Beebe, the Reverend Cuthbert
   Eager, Mr Emerson, Mr George Emerson, Miss
   Eleanor Lavish, Miss Charlotte Bartlett and Miss
   Lucy Honeychurch Drive out in Carriages to See a
   View; Italians Drive them   58
7 They Return   69

Part 2

8   Medieval   82
9   Lucy as a Work of Art   96
10 Cecil as a Humorist   109
11 In Mrs Vyse's Well-Appointed Flat   118
12 Twelfth Chapter   124
13 How Miss Bartlett's Boiler was so Tiresome   134

14 How Lucy Faced the External Situation Bravely   142
15 The Disaster Within   148
16 Lying to George   161
17 Lying to Cecil   169
18 Lying to Mr Beebe, Mrs Honeychurch, Freddy
      and the Servants   175
19 Lying to Mr Emerson   190
20 The End of the Middle Ages   205

A Room with
a View

Part One

Chapter 1
The Bertolini

"The Signora had no business to do it," said Miss Bartlett, "no business at all. She promised us south rooms with a view, close together, instead of which here are north rooms, here are north rooms, looking into a courtyard, and a long way apart. Oh, Lucy!"

"And a Cockney, besides!" said Lucy, who had been further saddened by the Signora's unexpected accent. "It might be London." She looked at the two rows of English people who were sitting at the table; at the row of white bottles of water and red bottles of wine that ran between the English people; at the portraits of the late Queen and the late Poet Laureate that hung behind the English people, heavily framed; at the notice of the English church (Rev. Cuthbert Eager, M.A. Oxon.), that was the only other decoration of the wall. "Charlotte, don't you feel, too, that we might be in London? I can hardly believe that all kinds of other things are just outside. I suppose it is one's being so tired."

"This meat has surely been used for soup," said Miss Bartlett, laying down her fork.

"I wanted so to see the Arno. The rooms the Signora promised us in her letter would have looked over the Arno. The Signora had no business to do it at all. Oh, it is a shame!"

"Any nook does for me," Miss Bartlett continued; "but it does seem hard that you shouldn't have a view."

Lucy felt that she had been selfish. "Charlotte, you mustn't spoil me: of course, you must look over the Arno, too. I meant that. The first vacant room in the front—"

"You must have it," said Miss Bartlett, part of whose travelling expenses were paid by Lucy's mother—a piece of generosity to which she made many a tactful allusion.

"No, no. You must have it."

"I insist on it. Your mother would never forgive me, Lucy."

"She would never forgive *me*."

The ladies' voices grew animated, and—if the sad truth be owned—a little peevish. They were tired, and under the guise of unselfishness they wrangled. Some of their neighbours interchanged glances, and one of them—one of the ill-bred people whom one does meet abroad—leant forward over the table and actually intruded into their argument. He said:

"I have a view, I have a view."

Miss Bartlett was startled. Generally at a pension people looked them over for a day or two before speaking, and often did not find out that they would "do" till they had gone. She knew that the intruder was ill-bred, even before she glanced at him. He was an old man, of heavy build, with a fair, shaven face and large eyes. There was something childish in those eyes, though it was not the childishness of senility. What exactly it was Miss Bartlett did not stop to consider, for her glance passed on to his clothes. These did not attract her. He was probably trying to become acquainted with them before they got into the swim. So she assumed a dazed expression when he spoke to her, and then said: "A view? Oh, a view! How delightful a view is!"

"This is my son," said the old man; "his name's George. He has a view, too."

"Ah," said Miss Bartlett, repressing Lucy, who was about to speak.

"What I mean," he continued, "is that you can have our rooms, and we'll have yours. We'll change."

The better class of tourist was shocked at this, and sympathized with the newcomers. Miss Bartlett, in reply, opened her mouth as little as possible, and said:

"Thank you very much indeed; that is out of the question."

"Why?" said the old man, with both fists on the table.

"Because it is quite out of the question, thank you."

"You see, we don't like to take—" began Lucy.

3

Her cousin again repressed her.

"But why?" he persisted. "Women like looking at a view; men don't." And he thumped with his fists like a naughty child, and turned to his son, saying, "George, persuade them!"

"It's so obvious they should have the rooms," said the son. "There's nothing else to say."

He did not look at the ladies as he spoke, but his voice was perplexed and sorrowful. Lucy, too, was perplexed; but she saw that they were in for what is known as "quite a scene", and she had an odd feeling that whenever these ill-bred tourists spoke the contest widened and deepened till it dealt, not with rooms and views, but with—well, with something quite different, whose existence she had not realized before. Now the old man attacked Miss Bartlett almost violently: Why should she not change? What possible objection had she? They would clear out in half an hour.

Miss Bartlett, though skilled in the delicacies of conversation, was powerless in the presence of brutality. It was impossible to snub anyone so gross. Her face reddened with displeasure. She looked around as much as to say, "Are you all like this?" And two little old ladies, who were sitting further up the table, with shawls hanging over the backs of the chairs, looked back, clearly indicating, "We are not; we are genteel."

"Eat your dinner, dear," she said to Lucy, and began to toy again with the meat that she had once censured.

Lucy mumbled that those seemed very odd people opposite.

"Eat your dinner, dear. This pension is a failure. To-morrow we will make a change."

Hardly had she announced this fell decision when she reversed it. The curtains at the end of the room parted, and revealed a clergyman, stout but attractive, who hurried forward to take his place at the table, cheerfully apologizing for his lateness. Lucy, who had not yet acquired decency, at once rose to her feet, exclaiming: "Oh, oh! Why, it's Mr

4

Beebe! Oh, how perfectly lovely! Oh, Charlotte, we must stop now, however bad the rooms are. Oh!"

Miss Bartlett said, with more restraint:

"How do you do, Mr Beebe? I expect that you have forgotten us: Miss Bartlett and Miss Honeychurch, who were at Tunbridge Wells when you helped the vicar of St Peter's that very cold Easter."

The clergyman, who had the air of one on a holiday, did not remember the ladies quite as clearly as they remembered him. But he came forward pleasantly enough and accepted the chair into which he was beckoned by Lucy.

" I *am* so glad to see you," said the girl, who was in a state of spiritual starvation, and would have been glad to see the waiter if her cousin had permitted it. "Just fancy how small the world is. Summer Street, too, makes it so specially funny."

"Miss Honeychurch lives in the parish of Summer Street," said Miss Bartlett, filling up the gap, "and she happened to tell me in the course of conversation that you have just accepted the living—"

"Yes, I heard from mother so last week. She didn't know that I knew you at Tunbridge Wells; but I wrote back at once, and I said: 'Mr Beebe is—' "

"Quite right," said the clergyman. "I move into the rectory at Summer Street next June. I am lucky to be appointed to such a charming neighbourhood."

"Oh, how glad I am! The name of our house is Windy Corner."

Mr Beebe bowed.

"There is mother and me generally, and my brother, though it's not often we get him to ch—the church is rather far off, I mean."

"Lucy dearest, let Mr Beebe eat his dinner."

"I am eating it, thank you, and enjoying it."

He preferred to talk to Lucy, whose playing he remembered, rather than to Miss Bartlett, who probably remembered his sermons. He asked the girl whether she knew Florence well, and was informed at some length that she had never been there before. It is delightful to advise a newcomer, and he was first in the field.

"Don't neglect the country round," his advice concluded. "The first fine afternoon drive up to Fiesole, and round by Settignano, or something of that sort."

"No!" cried a voice from the top of the table. "Mr Beebe, you are wrong. The first fine afternoon your ladies must go to Prato."

"That lady looks so clever," whispered Miss Bartlett to her cousin. "We are in luck."

And, indeed, a perfect torrent of information burst on them. People told them what to see, when to see it, how to stop the electric trams, how to get rid of the beggars, how much to give for a vellum blotter, how much the place would grow upon them. The Pension Bertolini had decided, almost enthusiastically, that they would do. Whichever way they looked, kind ladies smiled and shouted at them. And above all rose the voice of the clever lady, crying: "Prato! They must go to Prato. That place is too sweetly squalid for words. I love it; I revel in shaking off the trammels of respectability, as you know."

The young man named George glanced at the clever lady, and then returned moodily to his plate. Obviously he and his father did not do. Lucy, in the midst of her success, found time to wish they did. It gave her no extra pleasure that any-one should be left in the cold; and when she rose to go she turned back and gave the two outsiders a nervous little bow.

The father did not see it; the son acknowledged it, not by another bow, but by raising his eyebrows and smiling; he seemed to be smiling across something.

She hastened after her cousin, who had already dis-appeared through the curtains—curtains which smote one in the face, and seemed heavy with more than cloth. Beyond them stood the unreliable Signora, bowing good-evening to her guests, and supported by 'Enery, her little boy, and Victorier, her daughter. It made a curious little scene, this attempt of the Cockney to convey the grace and geniality of the South. And even more curious was the drawing-room,

6

which attempted to rival the solid comfort of a Bloomsbury boarding-house. Was this really Italy?

Miss Bartlett was already seated on a tightly stuffed armchair, which had the colour and the contours of a tomato. She was talking to Mr Beebe, and as she spoke her long narrow head drove backwards and forwards, slowly, regularly, as though she were demolishing some invisible obstacle. "We are most grateful to you," she was saying. "The first evening means so much. When you arrived we were in for a peculiarly *mauvais quart d'heure*."

He expressed his regret.

"Do you, by any chance, know the name of an old man who sat opposite us at dinner?"

"Emerson."

"Is he a friend of yours?"

"We are friendly—as one is in pensions."

"Then I will say no more."

He pressed her very slightly, and she said more.

"I am, as it were," she concluded, "the chaperon of my young cousin, Lucy, and it would be a serious thing if I put her under an obligation to people of whom we knew nothing. His manner was somewhat unfortunate. I hope I acted for the best."

"You acted very naturally," said he. He seemed thoughtful, and after a few moments added: "All the same, I don't think much harm would have come of accepting."

"No *harm*, of course. But we could not be under an obligation."

"He is rather a peculiar man." Again he hesitated, and then said gently: "I think he would not take advantage of your acceptance, nor expect you to show gratitude. He has the merit—if it is one—of saying exactly what he means. He has rooms he does not value, and he thinks you would value them. He no more thought of putting you under an obligation than he thought of being polite. It is so difficult—at least, I find it difficult—to understand people who speak the truth."

Lucy was pleased, and said: "I was hoping that he was nice; I do so always hope that people will be nice."

7

"I think he is; nice and tiresome. I differ from him on almost every point of any importance, and so, I expect—I may say I hope—you will differ. But his is a type one disagrees with rather than deplores. When he first came here he not unnaturally put people's backs up. He has no tact and no manners—I don't mean by that that he has bad manners—and he will not keep his opinions to himself. We nearly complained about him to our depressing Signora, but I am glad to say we thought better of it."

"Am I to conclude," said Miss Bartlett, "that he is a Socialist?"

Mr Beebe accepted the convenient word, not without a slight twitching of the lips.

"And presumably he has brought up his son to be a Socialist, too?"

"I hardly know George, for he hasn't learned to talk yet. He seems a nice creature, and I think he has brains. Of course, he has all his father's mannerisms, and it is quite possible that he, too, may be a Socialist."

"Oh, you relieve me," said Miss Bartlett. "So you think I ought to have accepted their offer? You feel I have been narrow-minded and suspicious?"

"Not at all," he answered; "I never suggested that."

"But ought I not to apologize, at all events, for my apparent rudeness?"

He replied, with some irritation, that it would be quite unnecessary, and got up from his seat to go to the smoking-room.

"Was I a bore?" said Miss Bartlett, as soon as he had disappeared. "Why didn't you talk, Lucy? He prefers young people, I'm sure. I do hope I haven't monopolized him. I hoped you would have him all the evening, as well as all dinner-time."

"He is nice," exclaimed Lucy. "Just what I remember. He seems to see good in everyone. No one would take him for a clergyman."

"My dear Lucia—"

"Well, you know what I mean. And you know how

clergymen generally laugh; Mr Beebe laughs just like an ordinary man."

"Funny girl! How you do remind me of your mother. I wonder if she will approve of Mr Beebe."

"I'm sure she will; and so will Freddy."

"I think everyone at Windy Corner will approve; it is the fashionable world. I am used to Tunbridge Wells, where we are all hopelessly behind the times."

"Yes," said Lucy despondently.

There was a haze of disapproval in the air, but whether the disapproval was of herself, or of Mr Beebe, or of the fashionable world at Windy Corner, or of the narrow world at Tunbridge Wells, she could not determine. She tried to locate it, but as usual she blundered. Miss Bartlett sedulously denied disapproving of anyone, and added: "I am afraid you are finding me a very depressing companion."

And the girl again thought: "I must have been selfish or unkind; I must be more careful. It is so dreadful for Charlotte, being poor."

Fortunately one of the little old ladies, who for some time had been smiling very benignly, now approached and asked if she might be allowed to sit where Mr Beebe had sat. Permission granted, she began to chatter gently about Italy, the plunge it had been to come there, the gratifying success of the plunge, the improvement in her sister's health, the necessity of closing the bedroom windows at night, and of thoroughly emptying the water-bottles in the morning. She handled her subjects agreeably, and they were, perhaps, more worthy of attention than the high discourse upon Guelfs and Ghibellines which was proceeding tempestuously at the other end of the room. It was a real catastrophe, not a mere episode, that evening of hers at Venice, when she had found in her bedroom something that is one worse than a flea, though one better than something else.

"But here you are as safe as in England; Signora Bertolini is so English."

"Yet our rooms smell," said poor Lucy. "We dread going to bed."

"Ah, then you look into the court." She sighed. "If only Mr Emerson was more tactful! We were so sorry for you at dinner."

"I think he was meaning to be kind."

"Undoubtedly he was," said Miss Bartlett. "Mr Beebe has just been scolding me for my suspicious nature. Of course, I was holding back on my cousin's account."

"Of course," said the little old lady; and they murmured that one could not be too careful with a young girl.

Lucy tried to look demure, but could not help feeling a great fool. No one was careful with her at home; or, at all events, she had not noticed it.

"About old Mr Emerson—I hardly know. No, he is not tactful; yet, have you ever noticed that there are people who do things which are most indelicate, and yet at the same time—beautiful?"

"Beautiful?" said Miss Bartlett, puzzled at the word. "Are not beauty and delicacy the same?"

"So one would have thought," said the other helplessly. "But things are so difficult, I sometimes think."

She proceeded no further into things, for Mr Beebe reappeared, looking extremely pleasant.

"Miss Bartlett," he cried, "it's all right about the rooms. I'm so glad. Mr Emerson was talking about it in the smoking-room, and, knowing what I did, I encouraged him to make the offer again. He has let me come and ask you. He would be so pleased."

"Oh, Charlotte," cried Lucy to her cousin, "we must have the rooms now. The old man is just as nice and kind as he can be."

Miss Bartlett was silent.

"I fear," said Mr Beebe, after a pause, "that I have been officious. I must apologize for my interference."

Gravely displeased, he turned to go. Not till then did Miss Bartlett reply: "My own wishes, dearest Lucy, are unimportant in comparison with yours. It would be hard indeed if I stopped you doing as you liked at Florence, when I am only here through your kindness. If you wish me to turn these gentlemen out of their rooms, I will do it. Would you then, Mr Beebe, kindly tell Mr Emerson that I accept his kind offer, and then conduct him to me, in order that I may thank him personally?"

She raised her voice as she spoke; it was heard all over the drawing-room, and silenced the Guelfs and the Ghibellines. The clergyman, inwardly cursing the female sex, bowed and departed with her message.

"Remember, Lucy, I alone am implicated in this. I do not wish the acceptance to come from you. Grant me that, at all events."

Mr Beebe was back, saying rather nervously:

"Mr Emerson is engaged, but here is his son instead."

The young man gazed down on the three ladies, who felt seated on the floor, so low were their chairs.

"My father," he said, "is in his bath, so you cannot thank him personally. But any message given by you to me will be given by me to him as soon as he comes out."

Miss Bartlett was unequal to the bath. All her barbed civilities came forth wrong end first. Young Mr Emerson scored a notable triumph, to the delight of Mr Beebe and to the secret delight of Lucy.

"Poor young man!" said Miss Bartlett, as soon as he had gone. "How angry he is with his father about the rooms! It is all he can do to keep polite."

"In half an hour or so your rooms will be ready," said Mr Beebe. Then, looking rather thoughtfully at the two cousins, he retired to his own room, to write up his philosophic diary.

"Oh dear!" breathed the little old lady, and shuddered as if all the winds of heaven had entered the apartment. "Gentlemen sometimes do not realize—" Her voice faded away, but Miss Bartlett seemed to understand, and a conversation developed, in which gentlemen who did not thoroughly realize played a principal part. Lucy, not realizing either, was reduced to literature. Taking up Baedeker's *Handbook to Northern Italy*, she committed to memory the most important dates of Florentine history. For she was determined to enjoy herself on the morrow. Thus the half-hour crept profitably away, and at last Miss Bartlett rose with a sigh, and said:

"I think one might venture now. No, Lucy, do not stir. I will superintend the move."

"How you do do everything," said Lucy.

"Naturally, dear. It is my affair."

"But I would like to help you."

"No, dear."

Charlotte's energy! And her unselfishness! She had been thus all her life, but really, on this Italian tour, she was surpassing herself. So Lucy felt, or strove to feel. And yet—there was a rebellious spirit in her which wondered whether the acceptance might not have been less delicate and more beautiful. At all events, she entered her own room without any feeling of joy.

"I want to explain," said Miss Bartlett, "why it is that I have taken the largest room. Naturally, of course, I should have given it to you; but I happen to know that it belongs to the young man, and I was sure your mother would not like it."

Lucy was bewildered.

"If you are to accept a favour, it is more suitable you should be under an obligation to his father than to him. I am a woman of the world, in my small way, and I know where things lead to. However, Mr Beebe is a guarantee of a sort that they will not presume on this."

"Mother wouldn't mind, I'm sure," said Lucy, but again had the sense of larger and unsuspected issues.

Miss Bartlett only sighed, and enveloped her in a protecting embrace as she wished her goodnight. It gave Lucy the sensation of a fog, and when she reached her own room she opened the window and breathed the clean night air, thinking of the kind old man who had enabled her to see the lights dancing in the Arno, and the cypresses of San Miniato, and the foothills of the Apennines, black against the rising moon.

Miss Bartlett, in her room, fastened the window-shutters

and locked the door, and then made a tour of the apartment to see where the cupboards led, and whether there were any oubliettes or secret entrances. It was then that she saw, pinned up over the wash-stand, a sheet of paper on which was scrawled an enormous note of interrogation. Nothing more.

"What does it mean?" she thought, and she examined it carefully by the light of a candle. Meaningless at first, it gradually became menacing, obnoxious, portentous with evil. She was seized with an impulse to destroy it, but fortunately remembered that she had no right to do so, since it must be the property of young Mr Emerson. So she unpinned it carefully, and put it between two pieces of blotting-paper to keep it clean for him. Then she completed her inspection of the room, sighed heavily according to her habit, and went to bed.

Chapter 2
In Santa Croce with no Baedeker

It was pleasant to wake up in Florence, to open the eyes upon a bright bare room, with a floor of red tiles which look clean though they are not; with a painted ceiling whereon pink griffins and blue amorini sport in a forest of yellow violins and bassoons. It was pleasant, too, to fling wide the windows, pinching the fingers in unfamiliar fastenings, to lean out into sunshine with beautiful hills and trees and marble churches opposite, and, close below, the Arno, gurgling against the embankment of the road.

Over the river men were at work with spades and sieves on the sandy foreshore, and on the river was a boat, also diligently employed for some mysterious end. An electric tram came rushing underneath the window. No one was inside it, except one tourist; but its platforms were overflowing with Italians, who preferred to stand. Children tried to hang on behind, and the conductor, with no malice, spat in their faces to make them let go. Then soldiers appeared—good-looking, undersized men—wearing each a knapsack covered with mangy fur, and a greatcoat which had been cut for some larger soldier. Beside them walked officers, looking foolish and fierce, and before them went little boys, turning somersaults in time with the band. The tram-car became entangled in their ranks, and moved on painfully, like a caterpillar in a swarm of ants. One of the little boys fell down, and some white bullocks came out of an archway. Indeed, if it had not been for the good advice of an old man who was selling buttonhooks, the road might never have got clear.

Over such trivialities as these many a valuable hour may slip away, and the traveller who has gone to Italy to study the tactile values of Giotto, or the corruption of the Papacy, may return remembering nothing but the blue sky and the men and women who live under it. So it was as well that Miss Bartlett should tap and come in, and having commented on Lucy's leaving the door unlocked, and on her leaning out of the window before she was fully dressed, should urge her to hasten herself, or the best of the day would be gone. By the time Lucy was ready her cousin had done her breakfast, and was listening to the clever lady among the crumbs.

A conversation then ensued, on not unfamiliar lines. Miss Bartlett was, after all, a wee bit tired, and thought they had better spend the morning settling in; unless Lucy would at all like to go out? Lucy would rather like to go out, as it was her first day in Florence, but, of course, she could go alone. Miss Bartlett could not allow this. Of course she would accompany Lucy everywhere. Oh, certainly not; Lucy would stop with her cousin. Oh no! That would never do! Oh yes!

At this point the clever lady broke in.

"If it is Mrs Grundy who is troubling you, I do assure you that you can neglect the good person. Being English, Miss Honeychurch will be perfectly safe. Italians understand. A dear friend of mine, Contessa Baroncelli, has two daughters, and when she cannot send a maid to school with them she lets them go in sailor-hats instead. Everyone takes them for English, you see, especially if their hair is strained tightly behind."

Miss Bartlett was unconvinced by the safety of Contessa Baroncelli's daughters. She was determined to take Lucy herself, her head not being so very bad. The clever lady then said that she was going to spend a long morning in Santa Croce, and if Lucy would come too she would be delighted.

"I will take you by a dear dirty back way, Miss Honeychurch, and if you bring me luck we shall have an adventure."

Lucy said that this was most kind, and at once opened the Baedeker, to see where Santa Croce was.

"Tut, tut! Miss Lucy! I hope we shall soon emancipate you from Baedeker. He does but touch the surface of things.

As to the true Italy—he does not even dream of it. The true Italy is only to be found by patient observation."

This sounded very interesting, and Lucy hurried over her breakfast, and started with her new friend in high spirits. Italy was coming at last. The Cockney Signora and her works had vanished like a bad dream.

Miss Lavish—for that was the clever lady's name— turned to the right along the sunny Lungarno. How delightfully warm! But a wind down the side-streets that cut like a knife, didn't it? Ponte alle Grazie—particularly interesting, mentioned by Dante. San Miniato—beautiful as well as interesting; the crucifix that kissed a murderer— Miss Honeychurch would remember the story. The men on the river were fishing. (Untrue; but then so is most information.) Then Miss Lavish darted under the archway of the white bullocks, and she stopped, and she cried:

"A smell! A true Florentine smell! Every city, let me teach you, has its own smell."

"Is it a very nice smell?" said Lucy, who had inherited from her mother a distaste to dirt.

"One doesn't come to Italy for niceness," was the retort; "one comes for life. Buon giorno! Buon giorno!" bowing right and left. "Look at that adorable wine-cart! How the driver stares at us, dear, simple soul!"

So Miss Lavish proceeded through the streets of the city of Florence, short, fidgety, and playful as a kitten, though without a kitten's grace. It was a treat for the girl to be with anyone so clever and so cheerful; and a blue military cloak, such as an Italian officer wears, only increased the sense of festivity.

"Buon giorno! Take the word of an old woman, Miss Lucy: you will never repent of a little civility to your inferiors. *That* is the true democracy. Though I am a real Radical as well. There, now you're shocked."

"Indeed, I'm not!" exclaimed Lucy. "We are Radicals, too, out and out. My father always voted for Mr Gladstone, until he was so dreadful about Ireland."

"I see, I see. And now you have gone over to the enemy."

"Oh, please—! If my father was alive, I am sure he would vote Radical again now that Ireland is all right. And as it is, the glass over our front door was broken last election, and Freddy is sure it was the Tories; but mother says nonsense, a tramp."

"Shameful! A manufacturing district, I suppose?"

"No—in the Surrey hills. About five miles from Dorking, looking over the Weald."

Miss Lavish seemed interested, and slackened her trot.

"What a delightful part; I know it so well. It is full of the very nicest people. Do you know Sir Harry Otway—a Radical if ever there was?"

"Very well indeed."

"And old Mrs Butterworth the philanthropist?"

"Why, she rents a field of us! How funny!"

Miss Lavish looked at the narrow ribbon of sky, and murmured:

"Oh, you have property in Surrey?"

"Hardly any," said Lucy, fearful of being thought a snob. "Only thirty acres—just the garden, all downhill, and some fields."

Miss Lavish was not disgusted, and said it was just the size of her aunt's Suffolk estate. Italy receded. They tried to remember the last name of Lady Louisa someone, who had taken a house near Summer Street the other year, but she had not liked it, which was odd of her. And just as Miss Lavish had got the name she broke off and exclaimed:

"Bless us! Bless us and save us! We've lost the way."

Certainly they had seemed a long time in reaching Santa Croce, the tower of which had been plainly visible from the landing window. But Miss Lavish had said so much about knowing her Florence by heart, that Lucy had followed her with no misgivings.

"Lost! Lost! My dear Miss Lucy, during our political diatribes we have taken a wrong turning. How those horrid Conservatives would jeer at us! What are we to do? Two lone females in an unknown town. Now, this is what *I* call an adventure."

Lucy, who wanted to see Santa Croce, suggested, as a possible solution, that they should ask the way there.

"Oh, but that is the word of a craven! And no, you are not, not, *not* to look at your Baedeker. Give it to me; I shan't let you carry it. We will simply drift."

Accordingly they drifted through a series of those gray-brown streets, neither commodious nor picturesque, in which the eastern quarter of the city abounds. Lucy soon lost interest in the discontent of Lady Louisa, and became discontented herself. For one ravishing moment Italy appeared. She stood in the Square of the Annunziata and saw in the living terracotta those divine babies whom no cheap reproduction can ever stale. There they stood, with their shining limbs bursting from the garments of charity, and their strong white arms extended against circlets of heaven. Lucy thought she had never seen anything more beautiful; but Miss Lavish, with a shriek of dismay, dragged her forward, declaring that they were out of their path now by at least a mile.

The hour was approaching at which the continental breakfast begins, or rather ceases, to tell, and the ladies bought some hot chestnut paste out of a little shop, because it looked so typical. It tasted partly of the paper in which it was wrapped, partly of hair-oil, partly of the great unknown. But it gave them strength to drift into another piazza, large and dusty, on the further side of which rose a black-and-white façade of surpassing ugliness. Miss Lavish spoke to it dramatically. It was Santa Croce. The adventure was over.

"Stop a minute; let those two people go on, or I shall have to speak to them. I do detest conventional intercourse. Nasty! They are going into the church, too. Oh, the Britisher abroad!"

"We sat opposite them at dinner last night. They have given us their rooms. They were so very kind."

"Look at their figures!" laughed Miss Lavish. "They walk through my Italy like a pair of cows. It's very naughty of me, but I would like to set an examination paper at Dover, and turn back every tourist who couldn't pass it."

"What would you ask us?"

Miss Lavish laid her hand pleasantly on Lucy's arm, as if to suggest that she, at all events, would get full marks. In this exalted mood they reached the steps of the great church, and were about to enter it when Miss Lavish stopped, squeaked, flung up her arms, and cried:

"There goes my local-colour box! I must have a word with him!"

And in a moment she was away over the Piazza, her military cloak flapping in the wind; nor did she slacken speed till she caught up an old man with white whiskers, and nipped him playfully upon the arm.

Lucy waited for nearly ten minutes. Then she began to get tired. The beggars worried her, the dust blew in her eyes, and she remembered that a young girl ought not to loiter in public places. She descended slowly into the Piazza with the intention of rejoining Miss Lavish, who was really almost too original. But at that moment Miss Lavish and her local-colour box moved also, and disappeared down a side-street, both gesticulating largely.

Tears of indignation came to Lucy's eyes—partly because Miss Lavish had jilted her, partly because she had taken her Baedeker. How could she find her way home? How could she find her way about in Santa Croce? Her first morning was ruined, and she might never be in Florence again. A few minutes ago she had been all high spirits, talking as a woman of culture, and half-persuading herself that she was full of originality. Now she entered the church depressed and humiliated, not even able to remember whether it was built by the Franciscans or the Dominicans.

Of course, it must be a wonderful building. But how like a barn! And how very cold! Of course, it contained frescoes by Giotto, in the presence of whose tactile values she was capable of feeling what was proper. But who was to tell her which they were? She walked about disdainfully, unwilling to be enthusiastic over monuments of uncertain authorship or date. There was no one even to tell her which, of all the sepulchral slabs that paved the nave and transepts, was the one that was really beautiful, the one that had been most praised by Mr Ruskin.

Then the pernicious charm of Italy worked on her, and, instead of acquiring information, she began to be happy. She puzzled out the Italian notices—the notice that forbade people to introduce dogs into the church—the notice that prayed people, in the interests of health and out of respect to the sacred edifice in which they found themselves, not to spit. She watched the tourists: their noses were as red as their Baedekers, so cold was Santa Croce. She beheld the horrible fate that overtook three Papists—two he-babies and a she-baby—who began their career by sousing each other with the Holy Water, and then proceeded to the Machiavelli memorial, dripping, but hallowed. Advancing towards it very slowly and from immense distances, they touched the stone with their fingers, with their handkerchiefs, with their heads, and then retreated. What could this mean? They did it again and again. Then Lucy realized that they had mistaken Machiavelli for some saint, and by continual contact with his shrine were hoping to acquire virtue. Punishment followed quickly. The smallest he-baby stumbled over one of the sepulchral slabs so much admired by Mr Ruskin, and entangled his feet in the features of a recumbent bishop. Protestant as she was, Lucy darted forward. She was too late. He fell heavily upon the prelate's upturned toes.

"Hateful bishop!" exclaimed the voice of old Mr Emerson, who had darted forward also. "Hard in life, hard in death. Go out into the sunshine, little boy, and kiss your hand to the sun, for that is where you ought to be. Intolerable bishop!"

The child screamed frantically at these words, and at these dreadful people who picked him up, dusted him, rubbed his bruises, and told him not to be superstitious.

"Look at him!" said Mr Emerson to Lucy. "Here's a mess: a baby hurt, cold and frightened! But what else can you expect from a church?"

The child's legs had become as melting wax. Each time that old Mr Emerson and Lucy set it erect it collapsed with a roar. Fortunately an Italian lady, who ought to have been saying her prayers, came to the rescue. By some mysterious virtue, which mothers alone possess, she stiffened the little boy's backbone and imparted strength to his knees. He stood. Still gibbering with agitation, he walked away.

"You are a clever woman," said Mr Emerson. "You have done more than all the relics in the world. I am not of your creed, but I do believe in those who make their fellow creatures happy. There is no scheme of the universe—"

He paused for a phrase.

"Niente," said the Italian lady, and returned to her prayers.

"I'm not sure she understands English," suggested Lucy.

In her chastened mood she no longer despised the Emersons. She was determined to be gracious to them, beautiful rather than delicate, and, if possible, to erase Miss Bartlett's civility by some gracious reference to the pleasant rooms.

"That woman understands everything," was Mr Emerson's reply. "But what are you doing here? Are you doing the church? Are you through with the church?"

"No," cried Lucy, remembering her grievance. "I came here with Miss Lavish, who was to explain everything; and just by the door—it is too bad!—she simply ran away, and after waiting quite a time I had to come in by myself."

"Why shouldn't you?" said Mr Emerson.

"Yes, why shouldn't you come by yourself?" said the son, addressing the young lady for the first time.

"But Miss Lavish has even taken away Baedeker."

"Baedeker?" said Mr Emerson. "I'm glad it's *that* that you minded. It's worth minding, the loss of a Baedeker. *That*'s worth minding."

Lucy was puzzled. She was again conscious of some new idea, and was not sure whither it would lead her.

"If you've no Baedeker," said the son, "you'd better join us."

Was this where the idea would lead? She took refuge in her dignity.

"Thank you very much, but I could not think of that. I hope you do not suppose that I came to join on to you. I really came to help with the child, and to thank you for so kindly giving us your rooms last night. I hope that you have not been put to any great inconvenience."

"My dear," said the old man gently, "I think that you are repeating what you have heard older people say. You are pretending to be touchy; but you are not really. Stop being so tiresome, and tell me instead what part of the church you want to see. To take you to it will be a real pleasure."

Now, this was abominably impertinent, and she ought to have been furious. But it is sometimes as difficult to lose one's temper as it is difficult at other times to keep it. Lucy could not get cross. Mr Emerson was an old man, and surely a girl might humour him. On the other hand, his son was a young man, and she felt that a girl ought to be offended with him, or at all events be offended before him. It was at him that she gazed before replying.

"I am not touchy, I hope. It is the Giottos that I want to see, if you will kindly tell me which they are."

The son nodded. With a look of sombre satisfaction, he led the way to the Peruzzi Chapel. There was a hint of the teacher about him. She felt like a child in school who had answered a question rightly.

The chapel was already filled with an earnest congregation, and out of them rose the voice of a lecturer, directing them how to worship Giotto, not by tactile valuations, but by the standards of the spirit.

"Remember," he was saying, "the facts about this church of Santa Croce; how it was built by faith in the full fervour of medievalism, before any taint of the Renaissance had appeared. Observe how Giotto in these frescoes—now, unhappily, ruined by restoration—is untroubled by the snares of anatomy and perspective. Could anything be more majestic, more pathetic, beautiful, true? How little, we feel, avails knowledge and technical cleverness against a man who truly feels!"

"No!" exclaimed Mr Emerson, in much too loud a voice

for church. "Remember nothing of the sort! Built by faith indeed! That simply means the workmen weren't paid properly. And as for the frescoes, I see no truth in them. Look at that fat man in blue! He must weigh as much as I do, and he is shooting into the sky like an air-balloon."

He was referring to the fresco of the Ascension of St John. Inside, the lecturer's voice faltered, as well it might. The audience shifted uneasily, and so did Lucy. She was sure that she ought not to be with these men; but they had cast a spell over her. They were so serious and so strange that she could not remember how to behave.

"Now, did this happen, or didn't it? Yes or no?"

George replied:

"It happened like this, if it happened at all. I would rather go up to heaven by myself than be pushed by cherubs; and if I got there I should like my friends to lean out of it, just as they do here."

"You will never go up," said his father. "You and I, dear boy, will lie at peace in the earth that bore us, and our names will disappear as surely as our work survives."

"Some of the people can only see the empty grave, not the saint, whoever he is, going up. It did happen like that, if it happened at all."

"Pardon me," said a frigid voice. "The chapel is somewhat small for two parties. We will incommode you no longer."

The lecturer was a clergyman, and his audience must be also his flock, for they held prayerbooks as well as guidebooks in their hands. They filed out of the chapel in silence. Amongst them were the two little old ladies of the Pension Bertolini—Miss Teresa and Miss Catharine Alan.

"Stop!" cried Mr Emerson. "There's plenty of room for us all. Stop!"

The procession disappeared without a word. Soon the lecturer could be heard in the next chapel, describing the life of St Francis.

"George, I do believe that clergyman is the Brixton curate."

George went into the next chapel and returned, saying: "Perhaps he is. I don't remember."

"Then I had better speak to him and remind him who I am. It's that Mr Eager. Why did he go? Did we talk too loud? How vexatious! I shall go and say we are sorry. Hadn't I better? Then perhaps he will come back."

"He will not come back," said George.

But Mr Emerson, contrite and unhappy, hurried away to apologize to the Rev. Cuthbert Eager. Lucy, apparently absorbed in a lunette, could hear the lecture again interrupted, the anxious, aggressive voice of the old man, the curt, injured replies of his opponent. The son, who took every little contretemps as if it were a tragedy, was listening also.

"My father has that effect on nearly everyone," he informed her. "He will try to be kind."

"I hope we all try," said she, smiling nervously.

"Because we think it improves our characters. But he is kind to people because he loves them; and they find him out, and are offended, or frightened."

"How silly of them!" said Lucy, though in her heart she sympathized; "I think that a kind action done tactfully—"

"Tact!"

He threw up his head in disdain. Apparently she had given the wrong answer. She watched the singular creature pace up and down the chapel. For a young man his face was rugged, and—until the shadows fell upon it—hard. Enshadowed, it sprang into tenderness. She saw him once again at Rome, on the ceiling of the Sistine Chapel, carrying a burden of acorns. Healthy and muscular, he yet gave her the feeling of grayness, of tragedy that might only find solution in the night. The feeling soon passed; it was unlike her to have entertained anything so subtle. Born of silence and of unknown emotion, it passed when Mr Emerson returned, and she could re-enter the world of rapid talk, which was alone familiar to her.

"Were you snubbed?" asked his son tranquilly.

"But we have spoilt the pleasure of I don't know how many people. They won't come back."

24

". . . full of innate sympathy . . . quickness to perceive good in others . . . vision of the brotherhood of man. . . ." Scraps of the lecture on St Francis came floating round the partition wall.

"Don't let us spoil yours," he continued to Lucy. "Have you looked at those saints?"

"Yes," said Lucy. "They are lovely. Do you know which is the tombstone that is praised in Ruskin?"

He did not know, and suggested that they should try to guess it. George, rather to her relief, refused to move, and she and the old man wandered not unpleasantly about Santa Croce, which, though it is like a barn, has harvested many beautiful things inside its walls. There were also beggars to avoid, and guides to dodge round the pillars, and an old lady with her dog, and here and there was a priest modestly edging to his Mass through the groups of tourists. But Mr Emerson was only half-interested. He watched the lecturer, whose success he believed that he had impaired, and then he anxiously watched his son.

"Why will he look at that fresco?" he said uneasily. "I saw nothing in it."

"I like Giotto," she replied. "It is so wonderful what they say about his tactile values. Though I like things like the Della Robbia babies better."

"So you ought. A baby is worth a dozen saints. And my baby's worth the whole of Paradise, and as far as I can see he lives in Hell."

Lucy again felt that this did not do.

"In Hell," he repeated. "He's unhappy."

"Oh dear!" said Lucy.

"How can he be unhappy when he is strong and alive? What more is one to give him? And think how he has been brought up—free from all the superstition and ignorance that lead men to hate one another in the name of God. With such an education as that, I thought he was bound to grow up happy."

She was no theologian, but she felt that here was a very foolish old man, as well as a very irreligious one. She also

25

felt that her mother might not like her talking to that kind of person, and that Charlotte would object most strongly.

"What are we to do with him?" he asked. "He comes out for his holiday to Italy, and behaves—like that; like the little child who ought to have been playing, and who hurt himself upon the tombstone. Eh? What did you say?"

Lucy had made no suggestion. Suddenly he said:

"Now, don't be stupid over this. I don't require you to fall in love with my boy, but I do think you might try and understand him. You are nearer his age, and if you let yourself go I am sure you are sensible. You might help me. He has known so few women, and you have the time. You stop here several weeks, I suppose? But let yourself go. You are inclined to get muddled, if I may judge from last night. Let yourself go. Pull out from the depths those thoughts that you do not understand, and spread them out in the sunlight and know the meaning of them. By understanding George you may learn to understand yourself. It will be good for both of you."

To this extraordinary speech Lucy found no answer.

"I only know what it is that's wrong with him; not why it is."

"And what is it?" asked Lucy fearfully, expecting some harrowing tale.

"The old trouble: things won't fit."

"What things?"

"The things of the universe. It is quite true. They don't."

"Oh, Mr Emerson, what ever do you mean?"

In his ordinary voice, so that she scarcely realized he was quoting poetry, he said:

> "From far, from eve and morning
>   And yon twelve-winded sky,
> The stuff of life to knit me
>   Blew hither: here am I.

George and I both know this, but why does it distress him? We know that we come from the winds, and that we shall return to them; that all life is perhaps a knot, a tangle, a blemish in the eternal smoothness. But why should this make us unhappy? Let us rather love one another, and work and rejoice. I don't believe in this world-sorrow."

Miss Honeychurch assented.

"Then make my boy think like us. Make him realize that by the side of the everlasting Why there is a Yes—a transitory Yes if you like, but a Yes."

Suddenly she laughed; surely one ought to laugh. A young man melancholy because the universe wouldn't fit, because life was a tangle or a wind, or a Yes, or something!

"I'm very sorry," she cried. "You'll think me unfeeling, but—but—" Then she became matronly. "Oh, but your son wants employment. Has he no particular hobby? Why, I myself have worries, but I can generally forget them at the piano; and collecting stamps did no end of good for my brother. Perhaps Italy bores him; you ought to try the Alps or the Lakes."

The old man's face saddened, and he touched her gently with his hand. This did not alarm her; she thought that her advice had impressed him, and that he was thanking her for it. Indeed, he no longer alarmed her at all; she regarded him as a kind thing, but quite silly. Her feelings were as inflated spiritually as they had been an hour ago aesthetically, before she lost Baedeker. The dear George, now striding towards them over the tombstones, seemed both pitiable and absurd. He approached, his face in the shadow. He said:

"Miss Bartlett."

"Oh, good gracious me!" said Lucy, suddenly collapsing and again seeing the whole of life in a new perspective. "Where? Where?"

"In the nave."

"I see. Those gossiping little old Miss Alans must have—" She checked herself.

"Poor girl!" exploded old Mr Emerson. "Poor girl!"

She could not let this pass, for it was just what she was feeling herself.

"Poor girl? I fail to understand the point of that remark. I think myself a very fortunate girl, I assure you. I'm thoroughly happy, and having a splendid time. Pray don't waste time mourning over *me*. There's enough sorrow in the world, isn't there, without trying to invent it. Goodbye. Thank you both so much for all your kindness. Ah yes! There does come my cousin. A delightful morning! Santa Croce is a wonderful church."

She rejoined her cousin.

Chapter 3
Music, Violets and
the Letter S

It so happened that Lucy, who found daily life rather chaotic, entered a more solid world when she opened the piano. She was then no longer either deferential or patronizing; no longer either a rebel or a slave. The kingdom of music is not the kingdom of this world; it will accept those whom breeding and intellect and culture have alike rejected. The commonplace person begins to play, and shoots into the empyrean without effort, whilst we look up, marvelling how he has escaped us, and thinking how we could worship him and love him, would he but translate his visions into human words, and his experiences into human actions. Perhaps he cannot; certainly he does not, or does so very seldom. Lucy had done so never.

She was no dazzling *exécutante*; her runs were not at all like strings of pearls, and she struck no more right notes than was suitable for one of her age and situation. Nor was she the passionate young lady, who performs so tragically on a summer's evening with the window open. Passion was there, but it could not be easily labelled; it slipped between love and hatred and jealousy, and all the furniture of the pictorial style. And she was tragical only in the sense that she was great, for she loved to play on the side of Victory. Victory of what and over what—that is more than the words of daily life can tell us. But that some sonatas of Beethoven are written tragic no one can gainsay; yet they can triumph or despair as the player decides, and Lucy had decided that they should triumph.

A very wet afternoon at the Bertolini permitted her to do the thing she really liked, and after lunch she opened the little draped piano. A few people lingered round and praised her playing, but, finding that she made no reply, dispersed to their rooms to write up their diaries or to sleep. She took no notice of Mr Emerson looking for his son, nor of Miss Bartlett looking for Miss Lavish, nor of Miss Lavish looking for her cigarette-case. Like every true performer, she was intoxicated by the mere feel of the notes: they were fingers caressing her own; and by touch, not by sound alone, did she come to her desire.

Mr Beebe, sitting unnoticed in the window, pondered over this illogical element in Miss Honeychurch, and recalled the occasion at Tunbridge Wells when he had discovered it. It was at one of those entertainments where the upper classes entertain the lower. The seats were filled with a respectful audience, and the ladies and gentlemen of the parish, under the auspices of their vicar, sang, or recited, or imitated the drawing of a champagne-cork. Among the promised items was "Miss Honeychurch. Piano. Beethoven", and Mr Beebe was wondering whether it would be *Adelaide* or the march of *The Ruins of Athens*, when his composure was disturbed by the opening bars of Opus 111. He was in suspense all through the introduction, for not until the pace quickens does one know what the performer intends. With the roar of the opening theme he knew that things were going extraordinarily; in the chords that herald the conclusion he heard the hammer-strokes of victory. He was glad that she only played the first movement, for he could have paid no attention to the winding intricacies of the measure of nine-sixteen. The audience clapped, no less respectful. It was Mr Beebe who started the stamping; it was all that one could do.

"Who is she?" he asked the vicar afterwards.

"Cousin of one of my parishioners. I do not consider her choice of a piece happy. Beethoven is usually so simple and direct in his appeal that it is sheer perversity to choose a thing like that, which, if anything, disturbs."

"Introduce me."

"She will be delighted. She and Miss Bartlett are full of the praises of your sermon."

"My sermon?" cried Mr Beebe. "Why ever did she listen to it?"

When he was introduced he understood why, for Miss Honeychurch, disjoined from her music-stool, was only a young lady with a quantity of dark hair and a very pretty, pale, undeveloped face. She loved going to concerts, she loved stopping with her cousin, she loved iced coffee and meringues. He did not doubt that she loved his sermon also. But before he left Tunbridge Wells he made a remark to the vicar, which he now made to Lucy herself when she closed the little piano and moved dreamily towards him.

"If Miss Honeychurch ever takes to live as she plays, it will be very exciting—both for us and for her."

Lucy at once re-entered daily life.

"Oh, what a funny thing! Someone said just the same to mother, and she said she trusted I should never live a duet."

"Doesn't Mrs Honeychurch like music?"

"She doesn't mind it. But she doesn't like one to get excited over anything; she thinks I am silly about it. She thinks—I can't make out. Once, you know, I said that I liked my own playing better than anyone's. She has never got over it. Of course, I didn't mean that I played well; I only meant—"

"Of course," said he, wondering why she bothered to explain.

"Music—" said Lucy, as if attempting some generality. She could not complete it, and looked out absently upon Italy in the wet. The whole life of the South was disorganized, and the most graceful nation in Europe had turned into formless lumps of clothes. The street and the river were dirty yellow, the bridge was dirty gray, and the hills were dirty purple. Somewhere in their folds were concealed Miss Lavish and Miss Bartlett, who had chosen this afternoon to visit the Torre del Gallo.

"What about music?" said Mr Beebe.

"Poor Charlotte will be sopped," was Lucy's reply.

The expedition was typical of Miss Bartlett, who would return cold, tired, hungry and angelic, with a ruined skirt, a pulpy Baedeker, and a tickling cough in her throat. On another day, when the whole world was singing and the air ran into the mouth like wine, she would refuse to stir from the drawing-room, saying that she was an old thing, and no fit companion for a hearty girl.

"Miss Lavish has led your cousin astray. She hopes to find the true Italy in the wet, I believe."

"Miss Lavish is so original," murmured Lucy. This was the stock remark, the supreme achievement of the Pension Bertolini in the way of definition. Miss Lavish was so original. Mr Beebe had his doubts, but they would have been put down to clerical narrowness. For that and for other reasons, he held his peace.

"Is it true," continued Lucy in awestruck tones, "that Miss Lavish is writing a book?"

"They do say so."

"What is it about?"

"It will be a novel," replied Mr Beebe, "dealing with modern Italy. Let me refer you for an account to Miss Catharine Alan, who uses words herself more admirably than anyone I know."

"I wish Miss Lavish would tell me herself. We started such friends. But I don't think she ought to have run away with Baedeker that morning in Santa Croce. Charlotte was most annoyed at finding me practically alone, and so I couldn't help being a little annoyed with Miss Lavish."

"The two ladies, at all events, have made it up."

He was interested in the sudden friendship between women so apparently dissimilar as Miss Bartlett and Miss Lavish. They were always in each other's company, with Lucy a slighted third. Miss Lavish he believed he understood, but Miss Bartlett might reveal unknown depths of strangeness, though not, perhaps, of meaning. Was Italy deflecting her from the path of prim chaperon, which he had assigned to her at Tunbridge Wells? All his life he had loved to study maiden ladies; they were his speciality, and his profession had provided him with ample opportunities for the work. Girls like Lucy were charming to look at, but Mr Beebe was, from rather profound reasons, somewhat chilly in his attitude towards the other sex, and preferred to be interested rather than enthralled.

Lucy, for the third time, said that poor Charlotte would be sopped. The Arno was rising in flood, washing away the traces of the little carts upon the foreshore. But in the south-west there had appeared a dull haze of yellow, which might mean better weather if it did not mean worse. She opened the window to inspect, and a cold blast entered the room, drawing a plaintive cry from Miss Catharine Alan, who entered at the same moment by the door.

"Oh, dear Miss Honeychurch, you will catch a chill! And Mr Beebe here besides. Who would suppose this is Italy? There is my sister actually nursing the hot-water can; no comforts or proper provisions."

She sidled towards them and sat down, self-conscious as she always was on entering a room which contained one man, or a man and one woman.

"I could hear your beautiful playing, Miss Honeychurch, though I was in my room with the door shut. Doors shut; indeed, most necessary. No one has the least idea of privacy in this country. And one person catches it from another."

Lucy answered suitably. Mr Beebe was not able to tell the ladies of his adventure at Modena, where the chambermaid burst in upon him in his bath, exclaiming cheerfully, "Fa niente, sono vecchia." He contented himself with saying: "I quite agree with you, Miss Alan. The Italians are a most unpleasant people. They pry everywhere, they see every-thing, and they know what we want before we know it ourselves. We are at their mercy. They read our thoughts, they foretell our desires. From the cab-driver down to—to Giotto, they turn us inside out, and I resent it. Yet in their heart of hearts they are—how superficial! They have no conception of the intellectual life. How right is Signora Bertolini, who exclaimed to me the other day: 'Ho, Mr Beebe, if you knew what I suffer over the children's edju-caishion! *Hi* won't 'ave my little Victorier taught by a hignorant Italian what can't explain nothink!'"

Miss Alan did not follow, but gathered that she was being mocked in an agreeable way. Her sister was a little dis-appointed in Mr Beebe, having expected better things from a clergyman whose head was bald and who wore a pair of russet whiskers. Indeed, who would have supposed that tolerance, sympathy and a sense of humour would inhabit that militant form?

In the midst of her satisfaction she continued to sidle, and at last the cause was disclosed. From the chair beneath her she extracted a gun-metal cigarette-case, on which were powdered in turquoise the initials E. L.

"That belongs to Lavish," said the clergyman. "A good fellow, Lavish, but I wish she'd start a pipe."

"Oh, Mr Beebe," said Miss Alan, divided between awe and mirth. "Indeed, though it is dreadful of her to smoke, it is not quite as dreadful as you suppose. She took to it, practically in despair, after her life's work was carried away in a landslip. Surely that makes it more excusable."

"What was that?" asked Lucy.

Mr Beebe sat back complacently, and Miss Alan began as follows:

"It was a novel—and I am afraid, from what I can gather, not a very nice novel. It is so sad when people who have abilities misuse them, and I must say they nearly always do. Anyhow, she left it almost finished in the Grotto of the Calvary at the Cappuccini Hotel at Amalfi while she went for a little ink. She said: 'Can I have a little ink, please?' But you know what Italians are, and meanwhile the Grotto fell roaring onto the beach, and the saddest thing of all is that she cannot remember what she has written. The poor thing was very ill after it, and so got tempted into cigarettes. It is a great secret, but I am glad to say that she is writing another novel. She told Teresa and Miss Pole the other day that she had got up all the local colour—this novel is to be about modern Italy; the other was historical—but that she could not start till she had an idea. First she tried Perugia for an inspiration, then she came here—this must on no account get round. And so cheerful through it all! I cannot help thinking that there is something to admire in everyone, even if you do not approve of them."

Miss Alan was always thus being charitable against her

34

better judgement. A delicate pathos perfumed her discon-
nected remarks, giving them unexpected beauty, just as in the
decaying autumn woods there sometimes rise odours reminiscent of spring. She felt she had made almost too many
allowances, and apologized hurriedly for her toleration.

"All the same, she is a little too—I hardly like to say
unwomanly, but she behaved most strangely when the
Emersons arrived."

Mr Beebe smiled as Miss Alan plunged into an anecdote
which he knew she would be unable to finish in the presence
of a gentleman.

"I don't know, Miss Honeychurch, if you have noticed
that Miss Pole, the lady who has so much rather yellow
hair, takes lemonade. That old Mr Emerson, who puts
things very strangely—"

Her jaw dropped. She was silent. Mr Beebe, whose social
resources were endless, went out to order some tea, and she
continued to Lucy in a hasty whisper:

"Stomach. He warned Miss Pole of her stomach—acidity,
he called it—and he may have meant to be kind. I must say
I forgot myself and laughed; it was so sudden. As Teresa
truly said, it was no laughing-matter. But the point is that
Miss Lavish was positively *attracted* by his mentioning S.,
and said that she liked plain speaking, and meeting different
grades of thought. She thought they were commercial
travellers—'drummers' was the word she used—and all
through dinner she tried to prove that England, our great
and beloved country, rests on nothing but commerce. Teresa
was very much annoyed and left the table before the cheese,
saying as she did so: 'There, Miss Lavish, is one who can
confute you better than I,' and pointed to that beautiful
picture of Lord Tennyson. Then Miss Lavish said: 'Tut!
The early Victorians.' Just imagine! 'Tut! The early
Victorians.' My sister had gone, and I felt bound to speak.
I said: 'Miss Lavish, *I* am an early Victorian; at least, that
is to say, I will hear no breath of censure against our dear
Queen.' It was horrible speaking. I reminded her how the
Queen had been to Ireland when she did not want to go,

and I must say she was dumbfoundered, and made no reply. But, unluckily, Mr Emerson overheard this part, and called in his deep voice: 'Quite so, quite so! I honour the woman for her Irish visit.' The woman! I tell things so badly; but you see what a tangle we were in by this time, all on account of S. having been mentioned in the first place. But that was not all. After dinner Miss Lavish actually came up and said: 'Miss Alan, I am going into the smoking-room to talk to those two nice men. Come too.' Needless to say, I refused such an unsuitable invitation, and she had the impertinence to tell me that it would broaden my ideas, and said that she had four brothers, all university men, except one who was in the Army, who always made a point of talking to commercial travellers."

"Let me finish the story," said Mr Beebe, who had returned. "Miss Lavish tried Miss Pole, myself, everyone, and finally said: 'I shall go alone.' She went. At the end of five minutes she returned unobtrusively with a green baize board, and began playing patience."

"What ever happened?" cried Lucy.

"No one knows. No one will ever know. Miss Lavish will never dare to tell, and Mr Emerson does not think it worth telling."

"Mr Beebe—old Mr Emerson, is he nice or not nice? I do so want to know."

Mr Beebe laughed and suggested that she should settle the question for herself.

"No; but it is so difficult. Sometimes he is so silly, and then I do not mind him. Miss Alan, what do you think? Is he nice?"

The little old lady shook her head, and sighed disapprovingly. Mr Beebe, whom the conversation amused, stirred her up by saying:

"I consider that you are bound to class him as nice, Miss Alan, after that business of the violets."

"Violets? Oh dear! Who told you about the violets? How do things get round? A pension is a sad place for gossips. No, I cannot forget how they behaved at Mr Eager's lecture at

Santa Croce. Oh, poor Miss Honeychurch! It really was too bad! No, I have quite changed. I do *not* like the Emersons. They are *not* nice."

Mr Beebe smiled nonchalantly. He had made a gentle effort to introduce the Emersons into Bertolini society, and the effort had failed. He was almost the only person who remained friendly to them. Miss Lavish, who represented intellect, was avowedly hostile, and now the Miss Alans, who stood for good breeding, were following her. Miss Bartlett, smarting under an obligation, would scarcely be civil. The case of Lucy was different. She had given him a hazy account of her adventures in Santa Croce, and he gathered that the two men had made a curious and possibly concerted attempt to annex her, to show her the world from their own strange standpoint, to interest her in their private sorrows and joys. This was impertinent; he did not wish their cause to be championed by a young girl; he would rather it should fail. After all, he knew nothing about them, and pension joys, pension sorrows, are flimsy things; whereas Lucy would be his parishioner.

Lucy, with one eye upon the weather, finally said that she thought the Emersons were nice; not that she saw anything of them now. Even their seats at dinner had been moved.

"But aren't they always waylaying you to go out with them, dear?" said the little lady inquisitively.

"Only once. Charlotte didn't like it, and said something —quite politely, of course."

"Most right of her. They don't understand our ways. They must find their level."

Mr Beebe rather felt that they had gone under. They had given up their attempt—if it was one—to conquer society, and now the father was almost as silent as the son. He wondered whether he would not plan a pleasant day for these folk before they left—some expedition, perhaps, with Lucy well chaperoned to be nice to them. It was one of Mr Beebe's chief pleasures to provide people with happy memories.

37

Evening approached while they chatted; the air became brighter; the colours on the trees and hills were purified, and the Arno lost its muddy solidity and began to twinkle. There were a few streaks of bluish-green among the clouds, a few patches of watery light upon the earth, and then the dripping façade of San Miniato shone brilliantly in the declining sun.

"Too late to go out," said Miss Alan in a voice of relief. "All the galleries are shut."

"I think I shall go out," said Lucy. "I want to go round the town in the circular tram—on the platform by the driver."

Her two companions looked grave. Mr Beebe, who felt responsible for her in the absence of Miss Bartlett, ventured to say:

"I wish we could. Unluckily I have letters. If you do want to go out alone, won't you be better on your feet?"

"Italians, dear, you know," said Miss Alan.

"Perhaps I shall meet someone who reads me through and through!"

But they still looked disapproval, and she so far conceded to Mr Beebe as to say that she would only go for a little walk, and keep to the streets frequented by tourists.

"She oughtn't really to go at all," said Mr Beebe, as they watched her from the window, "and she knows it. I put it down to too much Beethoven."

Chapter 4
Fourth Chapter

Mr Beebe was right. Lucy never knew her desires so clearly as after music. She had not really appreciated the clergyman's wit, nor the suggestive twitterings of Miss Alan. Conversation was tedious; she wanted something big, and she believed that it would have come to her on the windswept platform of an electric tram.

This she might not attempt. It was unladylike. Why? Why were most big things unladylike? Charlotte had once explained to her why. It was not that ladies were inferior to men; it was that they were different. Their mission was to inspire others to achievement rather than to achieve themselves. Indirectly, by means of tact and a spotless name, a lady could accomplish much. But if she rushed into the fray herself she would be first censured, then despised, and finally ignored. Poems had been written to illustrate this point.

There is much that is immortal in this medieval lady. The dragons have gone, and so have the knights, but still she lingers in our midst. She reigned in many an early Victorian castle, and was queen of much early Victorian song. It is sweet to protect her in the intervals of business, sweet to pay her honour when she has cooked our dinner well. But alas! the creature grows degenerate. In her heart also there are springing up strange desires. She too is enamoured of heavy winds, and vast panoramas, and green expanses of the sea. She has marked the kingdom of this world, how full it is of wealth, and beauty, and war—a radiant crust, built around the central fires, spinning towards the receding heavens. Men, declaring that she inspires them to it, move joyfully over the surface, having the most delightful meetings with other men, happy, not because they are masculine, but because they are alive.

Before the show breaks up she would like to drop the august title of the Eternal Woman, and go there as her transitory self.

Lucy does not stand for the medieval lady, who was rather an ideal to which she was bidden to lift her eyes when feeling serious. Nor has she any system of revolt. Here and there a restriction annoyed her particularly, and she would transgress it, and perhaps be sorry that she had done so. This afternoon she was peculiarly restive. She would really like to do something of which her well-wishers disapproved. As she might not go on the electric tram, she went to Alinari's shop.

There she bought a photograph of Botticelli's *Birth of Venus*. Venus, being a pity, spoiled the picture, otherwise so charming, and Miss Bartlett had persuaded her to do without it. (A pity in art of course signified the nude.) Giorgione's *Tempesta*, the *Idolino*, some of the Sistine frescoes and the Apoxyomenos were added to it. She felt a little calmer then, and bought Fra Angelico's *Coronation*, Giotto's *Ascension of St John*, some Della Robbia babies, and some Guido Reni Madonnas. For her taste was catholic, and she extended uncritical approval to every well-known name.

But though she spent nearly seven lire the gates of liberty seemed still unopened. She was conscious of her discontent; it was new to her to be conscious of it. "The world," she thought, "is certainly full of beautiful things, if only I could come across them." It was not surprising that Mrs Honeychurch disapproved of music, declaring that it always left her daughter peevish, unpractical and touchy.

"Nothing ever happens to me," she reflected, as she entered the Piazza Signoria and looked nonchalantly at its marvels, now fairly familiar to her. The great square was in shadow; the sunshine had come too late to strike it. Neptune was already unsubstantial in the twilight, half god, half ghost, and his fountain plashed dreamily to the men and satyrs who idled together on its marge. The Loggia showed as the triple entrance of a cave, wherein dwelt many a deity, shadowy but immortal, looking forth upon the arrivals and departures of mankind. It was the hour of unreality—the hour, that is, when unfamiliar things are real. An older person at such an hour and in such a place might think that sufficient was happening to him, and rest content. Lucy desired more.

She fixed her eyes wistfully on the tower of the palace, which rose out of the lower darkness like a pillar of roughened gold. It seemed no longer a tower, no longer supported by earth, but some unattainable treasure throbbing in the tranquil sky. Its brightness mesmerized her, still dancing before her eyes when she bent them to the ground and started towards home.

Then something did happen.

Two Italians by the Loggia had been bickering about a debt. "Cinque lire," they had cried, "cinque lire!" They sparred at each other, and one of them was hit lightly upon the chest. He frowned; he bent towards Lucy with a look of interest, as if he had an important message for her. He opened his lips to deliver it, and a stream of red came out between them and trickled down his unshaven chin.

That was all. A crowd rose out of the dusk. It hid this extraordinary man from her, and bore him away to the fountain. Mr George Emerson happened to be a few paces away, looking at her across the spot where the man had been. How very odd! Across something. Even as she caught sight of him he grew dim; the palace itself grew dim, swayed above her, fell onto her softly, slowly, noiselessly, and the sky fell with it.

She thought: "Oh, what have I done?"

"Oh, what have I done?" she murmured, and opened her eyes.

George Emerson still looked at her, but not across anything. She had complained of dullness, and lo! one man was stabbed, and another held her in his arms.

They were sitting on some steps in the Uffizi Arcade. He must have carried her. He rose when she spoke, and began to dust his knees. She repeated:

"Oh, what have I done?"

"You fainted."

"I—I am very sorry."

"How are you now?"

"Perfectly well—absolutely well." And she began to nod and smile.

"Then let us come home. There's no point in our stopping."

He held out his hand to pull her up. She pretended not to see it. The cries from the fountain—they had never ceased— rang emptily. The whole world seemed pale and void of its original meaning.

"How very kind you have been! I might have hurt myself falling. But now I am well. I can go alone, thank you."

His hand was still extended.

"Oh, my photographs!" she exclaimed suddenly.

"What photographs?"

"I bought some photographs at Alinari's. I must have dropped them out there in the square." She looked at him cautiously. "Would you add to your kindness by fetching them?"

He added to his kindness. As soon as he had turned his back, Lucy arose with the cunning of a maniac and stole down the arcade towards the Arno.

"Miss Honeychurch!"

She stopped with her hand on her heart.

"You sit still; you aren't fit to go home alone."

"Yes, I am, thank you so very much."

"No, you aren't. You'd go openly if you were."

"But I had rather—"

"Then I don't fetch your photographs."

"I had rather be alone."

He said imperiously: "The man is dead—the man is probably dead; sit down till you are rested." She was bewildered, and obeyed him. "And don't move till I come back."

In the distance she saw creatures with black hoods, such as appear in dreams. The palace tower had lost the reflection of the declining day, and joined itself to earth. How should she talk to Mr Emerson when he returned from the shadowy square? Again the thought occurred to her, "Oh, what have I done?"—the thought that she, as well as the dying man, had crossed some spiritual boundary.

He returned, and she talked of the murder. Oddly enough, it was an easy topic. She spoke of the Italian character; she became almost garrulous over the incident that had made her faint five minutes before. Being strong physically, she soon overcame the horror of blood. She rose without his assistance, and though wings seemed to flutter inside her she walked firmly enough towards the Arno. There a cabman signalled to them; they refused him.

"And the murderer tried to kiss him, you say—how very odd Italians are!—and gave himself up to the police! Mr Beebe was saying that Italians know everything, but I think they are rather childish. When my cousin and I were at the Pitti yesterday—what was that?"

He had thrown something into the stream.

"What did you throw in?"

"Things I didn't want," he said crossly.

"Mr Emerson!"

"Well?"

"Where are the photographs?"

He was silent.

"I believe it was my photographs that you threw away."

"I didn't know what to do with them," he cried, and his voice was that of an anxious boy. Her heart warmed towards him for the first time. "They were covered with blood. There! I'm glad I've told you; and all the time we were making conversation I was wondering what to do with them." He pointed downstream. "They've gone." The river swirled under the bridge. "I did mind them so, and one is so foolish, it seemed better that they should go out to the sea—I don't know; I may just mean that they frightened me." Then the boy verged into a man. "For something tremendous has happened; I must face it without getting muddled. It isn't exactly that a man has died."

43

Something warned Lucy that she must stop him.

"It has happened," he repeated, "and I mean to find out what it is."

"Mr Emerson—"

He turned towards her frowning, as if she had disturbed him in some abstract quest.

"I want to ask you something before we go in."

They were close to their pension. She stopped and leant her elbows against the parapet of the embankment. He did likewise. There is at times a magic in identity of position; it is one of the things that have suggested to us eternal comradeship. She moved her elbows before saying:

"I have behaved ridiculously."

He was following his own thoughts.

"I was never so much ashamed of myself in my life; I cannot think what came over me."

"I nearly fainted myself," he said; but she felt that her attitude repelled him.

"Well, I owe you a thousand apologies."

"Oh, all right."

"And—this is the real point—you know how silly people are gossiping—ladies especially, I am afraid—you understand what I mean?"

"I'm afraid I don't."

"I mean, would you not mention it to anyone, my foolish behaviour?"

"Your behaviour? Oh yes, all right—all right."

"Thank you so much. And would you—"

She could not carry her request any further. The river was gushing below them, almost black in the advancing night. He had thrown her photographs into it, and then he had told her the reason. It struck her that it was hopeless to look for chivalry in such a man. He would do her no harm by idle gossip; he was trustworthy, intelligent, and even kind; he might even have a high opinion of her. But he lacked chivalry; his thoughts, like his behaviour, would not be modified by awe. It was useless to say to him, "And would you—" and hope that he would complete the sentence for himself, averting his eyes from her nakedness like the knight in that beautiful picture. She had been in his arms, and he remembered it, just as he remembered the blood on the photographs that she had bought in Alinari's shop. It was not exactly that a man had died; something had happened to the living: they had come to a situation where character tells, and where Childhood enters upon the branching paths of Youth.

"Well, thank you so much," she repeated. "How quickly these accidents do happen, and then one returns to the old life!"

"I don't."

Anxiety moved her to question him.

His answer was puzzling: "I shall probably want to live."

"But why, Mr Emerson? What do you mean?"

"I shall want to live, I say."

Leaning her elbows on the parapet, she contemplated the River Arno, whose roar was suggesting some unexpected melody to her ears.

Chapter 5
Possibilities of a
Pleasant Outing

It was a family saying that "you never knew which way Charlotte Bartlett would turn". She was perfectly pleasant and sensible over Lucy's adventure, found the abridged account of it quite adequate, and paid suitable tribute to the courtesy of Mr George Emerson. She and Miss Lavish had had an adventure also. They had been stopped at the *dazio* coming back, and the young officials there, who seemed impudent and *désœuvré*, had tried to search their reticules for provisions. It might have been most unpleasant. Fortunately, Miss Lavish was a match for anyone.

For good or for evil, Lucy was left to face her problem alone. None of her friends had seen her, either in the Piazza or, later on, by the embankment. Mr Beebe, indeed, noticing her startled eyes at dinner-time, had again passed to himself the remark of "Too much Beethoven". But he only supposed that she was ready for an adventure, not that she had encountered it. This solitude oppressed her; she was accustomed to have her thoughts confirmed by others or, at all events, contradicted; it was too dreadful not to know whether she was thinking right or wrong.

At breakfast next morning she took decisive action. There were two plans between which she had to choose. Mr Beebe was walking up to the Torre del Gallo with the Emersons and some American ladies. Would Miss Bartlett and Miss Honeychurch join the party? Charlotte declined for herself; she had been there in the rain the previous afternoon. But she thought it an admirable idea for Lucy, who hated shopping, changing money, fetching letters, and other irksome duties—all of which Miss Bartlett must accomplish this morning, and could easily accomplish alone.

"No, Charlotte!" cried the girl, with real warmth. "It's

very kind of Mr Beebe, but I am certainly coming with you. I had much rather."

"Very well, dear," said Miss Bartlett, with a faint flush of pleasure that called forth a deep flush of shame on the cheeks of Lucy. How abominably she behaved to Charlotte, now as always! But now she should alter. All the morning she would be really nice to her.

She slipped her arm into her cousin's, and they started off along the Lungarno. The river was a lion that morning in strength, voice and colour. Miss Bartlett insisted on leaning over the parapet to look at it. She then made her usual remark, which was:

"How I do wish Freddy and your mother could see this, too!"

Lucy fidgeted; it was tiresome of Charlotte to have stopped exactly where she did.

"Look, Lucia! Oh, you are watching for the Torre del Gallo party. I feared you would repent you of your choice."

Serious as the choice had been, Lucy did not repent. Yesterday had been a muddle—queer and odd, the kind of thing one could not write down easily on paper—but she had a feeling that Charlotte and her shopping were preferable to George Emerson and the summit of the Torre del Gallo. Since she could not unravel the tangle, she must take care not to re-enter it. She could protest sincerely against Miss Bartlett's insinuations.

But, though she had avoided the chief actor, the scenery unfortunately remained. Charlotte, with the complacency of fate, led her from the river to the Piazza Signoria. She could not have believed that stones, a loggia, a fountain, a palace tower, would have such significance. For a moment she understood the nature of ghosts.

The exact site of the murder was occupied, not by a ghost, but by Miss Lavish, who had the morning newspaper in her hand. She hailed them briskly. The dreadful catastrophe of the previous day had given her an idea which she thought would work up into a book.

"Oh, let me congratulate you!" said Miss Bartlett. "After your despair of yesterday! What a fortunate thing!"

"Aha! Miss Honeychurch, come you here! I am in luck. Now, you are to tell me absolutely everything that you saw from the beginning."

Lucy poked at the ground with her parasol.

"But perhaps you would rather not?"

"I'm sorry—if you could manage without it, I think I would rather not."

The elder ladies exchanged glances, not of disapproval; it is suitable that a girl should feel deeply.

"It is I who am sorry," said Miss Lavish. "We literary hacks are shameless creatures. I believe there's no secret of the human heart into which we wouldn't pry."

She marched cheerfully to the fountain and back, and did a few calculations in realism. Then she said that she had been in the Piazza since eight o'clock collecting material. A good deal of it was unsuitable, but of course one always had to adapt. The two men had quarrelled over a five-franc note. For the five-franc note she should substitute a young lady, which would raise the tone of the tragedy, and at the same time furnish an excellent plot.

"What is the heroine's name?" asked Miss Bartlett.

"Leonora," said Miss Lavish; her own name was Eleanor.

"I do hope she's nice."

That desideratum would not be omitted.

"And what is the plot?"

Love, murder, abduction, revenge, was the plot. Out it all came while the fountain plashed to the satyrs in the morning sun.

"I hope you will excuse me for boring on like this," Miss Lavish concluded. "It is so tempting to talk to really sympathetic people. Of course, this is the barest outline. There will be a deal of local colouring, descriptions of Florence and the neighbourhood, and I shall also introduce some humorous characters. And let me give you all fair warning: I intend to be unmerciful to the British tourist."

"Oh, you wicked woman!" cried Miss Bartlett. "I am sure you are thinking of the Emersons."

Miss Lavish gave a Machiavellian smile.

"I confess that in Italy my sympathies are not with my own countrymen. It is the neglected Italians who attract me, and whose lives I am going to paint so far as I can. For I repeat and I insist, and I have always held most strongly, that a tragedy such as yesterday's is not the less tragic because it happened in humble life."

There was a fitting silence when Miss Lavish had concluded. Then the cousins wished success to her labours, and walked slowly away across the square.

"She is my idea of a really clever woman," said Miss Bartlett. "That last remark struck me as so particularly true. It should be a most pathetic novel."

Lucy assented. At present her great aim was not to get put into it. Her perceptions this morning were curiously keen, and she believed that Miss Lavish had her on trial for an *ingénue*.

"She is emancipated, but only in the very best sense of the word," continued Miss Bartlett slowly. "None but the superficial would be shocked at her. We had a long talk yesterday. She believes in justice and truth and human interest. She told me also that she has a high opinion of the destiny of woman—Mr Eager! Why, how nice! What a pleasant surprise!"

"Ah, not for me," said the chaplain blandly, "for I have been watching you and Miss Honeychurch for quite a little time."

"We were chatting to Miss Lavish."

His brow contracted.

"So I saw. Were you indeed? Andate via! Sono occupato!" The last remark was made to a vendor of panoramic photographs who was approaching with a courteous smile. "I am about to venture a suggestion. Would you and Miss Honeychurch be disposed to join me in a drive some day this week —a drive in the hills? We might go up by Fiesole and back by Settignano. There is a point on that road where we could get down and have an hour's ramble on the hillside. The view thence of Florence is most beautiful—far better than the hackneyed view from Fiesole. It is the view that Alessio Baldovinetti is fond of introducing into his pictures. That

49

man had a decided feeling for landscape. Decidedly. But who looks at it today? Ah, the world is too much with us."

Miss Bartlett had not heard of Alessio Baldovinetti, but she knew that Mr Eager was no commonplace chaplain. He was a member of the residential colony who had made Florence their home. He knew the people who never walked about with Baedekers, who had learned to take a siesta after lunch, who took drives the pension tourists had never heard of, and saw by private influence galleries which were closed to them. Living in delicate seclusion, some in furnished flats, others in Renaissance villas on Fiesole's slope, they read, wrote, studied and exchanged ideas, thus attaining to that intimate knowledge, or rather perception, of Florence which is denied to all who carry in their pockets the coupons of Cook.

Therefore an invitation from the chaplain was something to be proud of. Between the two sections of his flock he was often the only link, and it was his avowed custom to select those of his migratory sheep who seemed worthy, and give them a few hours in the pastures of the permanent. Tea at a Renaissance villa? Nothing had been said about it yet. But if it did come to that—how Lucy would enjoy it!

A few days ago and Lucy would have felt the same. But the joys of life were grouping themselves anew. A drive in the hills with Mr Eager and Miss Bartlett—even if culminating in a residential tea-party—was no longer the greatest of them. She echoed the raptures of Charlotte somewhat faintly. Only when she heard that Mr Beebe was also coming did her thanks become more sincere.

"So we shall be a *partie carrée*," said the chaplain. "In these days of toil and tumult one has great need of the country and its message of purity. Andate via! Andate presto, presto! Ah, the town! Beautiful as it is, it is the town."

They assented.

"This very square—so I am told—witnessed yesterday the most sordid of tragedies. To one who loves the Florence of Dante and Savonarola there is something portentous in such desecration—portentous and humiliating."

"Humiliating indeed," said Miss Bartlett. "Miss Honeychurch happened to be passing through as it happened. She can hardly bear to speak of it." She glanced at Lucy proudly.

"And how came we to have you here?" asked the chaplain paternally.

Miss Bartlett's recent liberalism oozed away at the question.

"Do not blame her, please, Mr Eager. The fault is mine: I left her unchaperoned."

"So you were here alone, Miss Honeychurch?" His voice suggested sympathetic reproof, but at the same time indicated that a few harrowing details would not be unacceptable. His dark, handsome face drooped mournfully towards her to catch her reply.

"Practically."

"One of our pension acquaintances kindly brought her home," said Miss Bartlett, adroitly concealing the sex of the preserver.

"For her also it must have been a terrible experience. I trust that neither of you were at all—that it was not in your immediate proximity."

Of the many things Lucy was noticing today, not the least remarkable was this: the ghoulish fashion in which respectable people will nibble after blood. George Emerson had kept the subject strangely pure.

"He died by the fountain, I believe," was her reply.

"And you and your friend—"

"Were over at the Loggia."

"That must have saved you much. You have not, of course, seen the disgraceful illustrations which the gutter press— This man is a public nuisance; he knows that I am a resident perfectly well, and yet he goes on worrying me to buy his vulgar views."

Surely the vendor of photographs was in league with Lucy—in the eternal league of Italy with youth. He had suddenly extended his book before Miss Bartlett and Mr Eager, binding their hands together by a long glossy ribbon of churches, pictures and views.

"This is too much!" cried the chaplain, striking petulantly at one of Fra Angelico's angels. She tore. A shrill cry arose from the vendor. The book, it seemed, was more valuable than one would have supposed.

"Willingly would I purchase—" began Miss Bartlett.

"Ignore him," said Mr Eager sharply, and they all walked rapidly away from the square.

But an Italian can never be ignored, least of all when he has a grievance. His mysterious persecution of Mr Eager became relentless; the air rang with his threats and lamentations. He appealed to Lucy; would not she intercede? He was poor—he sheltered a family—the tax on bread. He waited, he gibbered, he was recompensed, he was dissatisfied, he did not leave them until he had swept their minds clean of all thoughts, whether pleasant or unpleasant.

Shopping was the topic that now ensued. Under the chaplain's guidance they selected many hideous presents and mementoes—florid little picture-frames that seemed fashioned in gilded pastry; other little frames, more severe, that stood on little easels, and were carven out of oak; a blotting book of vellum; a Dante of the same material; cheap mosaic brooches, which the maids, next Christmas, would never tell from real; pins, pots, heraldic saucers, brown art-photographs; Eros and Psyche in alabaster; St Peter to match—all of which would have cost less in London.

This successful morning left no pleasant impressions on Lucy. She had been a little frightened, both by Miss Lavish and by Mr Eager, she knew not why. And as they frightened her she had, strangely enough, ceased to respect them. She doubted that Miss Lavish was a great artist. She doubted that Mr Eager was as full of spirituality and culture as she had been led to suppose. They were tried by some new test, and they were found wanting. As for Charlotte—as for Charlotte, she was exactly the same. It might be possible to be nice to her; it was impossible to love her.

"The son of a labourer; I happen to know it for a fact. A mechanic of some sort himself when he was young; then he took to writing for the Socialistic press. I came across him at Brixton."

They were talking about the Emersons.

"How wonderfully people rise in these days!" sighed Miss Bartlett, fingering a model of the leaning Tower of Pisa.

"Generally," replied Mr Eager, "one has only sympathy with their success. The desire for education and for social advance—in these things there is something not wholly vile. There are some working men whom one would be very willing to see out here in Florence—little as they would make of it."

"Is he a journalist now?" Miss Bartlett asked.

"He is not; he made an advantageous marriage."

He uttered this remark with a voice full of meaning, and ended it with a sigh.

"Oh, so he has a wife."

"Dead, Miss Bartlett, dead. I wonder—yes, I wonder how he has the effrontery to look me in the face, to dare to claim acquaintance with me. He was in my London parish long ago. The other day in Santa Croce, when he was with Miss Honeychurch, I snubbed him. Let him beware that he does not get more than a snub."

"What?" cried Lucy, flushing.

"Exposure!" hissed Mr Eager.

He tried to change the subject; but in scoring a dramatic point he had interested his audience more than he had intended. Miss Bartlett was full of very natural curiosity. Lucy, though she wished never to see the Emersons again, was not disposed to condemn them on a single word.

"Do you mean," she asked, "that he is an irreligious man? We know that already."

"Lucy dear—" said Miss Bartlett, gently reproving her cousin's penetration.

"I should be astonished if you knew all. The boy—an innocent child at the time—I will exclude. God knows what his education and his inherited qualities may have made him."

"Perhaps," said Miss Bartlett, "it is something that we had better not hear."

"To speak plainly," said Mr Eager, "it is. I will say no more."

For the first time Lucy's rebellious thoughts swept out in words—for the first time in her life.

"You have said very little."

"It was my intention to say very little," was his frigid reply.

He gazed indignantly at the girl, who met him with equal indignation. She turned towards him from the shop counter; her breast heaved quickly. He observed her brow, and the sudden strength of her lips. It was intolerable that she should disbelieve him.

"Murder, if you want to know," he cried angrily. "That man murdered his wife!"

"How?" she retorted.

"To all intents and purposes he murdered her. That day in Santa Croce—did they say anything against me?"

"Not a word, Mr Eager—not a single word."

"Oh, I thought they had been libelling me to you. But I suppose it is only their personal charms that makes you defend them."

"I'm not defending them," said Lucy, losing her courage, and relapsing into the old chaotic methods. "They're nothing to me."

"How could you think she was defending them?" said Miss Bartlett, much discomfited by the unpleasant scene. The shop-man was possibly listening.

"She will find it difficult. For that man has murdered his wife in the sight of God."

The addition of God was striking. But the chaplain was really trying to qualify a rash remark. A silence followed which might have been impressive, but was merely awkward. Then Miss Bartlett hastily purchased the Leaning Tower, and led the way into the street.

"I must be going," said he, shutting his eyes and taking out his watch.

Miss Bartlett thanked him for his kindness, and spoke with enthusiasm of the approaching drive.

"Drive? Oh, is our drive to come off?"

Lucy was recalled to her manners, and after a little exertion the complacency of Mr Eager was restored.

"Bother the drive!" exclaimed the girl, as soon as he had departed. "It is just the drive we had arranged with Mr Beebe without any fuss at all. Why should he invite us in that absurd manner? We might as well invite him. We are each paying for ourselves."

Miss Bartlett, who had intended to lament over the Emersons, was launched by this remark into unexpected thoughts.

"If that is so, dear—if the drive we and Mr Beebe are going with Mr Eager is really the same as the one we were going with Mr Beebe, then I foresee a sad kettle of fish."

"How?"

"Because Mr Beebe has asked Eleanor Lavish to come, too."

"That will mean another carriage."

"Far worse. Mr Eager does not like Eleanor. She knows it herself. The truth must be told: she is too unconventional for him."

They were now in the newspaper-room at the English bank. Lucy stood by the central table, heedless of *Punch* and the *Graphic*, trying to answer, or at all events to formulate, the questions rioting in her brain. The well-known world had broken up, and there emerged Florence, a magic city where people thought and did the most extraordinary things. Murder, accusations of murder, a lady clinging to one man and being rude to another—were these the daily incidents of her streets? Was there more in her frank beauty than met the eye—the power, perhaps, to evoke passions, good and bad, and to bring them speedily to a fulfilment?

Happy Charlotte, who, though greatly troubled over things that did not matter, seemed oblivious to things that did; who could conjecture with admirable delicacy "where things might lead to", but apparently lost sight of the goal as she approached it! Now she was crouching in the corner trying to extract a circular note from a kind of linen nosebag which hung in chaste concealment round her neck. She had been told that this was the only safe way to carry money in Italy; it must only be broached within the walls of the

English bank. As she groped she murmured: "Whether it is Mr Beebe who forgot to tell Mr Eager, or Mr Eager who forgot when he told us, or whether they have decided to leave Eleanor out altogether—which they could scarcely do—but in any case we must be prepared. It is you they really want; I am only asked for appearances. You shall go with the two gentlemen, and I and Eleanor will follow behind. A one-horse carriage would do for us. Yet how difficult it is!"

"It is indeed," replied the girl, with a gravity that sounded sympathetic.

"What do you think about it?" asked Miss Bartlett, flushed from the struggle, and buttoning up her dress.

"I don't know what I think, nor what I want."

"Oh dear, Lucy! I do hope Florence isn't boring you. Speak the word, and, as you know, I would take you to the ends of the earth tomorrow."

"Thank you, Charlotte," said Lucy, and pondered over the offer.

There were letters for her at the bureau—one from her brother, full of athletics and biology; one from her mother, delightful as only her mother's letters could be. She read in it of the crocuses which had been bought for yellow and were coming up puce, of the new parlourmaid, who had watered the ferns with essence of lemonade, of the semi-detached cottages which were ruining Summer Street, and breaking the heart of Sir Harry Otway. She recalled the free, pleasant life of her home, where she was allowed to do everything, and where nothing ever happened to her. The road up through the pine-woods, the clean drawing-room, the view over the Sussex Weald—all hung before her bright and distinct, but pathetic as the pictures in a gallery to which, after much experience, a traveller returns.

"And the news?" asked Miss Bartlett.

"Mrs Vyse and her son have gone to Rome," said Lucy, giving the news that interested her least. "Do you know the Vyses?"

"Oh, not that way back. We can never have too much of the dear Piazza Signoria."

"They're nice people, the Vyses. So clever—my idea of what's really clever. Don't you long to be in Rome?"

"I die for it!"

The Piazza Signoria is too stony to be brilliant. It has no grass, no flowers, no frescoes, no glittering walls of marble or comforting patches of ruddy brick. By an odd chance—unless we believe in a presiding genius of place—the statues that relieve its severity suggest, not the innocence of childhood nor the glorious bewilderment of youth, but the conscious achievements of maturity. Perseus and Judith, Hercules and Thusnelda, they have done or suffered something, and, though they are immortal, immortality has come to them after experience, not before. Here, not only in the solitude of Nature, might a hero meet a goddess, or a heroine a god.

"Charlotte!" cried the girl suddenly. "Here's an idea. What if we popped off to Rome tomorrow—straight—to the Vyses' hotel? For I do know what I want. I'm sick of Florence. Now, you said you'd go to the ends of the earth! Do! Do!"

Miss Bartlett, with equal vivacity, replied:

"Oh, you droll person! Pray, what would become of your drive in the hills?"

They passed together through the gaunt beauty of the square, laughing over the unpractical suggestion.

Chapter 6

The Reverend Arthur Beebe, the Reverend Cuthbert Eager, Mr Emerson, Mr George Emerson, Miss Eleanor Lavish, Miss Charlotte Bartlett, and Miss Lucy Honeychurch Drive out in Carriages to See a View; Italians Drive them

It was Phaethon who drove them to Fiesole that memorable day, a youth all irresponsibility and fire, recklessly urging his master's horses up the stony hill. Mr Beebe recognized him at once. Neither the Ages of Faith nor the Age of Doubt had touched him; he was Phaethon in Tuscany driving a cab. And it was Persephone whom he asked leave to pick up on the way, saying that she was his sister—Persephone, tall and slender and pale, returning with the spring to her mother's cottage, and still shading her eyes from the un-accustomed light. To her Mr Eager objected, saying that here was the thin edge of the wedge, and one must guard against imposition. But the ladies interceded, and, when it had been made clear that it was a very great favour, the goddess was allowed to mount beside the god.

Phaethon at once slipped the left rein over her head, thus enabling himself to drive with his arm round her waist. She did not mind. Mr Eager, who sat with his back to the horses, saw nothing of the indecorous proceeding, and continued his conversation with Lucy. The other two occupants of the carriage were old Mr Emerson and Miss Lavish. For a dreadful thing had happened: Mr Beebe, without consulting Mr Eager, had doubled the size of the party. And, though Miss Bartlett and Miss Lavish had planned all the morning how people were to sit, at the critical moment when the carriages came round they lost their heads, and Miss Lavish got in with Lucy, while Miss Bartlett, with George Emerson and Mr Beebe, followed on behind.

It was hard on the poor chaplain to have his *partie carrée* thus transformed. Tea at a Renaissance villa, if he had ever meditated it, was now impossible. Lucy and Miss Bartlett had a certain style about them, and Mr Beebe, though unreliable, was a man of parts. But a shoddy lady writer and a journalist who had murdered his wife in the sight of God—they should enter no villa at his introduction.

Lucy, elegantly dressed in white, sat erect and nervous amid these explosive ingredients, attentive to Mr Eager, repressive towards Miss Lavish, watchful of old Mr Emerson —hitherto fortunately asleep, thanks to a heavy lunch and the drowsy atmosphere of spring. She looked on the expedition as the work of Fate. But for it she would have avoided George Emerson successfully. In an open manner he had shown that he wished to continue their intimacy. She had refused, not because she disliked him, but because she did not know what had happened, and suspected that he did know. And this frightened her.

For the real event—whatever it was—had taken place, not in the Loggia, but by the river. To behave wildly at the sight of death is pardonable. But to discuss it afterwards, to pass from discussion into silence, and through silence into sympathy, that is an error, not of a startled emotion, but of the whole fabric. There was really something blameworthy (she thought) in their joint contemplation of the shadowy stream, in the common impulse which had turned them to the house without the passing of a look or word. This sense of wickedness had been slight at first. She had nearly joined the party to the Torre del Gallo. But each time that she avoided George it became more imperative that she should avoid him again. And now celestial irony, working through her cousin and two clergymen, did not suffer her to leave Florence till she had made this expedition with him through the hills.

Meanwhile Mr Eager held her in civil converse; their little tiff was over.

"So, Miss Honeychurch, you are travelling? As a student of art?"

"Oh, dear me, no—oh no!"

"Perhaps as a student of human nature," interposed Miss Lavish, "like myself?"

"Oh no. I am here as a tourist."

"Oh, indeed," said Mr Eager. "Are you indeed? If you will not think me rude, we residents sometimes pity you poor tourists not a little—handed about like a parcel of goods from Venice to Florence, from Florence to Rome, living herded together in pensions or hotels, quite unconscious of anything that is outside Baedeker, their one anxiety to get 'done' or 'through' and go on somewhere else. The result is, they mix up towns, rivers, palaces in one inextricable whirl. You know the American girl in *Punch* who says: 'Say, poppa, what did we see at Rome?' And the father replies: 'Why, guess Rome was the place where we saw the yaller dog.' There's travelling for you. Ha! ha! ha!"

"I quite agree," said Miss Lavish, who had several times tried to interrupt his mordant wit. "The narrowness and superficiality of the Anglo-Saxon tourist is nothing less than a menace."

"Quite so. Now, the English colony at Florence, Miss Honeychurch—and it is of considerable size, though, of course, not all equally—a few are here for trade, for example. But the greater part are students. Lady Helen Laverstock is at present busy over Fra Angelico. I mention her name because we are passing her villa on the left. No, you can only see it if you stand—no, do not stand; you will fall. She is very proud of that thick hedge. Inside, perfect seclusion. One might have gone back six hundred years. Some critics believe that her garden was the scene of *The Decameron*, which lends it an additional interest, does it not?"

"It does indeed!" cried Miss Lavish. "Tell me, where do they place the scene of that wonderful seventh day?"

But Mr Eager proceeded to tell Miss Honeychurch that on the right lived Mr Someone Something, an American of the best type—so rare!—and that the Somebody Elses were further down the hill. "Doubtless you know her monographs in the series of 'Mediaeval Byways'? He is working at

'Gemistus Pletho'. Sometimes as I take tea in their beautiful grounds I hear, over the wall, the electric tram squealing up the new road with its load of hot, dusty, unintelligent tourists who are going to 'do' Fiesole in an hour in order that they may say they have been there, and I think—I think—I think how little they think what lies so near them."

During this speech the two figures on the box were sporting with each other disgracefully. Lucy had a spasm of envy. Granted that they wished to misbehave, it was pleasant for them to be able to do so. They were probably the only people enjoying the expedition. The carriage swept with agonizing jolts up through the Piazza of Fiesole and into the Settignano road.

"Piano! Piano!" said Mr Eager, elegantly waving his hand over his head.

"Va bene, signore, va bene, va bene," crooned the driver, and whipped his horses up again.

Now Mr Eager and Miss Lavish began to talk against each other on the subject of Alessio Baldovinetti. Was he a cause of the Renaissance, or was he one of its manifestations? The other carriage was left behind. As the pace increased to a gallop the large, slumbering form of Mr Emerson was thrown against the chaplain with the regularity of a machine.

"Piano! Piano!" said he, with a martyred look at Lucy.

An extra lurch made him turn angrily in his seat. Phaethon, who for some time had been endeavouring to kiss Persephone, had just succeeded.

A little scene ensued, which, as Miss Bartlett said afterwards, was most unpleasant. The horses were stopped, the lovers were ordered to disentangle themselves, the boy was to lose his *pourboire*, the girl was immediately to get down.

"She is my sister," said he, turning round on them with piteous eyes.

Mr Eager took the trouble to tell him that he was a liar. Phaethon hung down his head, not at the matter of the accusation, but at its manner. At this point Mr Emerson, whom the shock of stopping had awoken, declared that the lovers must on no account be separated, and patted them on the back to signify his approval. And Miss Lavish, though unwilling to ally with him, felt bound to support the cause of bohemianism.

"Most certainly I would let them be," she cried. "But I dare say I shall receive scant support. I have always flown in the face of the conventions all my life. This is what *I* call an adventure."

"We must not submit," said Mr Eager. "I knew he was trying it on. He is treating us as if we were a party of Cook's tourists."

"Surely no!" said Miss Lavish, her ardour visibly decreasing.

The other carriage had drawn up behind, and sensible Mr Beebe called out that after this warning the couple would be sure to behave themselves properly.

"Leave them alone," Mr Emerson begged the chaplain, of whom he stood in no awe. "Do we find happiness so often that we should turn it off the box when it happens to sit there? To be driven by lovers—a king might envy us, and if we part them it's more like sacrilege than anything I know."

Here the voice of Miss Bartlett was heard saying that a crowd had begun to collect.

Mr Eager, who suffered from an over-fluent tongue rather than a resolute will, was determined to make himself heard. He addressed the driver again. Italian in the mouth of Italians is a deep-voiced stream, with unexpected cataracts and boulders to preserve it from monotony. In Mr Eager's mouth it resembled nothing so much as an acid whistling fountain which played ever higher and higher, and quicker and quicker, and more and more shrilly, till abruptly it was turned off with a click.

"Signorina!" said the man to Lucy, when the display had ceased. Why should he appeal to Lucy?

"Signorina!" echoed Persephone in her glorious contralto. She pointed at the other carriage. Why?

For a moment the two girls looked at each other. Then Persephone got down from the box.

"Victory at last!" said Mr Eager, smiting his hands together as the carriages started again.

"It is not victory," said Mr Emerson. "It is defeat. You have parted two people who were happy."

Mr Eager shut his eyes. He was obliged to sit next to Mr Emerson, but he would not speak to him. The old man was refreshed by sleep, and took up the matter warmly. He commanded Lucy to agree with him; he shouted for support to his son.

"We have tried to buy what cannot be bought with money. He has bargained to drive us, and he is doing it. We have no rights over his soul."

Miss Lavish frowned. It is hard when a person you have classed as typically British speaks out of his character.

"He was not driving us well," she said. "He jolted us."

"That I deny. It was as restful as sleeping. Aha! He is jolting us now. Can you wonder? He would like to throw us out, and most certainly he is justified. And if I were superstitious I'd be frightened of the girl, too. It doesn't do to injure young people. Have you ever heard of Lorenzo de' Medici?"

Miss Lavish bristled.

"Most certainly I have. Do you refer to Lorenzo il Magnifico, or to Lorenzo, Duke of Urbino, or to Lorenzo surnamed Lorenzino on account of his diminutive stature?"

"The Lord knows. Possibly he does know, for I refer to Lorenzo the poet. He wrote a line—so I heard yesterday—which runs like this: 'Don't go fighting against the spring.' "

Mr Eager could not resist the opportunity for erudition.

"Non fate guerra al Maggio," he murmured. " 'War not with the May' would render a correct meaning."

"The point is, we have warred with it. Look." He pointed to the Val d' Arno, which was visible far below them, through the budding trees. "Fifty miles of spring, and we've come up to admire them. Do you suppose there's any difference between spring in nature and spring in man? But there we go, praising the one and condemning the other as improper, ashamed that the same laws work eternally through both."

63

No one encouraged him to talk. Presently Mr Eager gave
a signal for the carriages to stop, and marshalled the party
for their ramble on the hill. A hollow like a great amphi-
theatre, full of terraced steps and misty olives, now lay
between them and the heights of Fiesole, and the road, still
following its curve, was about to sweep on to a promontory
which stood out into the plain. It was this promontory,
uncultivated, wet, covered with bushes and occasional trees,
which had caught the fancy of Alessio Baldovinetti nearly
five hundred years before. He had ascended it, that diligent
and rather obscure master, possibly with an eye to business,
possibly for the joy of ascending. Standing there, he had seen
that view of the Val d' Arno and distant Florence, which
he afterwards had introduced not very effectively into his
work. But where exactly had he stood? That was the question which Mr Eager hoped to solve now. And Miss Lavish,
whose nature was attracted by anything problematical, had
become equally enthusiastic.

But it is not easy to carry the pictures of Alessio Baldovinetti in your head, even if you have remembered to look
at them before starting. And the haze in the valley increased
the difficulty of the quest. The party sprang about from tuft
to tuft of grass, their anxiety to keep together being only
equalled by their desire to go in different directions. Finally
they split into groups. Lucy clung to Miss Bartlett and Miss
Lavish; the Emersons returned to hold laborious converse
with the drivers; while the two clergymen, who were expected
to have topics in common, were left to each other.

The two elder ladies soon threw off the mask. In the audible
whisper that was now so familiar to Lucy they began to
discuss, not Alessio Baldovinetti, but the drive. Miss Bartlett
had asked Mr George Emerson what his profession was, and
he had answered "the railway". She was very sorry that she
had asked him. She had no idea that it would be such a
dreadful answer, or she would not have asked him. Mr
Beebe had turned the conversation so cleverly, and she hoped
that the young man was not very much hurt at her asking
him.

"The railway!" gasped Miss Lavish. "Oh, but I shall die! Of course it was the railway!" She could not control her mirth. "He is the image of a porter—on, on the South-Eastern."

"Eleanor, be quiet," plucking at her vivacious companion. "Hush! They'll hear—the Emersons—"

"I can't stop. Let me go my wicked way. A porter—"

"Eleanor!"

"I'm sure it's all right," put in Lucy. "The Emersons won't hear, and they wouldn't mind if they did."

Miss Lavish did not seem pleased at this.

"Miss Honeychurch listening!" she said rather crossly. "Pouf! Wouf! You naughty girl! Go away!"

"Oh, Lucy, you ought to be with Mr Eager, I'm sure."

"I can't find them now, and I don't want to either."

"Mr Eager will be offended. It is your party."

"Please, I'd rather stop here with you."

"No, I agree," said Miss Lavish. "It's like a school feast; the boys have got separated from the girls. Miss Lucy, you are to go. We wish to converse on high topics unsuited for your ear."

The girl was stubborn. As her time at Florence drew to its close she was only at ease amongst those to whom she felt indifferent. Such a one was Miss Lavish, and such for the moment was Charlotte. She wished she had not called attention to herself; they were both annoyed at her remark and seemed determined to get rid of her.

"How tired one gets," said Miss Bartlett. "Oh, I do wish Freddy and your mother could be here."

Unselfishness with Miss Bartlett had entirely usurped the functions of enthusiasm. Lucy did not look at the view either. She would not enjoy anything till she was safe at Rome.

"Then sit you down," said Miss Lavish. "Observe my foresight."

With many a smile she produced two of those mackintosh squares that protect the frame of the tourist from damp grass or cold marble steps. She sat on one; who was to sit on the other?

"Lucy; without a moment's doubt, Lucy. The ground will do for me. Really I have not had rheumatism for years. If I do feel it coming on I shall stand. Imagine your mother's feelings if I let you sit in the wet in your white linen." She sat down heavily where the ground looked particularly moist. "Here we are, all settled delightfully. Even if my dress is thinner it will not show so much, being brown. Sit down, dear; you are too unselfish; you don't assert yourself enough." She cleared her throat. "Now don't be alarmed; this isn't a cold. It's the tiniest cough, and I have had it three days. It's nothing to do with sitting here at all."

There was only one way of treating the situation. At the end of five minutes Lucy departed in search of Mr Beebe and Mr Eager, vanquished by the mackintosh square.

She addressed herself to the drivers, who were sprawling in the carriages, perfuming the cushions with cigars. The miscreant, a bony young man scorched black by the sun, rose to greet her with the courtesy of a host and the assurance of a relative.

"*Dove?*" said Lucy, after much anxious thought.

His face lit up. Of course he knew where. Not so far either. His arm swept three-fourths of the horizon. He should just think he did know where. He pressed his finger-tips to his forehead and then pushed them towards her, as if oozing with visible extract of knowledge.

More seemed necessary. What was the Italian for "clergymen"?

"Dove buoni uomini?" said she at last.

Good? Scarcely the adjective for those noble beings! He showed her his cigar.

"Uno—piu—piccolo," was her next remark, implying "Has the cigar been given to you by Mr Beebe, the smaller of the two good men?"

She was correct as usual. He tied the horse to a tree, kicked it to make it stay quiet, dusted the carriage, arranged his hair, remoulded his hat, encouraged his moustache, and in rather less than a quarter of a minute was ready to conduct her. Italians are born knowing the way. It would seem that

66

the whole earth lay before them, not as a map, but as a chess-board, whereon they continually behold the changing pieces as well as the squares. Anyone can find places, but the finding of people is a gift from God.

He only stopped once, to pick her some great blue violets. She thanked him with real pleasure. In the company of this common man the world was beautiful and direct. For the first time she felt the influence of spring. His arm swept the horizon gracefully; violets, like other things, existed in great profusion there; would she like to see them?

"Ma buoni uomini."

He bowed. Certainly. Good men first, violets afterwards. They proceeded briskly through the undergrowth, which became thicker and thicker. They were nearing the edge of the promontory, and the view was stealing round them, but the brown network of the bushes shattered it into countless pieces. He was occupied in his cigar, and in holding back the pliant boughs. She was rejoicing in her escape from dull-ness. Not a step, not a twig, was unimportant to her.

"What is that?"

There was a voice in the wood, in the distance behind them. The voice of Mr Eager? He shrugged his shoulders. An Italian's ignorance is sometimes more remarkable than his knowledge. She could not make him understand that perhaps they had missed the clergymen. The view was forming at last; she could discern the river, the golden plain, other hills.

"Eccolo!" he exclaimed.

At the same moment the ground gave way, and with a cry she fell out of the wood. Light and beauty enveloped her. She had fallen onto a little open terrace, which was covered with violets from end to end.

"Courage!" cried her companion, now standing some six feet above. "Courage and love."

She did not answer. From her feet the ground sloped sharply into the view, and violets ran down in rivulets and streams and cataracts, irrigating the hillside with blue, eddying round the tree stems, collecting into pools in the

67

hollows, covering the grass with spots of azure foam. But never again were they in such profusion; this terrace was the well-head, the primal source whence beauty gushed out to water the earth.

Standing at its brink, like a swimmer who prepares, was the good man. But he was not the good man that she had expected, and he was alone.

George had turned at the sound of her arrival. For a moment he contemplated her, as one who had fallen out of heaven. He saw radiant joy in her face, he saw the flowers beat against her dress in blue waves. The bushes above them closed. He stepped quickly forward and kissed her.

Before she could speak, almost before she could feel, a voice called, "Lucy! Lucy! Lucy!" The silence of life had been broken by Miss Bartlett, who stood brown against the view.

Chapter 7
They Return

Some complicated game had been playing up and down the hillside all the afternoon. What it was and exactly how the players had sided, Lucy was slow to discover. Mr Eager had met them with a questioning eye. Charlotte had repulsed him with much small-talk. Mr Emerson, seeking his son, was told whereabouts to find him. Mr Beebe, who wore the heated aspect of a neutral, was bidden to collect the factions for the return home. There was a general sense of groping and bewilderment. Pan had been amongst them—not the great god Pan, who has been buried these two thousand years, but the little god Pan, who presides over social contretemps and unsuccessful picnics. Mr Beebe had lost everyone, and had consumed in solitude the tea-basket which he had brought up as a pleasant surprise. Miss Lavish had lost Miss Bartlett. Lucy had lost Mr Eager. Mr Emerson had lost George. Miss Bartlett had lost a mackintosh square. Phaethon had lost the game.

That last fact was undeniable. He climbed onto the box shivering, with his collar up, prophesying the swift approach of bad weather.

"Let us go immediately," he told them. "The signorino will walk."

"All the way? He will be hours," said Mr Beebe.

"Apparently. I told him it was unwise." He would look no one in the face; perhaps defeat was particularly mortifying for him. He alone had played skilfully, using the whole of his instinct, while the others had used scraps of their intelligence. He alone had divined what things were, and what he wished them to be. He alone had interpreted the message that Lucy had received five days before from the lips of a dying man. Persephone, who spends half her life in the grave—she could interpret it also. Not so these English. They gain knowledge slowly, and perhaps too late.

The thoughts of a cab-driver, however just, seldom affect the lives of his employers. He was the most competent of Miss Bartlett's opponents, but infinitely the least dangerous. Once back in the town, he and his insight and his knowledge would trouble English ladies no more. Of course, it was most unpleasant; she had seen his black head in the bushes; he might make a tavern story out of it. But, after all, what have we to do with taverns? Real menace belongs to the drawing-room. It was of drawing-room people that Miss Bartlett thought as she journeyed downwards towards the fading sun. Lucy sat beside her; Mr Eager sat opposite, trying to catch her eye; he was vaguely suspicious. They spoke of Alessio Baldovinetti.

Rain and darkness came on together. The two ladies huddled together under an inadequate parasol. There was a lightning flash, and Miss Lavish, who was nervous, screamed from the carriage in front. At the next flash, Lucy screamed also. Mr Eager addressed her professionally.

"Courage, Miss Honeychurch, courage and faith. If I might say so, there is something almost blasphemous in this horror of the elements. Are we seriously to suppose that all these clouds, all this immense electrical display, is simply called into existence to extinguish you or me?"

"No—of course—"

"Even from the scientific standpoint the chances against our being struck are enormous. The steel knives, the only articles which might attract the current, are in the other carriage. And, in any case, we are infinitely safer than if we were walking. Courage—courage and faith."

Under the rug, Lucy felt the kindly pressure of her cousin's hand. At times our need for a sympathetic gesture is so great that we care not what exactly it signifies or how much we may have to pay for it afterwards. Miss Bartlett, by this timely exercise of her muscles, gained more than she would have got in hours of preaching or cross-examination.

She renewed it when the two carriages stopped, half into Florence.

"Mr Eager!" called Mr Beebe. "We want your assistance. Will you interpret for us?"

"George!" cried Mr Emerson. "Ask your driver which way George went. The boy may lose his way. He may be killed."

"Go, Mr Eager," said Miss Bartlett. "No, don't ask our driver; our driver is no help. Go and support poor Mr Beebe; he is nearly demented."

"He may be killed!" cried the old man. "He may be killed!"

"Typical behaviour," said the chaplain, as he quitted the carriage. "In the presence of reality that kind of person invariably breaks down."

"What does he know?" whispered Lucy as soon as they were alone. "Charlotte, how much does Mr Eager know?"

"Nothing, dearest; he knows nothing. But"—she pointed at the driver—"*he* knows everything. Dearest, had we better? Shall I?" She took out her purse. "It is dreadful to be entangled with low-class people. He saw it all." Tapping Phaethon's back with her guidebook, she said, "Silenzio!" and offered him a franc.

"Va bene," he replied, and accepted it. As well this ending to his day as any. But Lucy, a mortal maid, was disappointed in him.

There was an explosion up the road. The storm had struck the overhead wire of the tramline, and one of the great supports had fallen. If they had not stopped perhaps they might have been hurt. They chose to regard it as a miraculous preservation, and the floods of love and sincerity, which might fructify every hour of life, burst forth in tumult. They descended from the carriages; they embraced each other. It was as joyful to be forgiven past unworthinesses as to forgive them. For a moment they realized vast possibilities of good.

The older people recovered quickly. In the very height of their emotion they knew it to be unmanly or unladylike. Miss Lavish calculated that, even if they had continued, they would not have been caught in the accident. Mr Eager mumbled a temperate prayer. But the drivers, through miles of dark squalid road, poured out their souls to the dryads and the saints, and Lucy poured out hers to her cousin.

"Charlotte, dear Charlotte, kiss me. Kiss me again. Only you can understand me. You warned me to be careful. And I —I thought I was developing."

"Do not cry, dearest. Take your time."

"I have been obstinate and silly—worse than you know, far worse. Once by the river—oh, but he isn't killed—he wouldn't be killed, would he?"

The thought disturbed her repentance. As a matter of fact, the storm was worst along the road; but she had been near danger, and so she thought it must be near to everyone.

"I trust not. One would always pray against that."

"He is really—I think he was taken by surprise, just as I was before. But this time I'm not to blame; I do want you to believe that. I simply slipped into those violets. No, I want to be really truthful. I am a little to blame. I had silly thoughts. The sky, you know, was gold, and the ground all blue, and for a moment he looked like someone in a book."

"In a book?"

"Heroes—gods—the nonsense of schoolgirls."

"And then?"

"But, Charlotte, you know what happened then."

Miss Bartlett was silent. Indeed, she had little more to learn. With a certain amount of insight she drew her young cousin affectionately to her. All the way back Lucy's body was shaken by deep sighs, which nothing could repress.

"I want to be truthful," she whispered. "It is so hard to be absolutely truthful."

"Don't be troubled, dearest. Wait till you are calmer. We will talk it over before bed-time in my room."

So they re-entered the city with hands clasped. It was a shock to the girl to find how far emotion had ebbed in others. The storm had ceased, and Mr Emerson was easier about his son. Mr Beebe had regained good humour, and Mr

Eager was already snubbing Miss Lavish. Charlotte alone she was sure of—Charlotte, whose exterior concealed so much insight and love.

The luxury of self-exposure kept her almost happy through the long evening. She thought not so much of what had happened as of how she should describe it. All her sensations, her spasms of courage, her moments of unreasonable joy, her mysterious discontent, should be carefully laid before her cousin. And together in divine confidence they would disentangle and interpret them all.

"At last," thought she, "I shall understand myself. I shan't again be troubled by things that come out of nothing, and mean I don't know what."

Miss Alan asked her to play. She refused vehemently. Music seemed to her the employment of a child. She sat close to her cousin, who, with commendable patience, was listening to a long story about lost luggage. When it was over she capped it by a story of her own. Lucy became rather hysterical with the delay. In vain she tried to check, or at all events to accelerate, the tale. It was not till a late hour that Miss Bartlett had recovered her luggage and could say in her usual tone of gentle reproach: "Well, dear, I at all events am ready for Bedfordshire. Come into my room, and I will give a good brush to your hair."

With some solemnity the door was shut, and a cane chair placed for the girl. Then Miss Bartlett said:

"So what is to be done?"

She was unprepared for the question. It had not occurred to her that she would have to do anything. A detailed exhibition of her emotions was all that she had counted upon.

"What is to be done? A point, dearest, which you alone can settle."

The rain was streaming down the black windows, and the great room felt damp and chilly. One candle burned trembling on the chest of drawers close to Miss Bartlett's toque, which cast monstrous and fantastic shadows on the bolted door. A tram roared by in the dark, and Lucy felt unaccountably sad, though she had long since dried her eyes. She lifted them to the ceiling, where the griffins and bassoons were colourless and vague, the very ghosts of joy.

"It has been raining for nearly four hours," she said at last.

Miss Bartlett ignored the remark.

"How do you propose to silence him?"

"The driver?"

"My dear girl, no; Mr George Emerson."

Lucy began to pace up and down the room.

"I don't understand," she said at last.

She understood very well, but she no longer wished to be absolutely truthful.

"How are you going to stop him talking about it?"

"I have a feeling that talk is a thing he will never do."

"I, too, intend to judge him charitably. But unfortunately I have met the type before. They seldom keep their exploits to themselves."

"Exploits?" cried Lucy, wincing under the horrible plural.

"My poor dear, did you suppose that this was his first? Come here and listen to me. I am only gathering it from his own remarks. Do you remember that day at lunch when he argued with Miss Alan that liking one person is an extra reason for liking another?"

"Yes," said Lucy, whom at the time the argument had pleased.

"Well, I am no prude. There is no need to call him a wicked young man, but obviously he is thoroughly un-refined. Let us put it down to his deplorable antecedents and education, if you wish. But we are no further on with our question. What do you propose to do?"

An idea rushed across Lucy's brain, which, had she thought of it sooner and made it part of her, might have proved victorious.

"I propose to speak to him," said she.

Miss Bartlett uttered a cry of genuine alarm.

"You see, Charlotte, your kindness—I shall never forget it. But—as you said—it is my affair. Mine and his."

74

"And you are going to *implore* him, to *beg* him to keep silence?"

"Certainly not. There would be no difficulty. Whatever you ask him he answers, yes or no; then it is over. I have been frightened of him. But now I am not one little bit."

"But we fear him for you, dear. You are so young and inexperienced, you have lived among such nice people, that you cannot realize what men can be—how they can take a brutal pleasure in insulting a woman whom her sex does not protect and rally round. This afternoon, for example, if I had not arrived, what would have happened?"

"I can't think," said Lucy gravely.

Something in her voice made Miss Bartlett repeat her question, intoning it more vigorously.

"What would have happened if I hadn't arrived?"

"I can't think," said Lucy again.

"When he insulted you, how would you have replied?"

"I hadn't time to think. You came."

"Yes, but won't you tell me now what you would have done?"

"I should have—" She checked herself, and broke the sentence off. She went up to the dripping window and strained her eyes into the darkness. She could not think what she would have done.

"Come away from the window, dear," said Miss Bartlett. "You will be seen from the road."

Lucy obeyed. She was in her cousin's power. She could not modulate out of the key of self-abasement in which she had started. Neither of them referred again to her suggestion that she should speak to George and settle the matter, whatever it was, with him.

Miss Bartlett became plaintive.

"O for a real man! We are only two women, you and I. Mr Beebe is hopeless. There is Mr Eager, but you do not trust him. O for your brother! He is young, but I know that his sister's insult would rouse in him a very lion. Thank God, chivalry is not yet dead. There are still left some men who can reverence woman."

75

As she spoke, she pulled off her rings, of which she wore several, and ranged them upon the pin-cushion. Then she blew into her gloves and said:

"It will be a push to catch the morning train, but we must try."

"What train?"

"The train to Rome." She looked at her gloves critically.

The girl received the announcement as easily as it had been given.

"When does the train to Rome go?"

"At eight."

"Signora Bertolini would be upset."

"We must face that," said Miss Bartlett, not liking to say that she had given notice already.

"She will make us pay for a whole week's pension."

"I expect she will. However, we shall be much more comfortable at the Vyses' hotel. Isn't afternoon tea given there for nothing?"

"Yes, but they pay extra for wine."

After this remark she remained motionless and silent. To her tired eyes Charlotte throbbed and swelled like a ghostly figure in a dream.

They began to sort their clothes for packing, for there was no time to lose, if they were to catch the train to Rome. Lucy, when admonished, began to move to and fro between the rooms, more conscious of the discomforts of packing by candlelight than of a subtler ill. Charlotte, who was practical without ability, knelt by the side of an empty trunk, vainly endeavouring to pave it with books of varying thickness and size. She gave two or three sighs, for the stooping posture hurt her back, and, for all her diplomacy, she felt that she was growing old. The girl heard her as she entered the room, and was seized with one of those emotional impulses to which she could never attribute a cause. She only felt that the candle would burn better, the packing go easier, the world be happier, if she could give and receive some human love. The impulse had come before today, but never so strongly. She knelt down by her cousin's side and took her in her arms.

Miss Bartlett returned the embrace with tenderness and warmth. But she was not a stupid woman, and she knew perfectly well that Lucy did not love her, but needed her to love. For it was in ominous tones that she said, after a long pause:

"Dearest Lucy, how will you ever forgive me?"

Lucy was on her guard at once, knowing by bitter experience what forgiving Miss Bartlett meant. Her emotion relaxed; she modified her embrace a little, and she said:

"Charlotte dear, what do you mean? As if I have anything to forgive!"

"You have a great deal, and I have a very great deal to forgive myself, too. I know well how much I vex you at every turn."

"But no—"

Miss Bartlett assumed her favourite role, that of the prematurely aged martyr.

"Ah, but yes! I feel that our tour together is hardly the success I had hoped. I might have known it would not do. You want someone younger and stronger and more in sympathy with you. I am too uninteresting and old-fashioned—only fit to pack and unpack your things."

"Please—"

"My only consolation was that you found people more to your taste, and were often able to leave me at home. I had my own poor ideas of what a lady ought to do, but I hope I did not inflict them on you more than was necessary. You had your own way about these rooms, at all events."

"You mustn't say these things," said Lucy softly.

She still clung to the hope that she and Charlotte loved each other, heart and soul. They continued to pack in silence.

"I have been a failure," said Miss Bartlett, as she struggled with the straps of Lucy's trunk instead of strapping her own. "Failed to make you happy; failed in my duty to your mother. She has been so generous to me; I shall never face her again after this disaster."

"But mother will understand. It is not your fault, this trouble, and it isn't a disaster either."

"It is my fault, it is a disaster. She will never forgive me, and rightly. For instance, what right had I to make friends with Miss Lavish?"

"Every right."

"When I was here for your sake? If I have vexed you it is equally true that I have neglected you. Your mother will see this as clearly as I do, when you tell her."

Lucy, from a cowardly wish to improve the situation, said:

"Why need mother hear of it?"

"But you tell her everything?"

"I suppose I do generally."

"I dare not break your confidence. There is something sacred in it. Unless you feel that it is a thing you could not tell her."

The girl would not be degraded to this.

"Naturally I should have told her. But in case she should blame you in any way, I promise I will not. I am very willing not to. I will never speak of it either to her or to anyone."

Her promise brought the long-drawn interview to a sudden close. Miss Bartlett pecked her smartly on both cheeks, wished her goodnight, and sent her to her own room.

For a moment the original trouble was in the background. George would seem to have behaved like a cad throughout; perhaps that was the view which one would take eventually. At present she neither acquitted nor condemned him; she did not pass judgement. At the moment when she was about to judge him her cousin's voice had intervened, and, ever since, it was Miss Bartlett who had dominated; Miss Bartlett who, even now, could be heard sighing into a crack in the partition wall; Miss Bartlett who had really been neither pliable nor humble nor inconsistent. She had worked like a great artist; for a time—indeed, for years—she had been meaningless, but at the end there was presented to the girl the complete picture of a cheerless, loveless world in which the young rush to destruction until they learn better—a shamefaced world of precautions and barriers which may

78

avert evil, but which do not seem to bring good, if we may judge from those who have used them most.

Lucy was suffering from the most grievous wrong which this world has yet discovered: diplomatic advantage had been taken of her sincerity, of her craving for sympathy and love. Such a wrong is not easily forgotten. Never again did she expose herself without due consideration and precaution against rebuff. And such a wrong may react disastrously upon the soul.

The doorbell rang, and she started to the shutters. Before she reached them she hesitated, turned, and blew out the candle. Thus it was that, though she saw someone standing in the wet below, he, though he looked up, did not see her.

To reach his room he had to go by hers. She was still dressed. It struck her that she might slip into the passage and just say that she would be gone before he was up, and that their extraordinary intercourse was over.

Whether she would have dared to do this was never proved. At the critical moment Miss Bartlett opened her own door, and her voice said:

"I wish one word with you in the drawing-room, Mr Emerson, please."

Soon their footsteps returned, and Miss Bartlett said: "Good night, Mr Emerson."

His heavy, tired breathing was the only reply; the chaperon had done her work.

Lucy cried aloud: "It isn't true. It can't all be true. I want not to be muddled. I want to grow older quickly."

Miss Bartlett tapped on the wall.

"Go to bed at once, dear. You need all the rest you can get."

In the morning they left for Rome.

Part Two

Chapter 8
Medieval

The drawing-room curtains at Windy Corner had been pulled to meet, for the carpet was new and deserved protection from the August sun. They were heavy curtains, reaching almost to the ground, and the light that filtered through them was subdued and varied. A poet—none was present—might have quoted, "Life like a dome of many-coloured glass", or might have compared the curtains to sluice-gates, lowered against the intolerable tides of heaven. Without was poured a sea of radiance; within, the glory, though visible, was tempered to the capacities of man.

Two pleasant people sat in the room. One—a boy of nineteen—was studying a small manual of anatomy, and peering occasionally at a bone which lay upon the piano. From time to time he bounced in his chair and puffed and groaned, for the day was hot and the print small, and the human frame fearfully made; and his mother, who was writing a letter, did continually read out to him what she had written. And continually did she rise from her seat and part the curtains so that a rivulet of light fell across the carpet, and make the remark that they were still there.

"Where aren't they?" said the boy, who was Freddy, Lucy's brother. "I tell you I'm getting fairly sick."

"For goodness' sake go out of my drawing-room, then!" cried Mrs Honeychurch, who hoped to cure her children of slang by taking it literally.

Freddy did not move or reply.

"I think things are coming to a head," she observed, rather wanting her son's opinion on the situation if she could obtain it without undue supplication.

"Time they did."

"I am glad that Cecil is asking her this once more."

"It's his third go, isn't it?"

"Freddy, I do call the way you talk unkind."

"I didn't mean to be unkind." Then he added: "But I do think Lucy might have got this off her chest in Italy. I don't know how girls manage things, but she can't have said 'No' properly before, or she wouldn't have to say it again now. Over the whole thing—I can't explain—I do feel so uncomfortable."

"Do you indeed, dear? How interesting!"

"I feel—never mind."

He returned to his work.

"Just listen to what I have written to Mrs Vyse. I said: 'Dear Mrs Vyse—'"

"Yes, mother, you told me. A jolly good letter."

"I said: 'Dear Mrs Vyse, Cecil has just asked my permission about it, and I should be delighted, if Lucy wishes it. But—'" She stopped reading. "I was rather amused at Cecil asking my permission at all. He has always gone in for unconventionality, and parents nowhere, and so forth. When it comes to the point, he can't get on without me."

"Nor me."

"You?"

Freddy nodded.

"What do you mean?"

"He asked me for my permission also."

She exclaimed: "How very odd of him!"

"Why so?" asked the son and heir. "Why shouldn't my permission be asked?"

"What do you know about Lucy or girls or anything? What ever did you say?"

"I said to Cecil, 'Take her or leave her; it's no business of mine!'"

"What a helpful answer!" But her own answer, though more normal in its wording, had been to the same effect.

"The bother is this," began Freddy.

Then he took up his work again, too shy to say what the bother was. Mrs Honeychurch went back to the window.

"Freddy, you must come. There they still are!"

"I don't see you ought to go peeping like that."

"Peeping like that! Can't I look out of my own window?"

But she returned to the writing-table, observing, as she passed her son, "Still page 322?" Freddy snorted, and turned over two leaves. For a brief space they were silent. Close by, beyond the curtains, the gentle murmur of a long conversation had never ceased.

"The bother is this: I have put my foot in it with Cecil most awfully." He gave a nervous gulp. "Not content with 'permission', which I did give—that is to say, I said, 'I don't mind'—well, not content with that, he wanted to know whether I wasn't off my head with joy. He practically put it like this: Wasn't it a splendid thing for Lucy and for Windy Corner generally if he married her? And he would have an answer—he said it would strengthen his hand."

"I hope you gave a careful answer, dear."

"I answered 'No'," said the boy, grinding his teeth. "There! Fly into a stew! I can't help it—I had to say it. I had to say no. He ought never to have asked me."

"Ridiculous child!" cried his mother. "You think you're so holy and truthful, but really it's only abominable conceit. Do you suppose that a man like Cecil would take the slightest notice of anything you say? I hope he boxed your ears. How dare you say no?"

"Oh, do keep quiet, mother! I had to say no when I couldn't say yes. I tried to laugh as if I didn't mean what I said, and, as Cecil laughed too, and went away, it may be all right. But I feel my foot's in it. Oh, do keep quiet, though, and let a man do some work."

"No," said Mrs Honeychurch, with the air of one who had considered the subject, "I shall not keep quiet. You know all that has passed between them in Rome; you know why he is down here, and yet you deliberately insult him, and try to turn him out of my house."

"Not a bit!" he pleaded. "I only let out I didn't like him. I don't hate him, but I don't like him. What I mind is that he'll tell Lucy."

He glanced at the curtains dismally.

"Well, *I* like him," said Mrs Honeychurch. "I know his mother; he's good, he's clever, he's rich, he's well connected —oh, you needn't kick the piano! He's well connected—I'll say it again if you like: he's well connected." She paused, as if rehearsing her eulogy, but her face remained dissatisfied. She added: "And he has beautiful manners."

"I liked him till just now. I suppose it's having him spoiling Lucy's first week at home; and it's also something that Mr Beebe said, not knowing."

"Mr Beebe?" said his mother, trying to conceal her interest. "I don't see how Mr Beebe comes in."

"You know Mr Beebe's funny way, when you never quite know what he means. He said: 'Mr Vyse is an ideal bachelor.' I was very cute. I asked him what he meant. He said: 'Oh, he's like me—better detached.' I couldn't make him say any more, but it set me thinking. Since Cecil has come after Lucy he hasn't been so pleasant, at least—I can't explain."

"You never can, dear. But I can. You are jealous of Cecil because he may stop Lucy knitting you silk ties."

The explanation seemed plausible, and Freddy tried to accept it. But at the back of his brain there lurked a dim mistrust. Cecil praised one too much for being athletic. Was that it? Cecil made one talk in his way, instead of letting one talk in one's own way. This tired one. Was that it? And Cecil was the kind of fellow who would never wear another fellow's cap. Unaware of his own profundity, Freddy checked himself. He must be jealous, or he would not dislike a man for such foolish reasons.

"Will this do?" called his mother. " 'Dear Mrs Vyse, Cecil has just asked my permission about it, and I should be delighted if Lucy wishes it.' Then I put in at the top, 'and I have told Lucy so.' I must write the letter out again— 'and I have told Lucy so. But Lucy seems very uncertain, and in these days young people must decide for themselves.' I said that because I didn't want Mrs Vyse to think us old-fashioned. She goes in for lectures and improving her mind, and all the time a thick layer of flue under the beds, and the maids' dirty thumb-marks where you turn on the electric light. She keeps that flat abominably—"

"Suppose Lucy marries Cecil, would she live in a flat, or in the country?"

"Don't interrupt so foolishly. Where was I? Oh yes— 'Young people must decide for themselves. I know that Lucy likes your son, because she tells me everything, and she wrote to me from Rome when he asked her first.' No, I'll cross that last bit out—it looks patronizing. I'll stop at 'because she tells me everything'. Or shall I cross that out, too?"

"Cross it out, too," said Freddy.

Mrs Honeychurch left it in.

"Then the whole thing runs: 'Dear Mrs Vyse, Cecil has just asked my permission about it, and I should be delighted if Lucy wishes it, and I have told Lucy so. But Lucy seems very uncertain, and in these days young people must decide for themselves. I know that Lucy likes your son, because she tells me everything. But I do not know—' "

"Look out!" cried Freddy.

The curtains parted.

Cecil's first movement was one of irritation. He couldn't bear the Honeychurch habit of sitting in the dark to save the furniture. Instinctively he gave the curtains a twitch, and sent them swinging down their poles. Light entered. There was revealed a terrace, such as is owned by many villas, with trees each side of it, and on it a little rustic seat, and two flower-beds. But it was transfigured by the view beyond, for Windy Corner was built on the range that over-looks the Sussex Weald. Lucy, who was in the little seat, seemed on the edge of a green magic carpet which hovered in the air above the tremulous world.

Cecil entered.

Appearing thus late in the story, Cecil must be at once described. He was medieval. Like a Gothic statue. Tall and refined, with shoulders that seemed braced square by an effort of the will, and a head that was tilted a little higher than the usual level of vision, he resembled those fastidious saints who guard the portals of a French cathedral. Well educated, well endowed, and not deficient physically, he remained in the grip of a certain devil whom the modern world knows as self-consciousness, and whom the medieval, with dimmer vision, worshipped as asceticism. A Gothic statue implies celibacy, just as a Greek statue implies fruition, and perhaps this was what Mr Beebe meant. And Freddy, who ignored history and art, perhaps meant the same when he failed to imagine Cecil wearing another fellow's cap.

Mrs Honeychurch left her letter on the writing-table and moved towards her young acquaintance.

"Oh, Cecil!" she exclaimed—"oh, Cecil, do tell me!"

"I promessi sposi," said he.

They stared at him anxiously.

"She has accepted me," he said, and the sound of the thing in English made him flush and smile with pleasure, and look more human.

"I am so glad," said Mrs Honeychurch, while Freddy proffered a hand that was yellow with chemicals. They wished that they also knew Italian, for our phrases of approval and of amazement are so connected with little occasions that we fear to use them on great ones. We are obliged to become vaguely poetic, or to take refuge in Scriptural reminiscence.

"Welcome as one of the family!" said Mrs Honeychurch, waving her hand at the furniture. "This is indeed a joyous day! I feel sure that you will make dear Lucy happy."

"I hope so," replied the young man, shifting his eyes to the ceiling.

"We mothers—" simpered Mrs Honeychurch, and then realized that she was affected, sentimental, bombastic—all the things she hated most. Why could she not be as Freddy, who stood stiff in the middle of the room, looking very cross and almost handsome?

"I say, Lucy!" called Cecil, for conversation seemed to flag.

Lucy rose from the seat. She moved across the lawn and smiled in at them, just as if she was going to ask them to play tennis. Then she saw her brother's face. Her lips parted, and she took him in her arms. He said, "Steady on!"

"Not a kiss for me?" asked her mother.

Lucy kissed her also.

"Would you take them into the garden and tell Mrs Honeychurch all about it?" Cecil suggested. "And I'd stop here and tell my mother."

"We go with Lucy?" said Freddy, as if taking orders.

"Yes, you go with Lucy."

They passed into the sunlight. Cecil watched them cross the terrace, and descend out of sight by the steps. They would descend—he knew their ways—past the shrubbery, and past the tennis lawn and the dahlia-bed, until they reached the kitchen-garden, and there, in the presence of the potatoes and the peas, the great event would be discussed.

Smiling indulgently, he lit a cigarette, and rehearsed the events that had led to such a happy conclusion.

He had known Lucy for several years, but only as a commonplace girl who happened to be musical. He could still remember his depression that afternoon at Rome, when she and her terrible cousin fell on him out of the blue, and demanded to be taken to St Peter's. That day she had seemed a typical tourist—shrill, crude, and gaunt with travel. But Italy worked some marvel in her. It gave her light, and—which he held more precious—it gave her shadow. Soon he detected in her a wonderful reticence. She was like a woman of Leonardo da Vinci's, whom we love not so much for herself as for the things that she will not tell us. The things are assuredly not of this life; no woman of Leonardo's could have anything so vulgar as a 'story'. She did develop most wonderfully day by day.

So it happened that from patronizing civility he had slowly passed, if not to passion, at least to a profound uneasiness. Already at Rome he had hinted to her that they might be suitable for each other. It had touched him greatly that she had not broken away at the suggestion. Her refusal had been clear and gentle; after it—as the horrid phrase went—she had been exactly the same to him as before. Three months later, on the margin of Italy, among the flower-clad Alps, he had asked her again in bald, traditional language. She reminded him of a Leonardo more than ever; her sunburnt features were shadowed by fantastic rocks; at his words she had turned and stood between him and the light with immeasurable plains behind her. He walked home with her unashamed, feeling not at all like a rejected suitor. The things that really mattered were unshaken.

So now he had asked her once more, and, clear and gentle as ever, she had accepted him, giving no coy reasons for her delay, but simply saying that she loved him and would do her best to make him happy. His mother, too, would be pleased; she had counselled the step; he must write her a long account.

Glancing at his hand, in case any of Freddy's chemicals had come off on it, he moved to the writing-table. There he saw "Dear Mrs Vyse", followed by many erasures. He recoiled without reading any more, and after a little hesitation sat down elsewhere, and pencilled a note on his knee.

Then he lit another cigarette, which did not seem quite as divine as the first, and considered what might be done to make the Windy Corner drawing-room more distinctive. With that outlook it should have been a successful room, but the trail of Tottenham Court Road was upon it; he could almost visualize the motor-vans of Messrs Shoolbred and Messrs Maple arriving at the door and depositing this chair, those varnished book-cases, that writing-table. The table recalled Mrs Honeychurch's letter. He did not want to read that letter—his temptations never lay in that direction; but he worried about it none the less. It was his own fault that she was discussing him with his mother; he had wanted her support in his third attempt to win Lucy; he wanted to feel that others, no matter who they were, agreed with him, and so he had asked their permission. Mrs Honeychurch had been civil, but obtuse in essentials, while as for Freddy—

"He is only a boy," he reflected. "I represent all that he despises. Why should he want me for a brother-in-law?"

The Honeychurches were a worthy family, but he began to realize that Lucy was of another clay; and perhaps—he did not put it very definitely—he ought to introduce her into more congenial circles as soon as possible.

"Mr Beebe!" said the maid, and the new rector of Summer Street was shown in; he had at once started on friendly relations, owing to Lucy's praise of him in her letters from Florence.

Cecil greeted him rather critically.

"I've come for tea, Mr Vyse. Do you suppose that I shall get it?"

"I should say so. Food is the thing one does get here—don't sit in that chair; young Honeychurch has left a bone in it."

"Pfui!"

"I know," said Cecil, "I know. I can't think why Mrs Honeychurch allows it."

For Cecil considered the bone and the Maple's furniture separately; he did not realize that, taken together, they kindled the room into the life that he desired.

"I've come for tea and for gossip. Isn't this news?"

"News? I don't understand you," said Cecil. "News?"

Mr Beebe, whose news was of a very different nature, prattled forward.

"I met Sir Harry Otway as I came up; I have every reason to hope that I am first in the field. He has bought Cissie and Albert from Mr Flack!"

"Has he indeed?" said Cecil, trying to recover himself. Into what a grotesque mistake had he fallen! Was it likely that a clergyman and a gentleman would refer to his engagement in a manner so flippant? But his stiffness remained, and, though he asked who Cissie and Albert might be, he still thought Mr Beebe rather a bounder.

"Unpardonable question! To have stopped a week at Windy Corner and not to have met Cissie and Albert, the semi-detached villas that have been run up opposite the church! I'll set Mrs Honeychurch after you."

"I'm shockingly stupid over local affairs," said the young

man languidly. "I can't even remember the difference between a Parish Council and a Local Government Board. Perhaps there is no difference, or perhaps those aren't the right names. I only go into the country to see my friends and to enjoy the scenery. It is very remiss of me. Italy and London are the only places where I don't feel to exist on sufferance."

Mr Beebe, distressed at this heavy reception of Cissie and Albert, determined to shift the subject.

"Let me see, Mr Vyse—I forget—what is your profession?"

"I have no profession," said Cecil. "It is another example of my decadence. My attitude—quite an indefensible one— is that so long as I am no trouble to anyone I have a right to do as I like. I know I ought to be getting money out of people, or devoting myself to things I don't care a straw about, but somehow I've not been able to begin."

"You are very fortunate," said Mr Beebe. "It is a wonderful opportunity, the possession of leisure."

His voice was rather parochial, but he did not quite see his way to answering naturally. He felt, as all who have regular occupation must feel, that others should have it also.

"I am glad that you approve. I daren't face the healthy person—for example, Freddy Honeychurch."

"Oh, Freddy's a good sort, isn't he?"

"Admirable. The sort who has made England what she is."

Cecil wondered at himself. Why, on this day of all others, was he so hopelessly contrary? He tried to get right by inquiring effusively after Mr Beebe's mother, an old lady for whom he had no particular regard. Then he flattered the clergyman, praised his liberal-mindedness, his enlightened attitude towards philosophy and science.

"Where are the others?" said Mr Beebe at last. "I insist on extracting tea before evening service."

"I suppose Anne never told them you were here. In this house one is so coached in the servants the day one arrives. The fault of Anne is that she begs your pardon when she hears you perfectly, and kicks the chair-legs with her feet.

The faults of Mary—I forget the faults of Mary, but they are very grave. Shall we look in the garden?"

"I know the faults of Mary. She leaves the dustpans standing on the stairs."

"The fault of Euphemia is that she will not, simply will not, chop the suet sufficiently small."

They both laughed, and things began to go better.

"The faults of Freddy—" Cecil continued.

"Ah, he has too many. No one but his mother can remember the faults of Freddy. Try the faults of Miss Honeychurch; they are not innumerable."

"She has none," said the young man, with grave sincerity.

"I quite agree. At present she has none."

"At present?"

"I'm not cynical. I'm only thinking of my pet theory about Miss Honeychurch. Does it seem reasonable that she should play so wonderfully, and live so quietly? I suspect that one day she will be wonderful in both. The watertight compartments in her will break down, and music and life will mingle. Then we shall have her heroically good, heroically bad—too heroic, perhaps, to be good or bad."

Cecil found his companion interesting.

"And at present you think her not wonderful as far as life goes?"

"Well, I must say I've only seen her at Tunbridge Wells, where she was not wonderful, and at Florence. Since I came to Summer Street she has been away. You saw her, didn't you, at Rome and in the Alps. Oh, I forgot; of course, you knew her before. No, she wasn't wonderful in Florence either, but I kept on expecting that she would be."

"In what way?"

Conversation had become agreeable to them, and they were pacing up and down the terrace.

"I could as easily tell you what tune she'll play next. There was simply the sense that she had found wings, and meant to use them. I can show you a beautiful picture in my Italian diary: Miss Honeychurch as a kite, Miss Bartlett holding the string. Picture number two: the string breaks."

The sketch was in his diary, but it had been made afterwards, when he viewed things artistically. At the time he had given surreptitious tugs to the string himself.

"But the string never broke?"

"No. I mightn't have seen Miss Honeychurch rise, but I should certainly have heard Miss Bartlett fall."

"It has broken now," said the young man in low, vibrating tones.

Immediately he realized that of all the conceited, ludicrous, contemptible ways of announcing an engagement this was the worst. He cursed his love of metaphor; had he suggested that he was a star and that Lucy was soaring up to reach him?

"Broken? What do you mean?"

"I meant," said Cecil stiffly, "that she is going to marry me."

The clergyman was conscious of some bitter disappointment which he could not keep out of his voice.

"I am sorry; I must apologize. I had no idea you were intimate with her, or I should never have talked in this flippant, superficial way. Mr Vyse, you ought to have stopped me." And down the garden he saw Lucy herself; yes, he was disappointed.

Cecil, who naturally preferred congratulations to apologies, drew down his mouth at the corners. Was this the reception his action would get from the world? Of course, he despised the world as a whole; every thoughtful man should; it is almost a test of refinement. But he was sensitive to the successive particles of it which he encountered.

Occasionally he could be quite crude.

"I am sorry I have given you a shock," he said dryly. "I fear that Lucy's choice does not meet with your approval."

"Not that. But you ought to have stopped me. I know Miss Honeychurch only a little as time goes. Perhaps I oughtn't to have discussed her so freely with anyone; certainly not with you."

"You are conscious of having said something indiscreet?"

Mr Beebe pulled himself together. Really, Mr Vyse had

the art of placing one in the most tiresome positions. He was driven to use the prerogatives of his profession.

"No, I have said nothing indiscreet. I foresaw at Florence that her quiet, uneventful childhood must end, and it has ended. I realized dimly enough that she might take some momentous step. She has taken it. She has learned—you will let me talk freely, as I have begun freely—she has learned what it is to love: the greatest lesson, some people will tell you, that our earthly life provides." It was now time for him to wave his hat at the approaching trio. He did not omit to do so. "She has learned through you," and if his voice was still clerical it was now also sincere; "let it be your care that her knowledge is profitable to her."

"Grazie tante!" said Cecil, who did not like parsons.

"Have you heard?" shouted Mrs Honeychurch as she toiled up the sloping garden. "Oh, Mr Beebe, have you heard the news?"

Freddy, now full of geniality, whistled the wedding march. Youth seldom criticizes the accomplished fact.

"Indeed I have!" he cried. He looked at Lucy. In her presence he could not act the parson any longer—at all events not without apology. "Mrs Honeychurch, I'm going to do what I am always supposed to do, but generally I'm too shy. I want to invoke every kind of blessing on them, grave and gay, great and small. I want them all their lives to be supremely good and supremely happy as husband and wife, as father and mother. And now I want my tea."

"You only asked for it just in time," the lady retorted. "How dare you be serious at Windy Corner?"

He took his tone from her. There was no more heavy beneficence, no more attempts to dignify the situation with poetry or the Scriptures. None of them dared or was able to be serious any more.

An engagement is so potent a thing that sooner or later it reduces all who speak of it to this state of cheerful awe. Away from it, in the solitude of their rooms, Mr Beebe, and even Freddy, might again be critical. But in its presence and in the presence of each other they were sincerely hilarious. It has a strange power, for it compels not only the lips, but the very heart. The chief parallel—to compare one great thing with another—is the power over us of a temple of some alien creed. Standing outside, we deride or oppose it, or at the most feel sentimental. Inside, though the saints and gods are not ours, we become true believers, in case any true believer should be present.

So it was that after the gropings and the misgivings of the afternoon they pulled themselves together and settled down to a very pleasant tea-party. If they were hypocrites they did not know it, and their hypocrisy had every chance of setting and of becoming true. Anne, putting down each plate as if it were a wedding present, stimulated them greatly. They could not lag behind that smile of hers which she gave them ere she kicked the drawing-room door. Mr Beebe chirruped. Freddy was at his wittiest, referring to Cecil as the "Fiasco"—family-honoured pun on fiancé. Mrs Honeychurch, amusing and portly, promised well as a mother-in-law. As for Lucy and Cecil, for whom the temple had been built, they also joined in the merry ritual, but waited, as earnest worshippers should, for the disclosure of some holier shrine of joy.

Chapter 9
Lucy as a Work of Art

A few days after the engagement was announced Mrs Honey-church made Lucy and her Fiasco come to a little garden party in the neighbourhood, for naturally she wanted to show people that her daughter was marrying a presentable man.

Cecil was more than presentable; he looked distinguished, and it was very pleasant to see his slim figure keeping step with Lucy, and his long, fair face responding when Lucy spoke to him. People congratulated Mrs Honeychurch, which is, I believe, a social blunder, but it pleased her, and she introduced Cecil rather indiscriminately to some stuffy dowagers.

At tea a misfortune took place: a cup of coffee was upset over Lucy's figured silk, and though Lucy feigned indiffer-ence her mother feigned nothing of the sort, but dragged her indoors to have the frock treated by a sympathetic maid. They were gone some time, and Cecil was left with the dowagers. When they returned he was not as pleasant as he had been.

"Do you go to much of this sort of thing?" he asked when they were driving home.

"Oh, now and then," said Lucy, who had rather enjoyed herself.

"Is it typical of county society?"

"I suppose so. Mother, would it be?"

"Plenty of society," said Mrs Honeychurch, who was trying to remember the hang of one of the dresses.

Seeing that her thoughts were elsewhere, Cecil bent towards Lucy and said:

"To me it seemed perfectly appalling, disastrous, por-tentous."

"I am so sorry that you were stranded."

"Not that, but the congratulations. It is so disgusting, the way an engagement is regarded as public property—a kind of waste place where every outsider may shoot his vulgar sentiment. All those old women smirking!"

"One has to go through it, I suppose. They won't notice us so much next time."

"But my point is that their whole attitude is wrong. An engagement—horrid word in the first place—is a private matter, and should be treated as such."

Yet the smirking old women, however wrong individually, were racially correct. The spirit of the generations had smiled through them, rejoicing in the engagement of Cecil and Lucy because it promised the continuance of life on earth. To Cecil and Lucy it promised something quite different—personal love. Hence Cecil's irritation and Lucy's belief that his irritation was just.

"How tiresome!" she said. "Couldn't you have escaped to tennis?"

"I don't play tennis—at least, not in public. The neighbourhood is deprived of the romance of me being athletic. Such romance as I have is that of the Inglese Italianato."

"Inglese Italianato?"

"È un diavolo incarnato! You know the proverb?"

She did not. Nor did it seem applicable to a young man who had spent a quiet winter in Rome with his mother. But Cecil, since his engagement, had taken to affect a cosmopolitan naughtiness which he was far from possessing.

"Well," said he, "I cannot help it if they do disapprove of me. There are certain irremovable barriers between myself and them, and I must accept them."

"We all have our limitations, I suppose," said wise Lucy.

"Sometimes they are forced on us, though," said Cecil, who saw from her remark that she did not quite understand his position.

"How?"

"It makes a difference, doesn't it, whether we fence ourselves in, or whether we are fenced out by the barriers of others?"

97

She thought a moment, and agreed that it did make a difference.

"Difference?" cried Mrs Honeychurch, suddenly alert. "I don't see any difference. Fences are fences, especially when they are in the same place."

"We were speaking of motives," said Cecil, on whom the interruption jarred.

"My dear Cecil, look here." She spread out her knees and perched her card-case on her lap. "This is me. That's Windy Corner. The rest of the pattern is the other people. Motives are all very well, but the fence comes here."

"We weren't talking of real fences," said Lucy, laughing.

"Oh, I see, dear—poetry."

She leant placidly back. Cecil wondered why Lucy had been amused.

"I tell you who has no 'fences', as you call them," she said, "and that's Mr Beebe."

"A parson fenceless would mean a parson defenceless."

Lucy was slow to follow what people said, but quick enough to detect what they meant. She missed Cecil's epigram, but grasped the feeling that prompted it.

"Don't you like Mr Beebe?" she asked thoughtfully.

"I never said so!" he cried. "I consider him far above the average. I only denied—" And he swept off on the subject of fences again, and was brilliant.

"Now, a clergyman that I do hate," said she, wanting to say something sympathetic, "a clergyman that does have fences, and the most dreadful ones, is Mr Eager, the English chaplain at Florence. He was truly insincere—not merely the manner unfortunate. He was a snob, and so conceited, and he did say such unkind things."

"What sort of things?"

"There was an old man at the Bertolini whom he said had murdered his wife."

"Perhaps he had."

"Why, no."

"Why 'no'?"

"He was such a nice old man, I'm sure."

98

Cecil laughed at her feminine inconsequence.

"Well, I did try to sift the thing. Mr Eager would never come to the point. He prefers it vague—said the old man had 'practically' murdered his wife—had murdered her in the sight of God."

"Hush, dear!" said Mrs Honeychurch absently.

"But isn't it intolerable that a person whom we're told to imitate should go round spreading slander? It was, I believe, chiefly owing to him that the old man was dropped. People pretended he was vulgar, but he certainly wasn't that."

"Poor old man! What was his name?"

"Harris," said Lucy glibly.

"Let's hope that Mrs Harris there warn't no sich person," said her mother.

Cecil nodded intelligently.

"Isn't Mr Eager a parson of the cultured type?" he asked.

"I don't know. I hate him. I've heard him lecture on Giotto. I hate him. Nothing can hide a petty nature. I *hate* him!"

"My goodness gracious me, child!" said Mrs Honeychurch. "You'll blow my head off! What ever is there to shout over? I forbid you and Cecil to hate any more clergymen."

He smiled. There was indeed something rather incongruous in Lucy's moral outburst over Mr Eager. It was as if one should see the Leonardo on the ceiling of the Sistine. He longed to hint to her that not here lay her vocation; that a woman's power and charm reside in mystery, not in muscular rant. But possibly rant is a sign of vitality: it mars the beautiful creature, but shows that she is alive. After a moment, he contemplated her flushed face and excited gestures with a certain approval. He forbore to repress the sources of youth.

Nature—simplest of topics, he thought—lay around them. He praised the pine-woods, the deep lakes of bracken, the crimson leaves that spotted the hurt-bushes, the serviceable beauty of the turnpike road. The outdoor world was not very familiar to him, and occasionally he went wrong in a question of fact. Mrs Honeychurch's mouth twitched when he spoke of the perpetual green of the larch.

"I count myself a lucky person," he concluded. "When I'm in London I feel I could never live out of it. When I'm in the country I feel the same about the country. After all, I do believe that birds and trees and the sky are the most wonderful things in life, and that the people who live amongst them must be the best. It's true that in nine cases out of ten they don't seem to notice anything. The country gentleman and the country labourer are each in their way the most depressing of companions. Yet they may have a tacit sympathy with the workings of Nature which is denied to us of the town. Do you feel that, Mrs Honeychurch?"

Mrs Honeychurch started and smiled. She had not been attending. Cecil, who was rather crushed on the front seat of the victoria, felt irritable, and determined not to say anything interesting again.

Lucy had not attended either. Her brow was wrinkled, and she still looked furiously cross—the result, he concluded, of too much moral gymnastics. It was sad to see her thus blind to the beauties of an August wood.

" 'Come down, O maid, from yonder mountain height,' " he quoted, and touched her knee with his own.

She flushed again and said: "What height?"

"Come down, O maid, from yonder mountain height:
  What pleasure lives in height (the shepherd sang),
  In height and in the splendour of the hills?

Let us take Mrs Honeychurch's advice and hate clergymen no more. What's this place?"

"Summer Street, of course," said Lucy, and roused herself.

The woods had opened to leave space for a sloping triangular meadow. Pretty cottages lined it on two sides, and the upper and third side was occupied by a new stone church, expensively simple, with a charming shingled spire. Mr Beebe's house was near the church. In height it scarcely exceeded the cottages. Some great mansions were at hand, but they were hidden in the trees. The scene suggested a Swiss alp rather than the shrine and centre of a leisured world, and was only marred by two ugly little villas—the villas that had competed with Cecil's engagement, having been acquired by Sir Harry Otway the very afternoon that Lucy had been acquired by him.

"Cissie" was the name of one of these villas, "Albert" of the other. These titles were not only picked out in shaded Gothic on the garden gates, but appeared a second time on the porches, where they followed the semicircular curve of the entrance arch in block capitals. Albert was inhabited. His tortured garden was bright with geraniums and lobelias and polished shells. His little windows were chastely swathed in Nottingham lace. Cissie was to let. Three noticeboards, belonging to Dorking agents, lolled on her fence and announced the not surprising fact. Her paths were already weedy; her pocket-handkerchief of a lawn was yellow with dandelions.

"The place is ruined!" said the ladies mechanically. "Summer Street will never be the same again."

As the carriage passed, Cissie's door opened, and a gentleman came out of her.

"Stop!" cried Mrs Honeychurch, touching the coachman with her parasol. "Here's Sir Harry. Now we shall know. Sir Harry, pull those things down at once!"

Sir Harry Otway—who need not be described—came to the carriage and said:

"Mrs Honeychurch, I meant to. I can't, I really can't turn out Miss Flack."

"Am I not always right? She ought to have gone before the contract was signed. Does she still live rent-free, as she did in her nephew's time?"

"But what can I do?" He lowered his voice. "An old lady, so very vulgar, and almost bedridden."

"Turn her out," said Cecil bravely.

Sir Harry sighed, and looked at the villas mournfully. He had had full warning of Mr Flack's intentions, and might have bought the plot before building commenced; but he was apathetic and dilatory. He had known Summer Street for so many years that he could not imagine it being spoilt. Not till Mrs Flack had laid the foundation stone, and the apparition of red and cream brick began to rise, did he take alarm. He called on Mr Flack, the local builder—a most reasonable and respectful man—who agreed that tiles would have made a more artistic roof, but pointed out that slates were cheaper. He ventured to differ, however, about the Corinthian columns which were to cling like leeches to the frames of the bow-windows, saying that, for his part, he liked to relieve the façade by a bit of decoration. Sir Harry hinted that a column, if possible, should be structural as well as decorative. Mr Flack replied that all the columns had been ordered, adding, "and all the capitals different—one with dragons in the foliage, another approaching to the Ionian style, another introducing Mrs Flack's initials—every one different." For he had read his Ruskin. He built his villas according to his desire; and not till he had inserted an immovable aunt into one of them did Sir Harry buy.

This futile and unprofitable transaction filled the knight with sadness as he leant on Mrs Honeychurch's carriage. He had failed in his duties to the countryside, and the countryside was laughing at him as well. He had spent money, and yet Summer Street was spoilt as much as ever. All he could do now was to find a desirable tenant for Cissie—someone really desirable.

"The rent is absurdly low," he told them, "and perhaps I am an easy landlord. But it is such an awkward size. It is too large for the peasant class, and too small for anyone the least like ourselves."

Cecil had been hesitating whether he should despise the villas or despise Sir Harry for despising them. The latter impulse seemed the more fruitful.

"You ought to find a tenant at once," he said maliciously. "It would be a perfect paradise for a bank-clerk."

"Exactly!" said Sir Harry excitedly. "That is exactly what I fear, Mr Vyse. It will attract the wrong type of people. The train service has improved—a fatal improvement, to my mind. And what are five miles from a station in these days of bicycles?"

"Rather a strenuous clerk it would be," said Lucy.

Cecil, who had his full share of medieval mischievousness, replied that the physique of the lower middle classes was improving at a most appalling rate. She saw that he was laughing at their harmless neighbour, and roused herself to stop him.

"Sir Harry!" she exclaimed, "I have an idea. How would you like spinsters?"

"My dear Lucy, it would be splendid. Do you know any such?"

"Yes; I met them abroad."

"Gentlewomen?" he asked tentatively.

"Yes, indeed, and at the present moment homeless. I heard from them last week. Miss Teresa and Miss Catharine Alan. I'm really not joking. They are quite the right people. Mr Beebe knows them, too. May I tell them to write to you?"

"Indeed you may!" he cried. "Here we are with the difficulty solved already. How delightful it is! Extra facilities— please tell them they shall have extra facilities, for I shall have no agents' fees. Oh, the agents! The appalling people they have sent me! One woman, when I wrote—a tactful letter, you know—asking her to explain her social position to me, replied that she would pay the rent in advance. As if one cares about that! And several references I took up were most unsatisfactory—people swindlers, or not respectable. And oh, the deceit! I have seen a good deal of the seamy side this last week. The deceit of the most promising people! My dear Lucy, the deceit!"

She nodded.

"My advice," put in Mrs Honeychurch, "is to have nothing to do with Lucy and her decayed gentlewomen at all. I know the type. Preserve me from people who have seen better days, and bring heirlooms with them that make the house smell stuffy. It's a sad thing, but I'd far rather let to someone who is going up in the world than to someone who has come down."

"I think I follow you," said Sir Harry; "but it is, as you say, a very sad thing."

"The Miss Alans aren't that!" cried Lucy.

"Yes, they are!" said Cecil. "I haven't met them, but I should say they were a highly unsuitable addition to the neighbourhood."

"Don't listen to him, Sir Harry—he's tiresome."

"It's I who am tiresome," he replied. "I oughtn't to come with my troubles to young people. But really I am so worried, and Lady Otway will only say that I cannot be too careful, which is quite true, but no real help."

"Then may I write to my Miss Alans?"

"Please!" he cried.

But his eye wavered when Mrs Honeychurch exclaimed:

"Beware! They are certain to have canaries. Sir Harry, beware of canaries: they spit the seed out through the bars of the cages, and then the mice come. Beware of women altogether. Only let to a man."

"Really—" he murmured gallantly, though he saw the wisdom of her remark.

"Men don't gossip over teacups. If they get drunk, there's an end of them—they lie down comfortably, and sleep it off. If they're vulgar, they somehow keep it to themselves. It doesn't spread so. Give me a man—of course, provided he's clean."

Sir Harry blushed. Neither he nor Cecil enjoyed these open compliments to their sex. Even the exclusion of the dirty did not leave them much distinction. He suggested that Mrs Honeychurch, if she had time, should descend from the carriage and inspect Cissie for herself. She was delighted. Nature had intended her to be poor and to live in such a house. Domestic arrangements always attracted her, especially when they were on a small scale.

Cecil pulled Lucy back as she followed her mother.

"Mrs Honeychurch," he said, "what if we two walk home and leave you?"

"Certainly!" was her cordial reply.

Sir Harry likewise seemed almost too glad to get rid of them. He beamed at them knowingly, said, "Aha! Young people, young people, young people!" and then hastened to unlock the house.

"Hopeless vulgarian!" exclaimed Cecil, almost before they were out of earshot.

"Oh, Cecil!"

"I can't help it. It would be wrong not to loathe that man."

"He isn't clever, but really he is nice."

"No, Lucy; he stands for all that is bad in country life. In London he would keep his place. He would belong to a brainless club, and his wife would give brainless dinner-parties. But down here he acts the little god with his gentility, and his patronage, and his sham aesthetics, and everyone—even your mother—is taken in."

"All that you say is quite true," said Lucy, though she felt discouraged. "I wonder whether—whether it matters so very much."

"It matters supremely. Sir Harry is the essence of that garden party. Oh, goodness, how cross I feel! How I do hope he'll get some vulgar tenant in that villa—some woman so really vulgar that he'll notice it. *Gentlefolks!* Ugh! With his bald head and retreating chin! But let's forget him."

This Lucy was glad enough to do. If Cecil disliked Sir Harry Otway and Mr Beebe, what guarantee was there that the people who really mattered to her would escape? For instance, Freddy. Freddy was neither clever nor subtle nor beautiful, and what prevented Cecil from saying, any minute, "It would be wrong not to loathe Freddy"? And what would she reply? Further than Freddy she did not go, but he gave her anxiety enough. She could only assure herself that Cecil had known Freddy some time, and that they had always got on pleasantly, except, perhaps, during the last few days, which was an accident, perhaps.

"Which way shall we go?" she asked him.

Nature—simplest of topics, she thought—was around them. Summer Street lay deep in the woods, and she had stopped where a footpath diverged from the highroad.

"Are there two ways?"

"Perhaps the road is more sensible, as we're got up smart."

"I'd rather go through the wood," said Cecil, with that subdued irritation that she had noticed in him all the afternoon. "Why is it, Lucy, that you always say the road? Do you know that you have never once been with me in the fields or the wood since we were engaged?"

"Haven't I? The wood, then," said Lucy, startled at his queerness, but pretty sure that he would explain later; it was not his habit to leave her in doubt as to his meaning.

She led the way into the whispering pines, and sure enough he did explain before they had gone a dozen yards.

"I had got an idea—I dare say wrongly—that you feel more at home with me in a room."

"A room?" she echoed, hopelessly bewildered.

"Yes. Or, at the most, in a garden, or on a road. Never in the real country like this."

"Oh, Cecil, what ever do you mean? I have never felt anything of the sort. You talk as if I was a kind of poetess sort of person."

"I don't know that you aren't. I connect you with a view—a certain type of view. Why shouldn't you connect me with a room?"

She reflected a moment, and then said, laughing:

"Do you know that you're right? I do. I must be a poetess after all. When I think of you it's always as in a room. How funny!"

To her surprise, he seemed annoyed.

"A drawing-room, pray? With no view?"

"Yes, with no view, I fancy. Why not?"

"I'd rather," he said reproachfully, "that you connected me with the open air."

She said again, "Oh, Cecil, what ever do you mean?"

As no explanation was forthcoming, she shook off the subject as too difficult for a girl, and led him further into the wood, pausing every now and then at some particularly beautiful or familiar combination of the trees. She had known the wood between Summer Street and Windy Corner ever since she could walk alone; she had played at losing Freddy in it, when Freddy was a purple-faced baby; and though she had now been to Italy it had lost none of its charm.

Presently they came to a little clearing among the pines—

another tiny green alp, solitary this time, and holding in its bosom a shallow pool.

She exclaimed, "The Sacred Lake!"

"Why you call it that?"

"I can't remember why. I suppose it comes out of some book. It's only a puddle now, but you see that stream going through it? Well, a good deal of water comes down after heavy rains, and can't get away at once, and the pool becomes quite large and beautiful. Then Freddy used to bathe there. He is very fond of it."

"And you?"

He meant, "Are you fond of it?" But she answered dreamily: "I bathed here, too, till I was found out. Then there was a row."

At another time he might have been shocked, for he had depths of prudishness within him. But now, with his momentary cult of the fresh air, he was delighted at her admirable simplicity. He looked at her as she stood by the pool's edge. She was got up smart, as she phrased it, and she reminded him of some brilliant flower that has no leaves of its own, but blooms abruptly out of a world of green.

"Who found you out?"

"Charlotte," she murmured. "She was stopping with us. Charlotte—Charlotte."

"Poor girl!"

She smiled gravely. A certain scheme, from which hitherto he had shrunk, now appeared practical.

"Lucy!"

"Yes, I suppose we ought to be going," was her reply.

"Lucy, I want to ask something of you that I have never asked before."

At the serious note in his voice she stepped frankly and kindly towards him.

"What, Cecil?"

"Hitherto never—not even that day on the lawn when you agreed to marry me—"

He became self-conscious and kept glancing round to see if they were observed. His courage had gone.

"Yes?"

"Up to now I have never kissed you."

She was as scarlet as if he had put the thing most indelicately.

"No—more you have," she stammered.

"Then I ask you—may I now?"

"Of course you may, Cecil. You might before. I can't run at you, you know."

At that supreme moment he was conscious of nothing but absurdities. Her reply was inadequate. She gave such a businesslike lift to her veil. As he approached her he found time to wish that he could recoil. As he touched her, his gold pince-nez became dislodged and was flattened between them.

Such was the embrace. He considered, with truth, that it had been a failure. Passion should believe itself irresistible. It should forget civility and consideration and all the other curses of a refined nature. Above all, it should never ask for leave where there is a right of way. Why could he not do as any labourer or navvy—nay, as any young man behind the counter would have done? He recast the scene. Lucy was standing flower-like by the water; he rushed up and took her in his arms; she rebuked him, permitted him, and revered him ever after for his manliness. For he believed that women revere men for their manliness.

They left the pool in silence, after this one salutation. He waited for her to make some remark which should show him her inmost thoughts. At last she spoke, and with fitting gravity.

"Emerson the name was, not Harris."

"What name?"

"The old man's."

"What old man?"

"That old man I told you about. The one Mr Eager was so unkind to."

He could not know that this was the most intimate conversation they had ever had.

Chapter 10
Cecil as a Humorist

The society out of which Cecil proposed to rescue Lucy was perhaps no very splendid affair, yet it was more splendid than her antecedents entitled her to. Her father, a prosperous local solicitor, had built Windy Corner as a speculation at the time the district was opening up, and, falling in love with his own creation, had ended by living there himself. Soon after his marriage, the social atmosphere began to alter. Other houses were built on the brow of that steep southern slope, and others, again, among the pine trees behind, and northward on the chalk barrier of the downs. Most of these houses were larger than Windy Corner, and were filled by people who came, not from the district, but from London, and who mistook the Honeychurches for the remnants of an indigenous aristocracy. He was inclined to be frightened, but his wife accepted the situation without either pride or humility. "I cannot think what people are doing," she would say, "but it is extremely fortunate for the children." She called everywhere; her calls were returned with enthusiasm, and by the time people found out that she was not exactly of their milieu they liked her, and it did not seem to matter. When Mr Honeychurch died, he had the satisfaction—which few honest solicitors despise—of leaving his family rooted in the best society obtainable.

The best obtainable. Certainly many of the immigrants were rather dull, and Lucy realized this more vividly since her return from Italy. Hitherto she had accepted their ideals without questioning—their kindly affluence, their inexplosive religion, their dislike of paper bags, orange-peel and broken bottles. A Radical out and out, she learned to speak with horror of Suburbia. Life, so far as she troubled to conceive it, was a circle of rich, pleasant people, with identical interests and identical foes. In this circle one thought, married and died. Outside it were poverty and vulgarity, for ever trying to enter, just as the London fog tries to enter the pinewoods, pouring through the gaps in the northern hills. But in Italy, where anyone who chooses may warm himself in equality, as in the sun, this conception of life vanished. Her senses expanded; she felt that there was no one whom she might not get to like, that social barriers were irremovable, doubtless, but not particularly high. You jump over them just as you jump into a peasant's olive-yard in the Apennines, and he is glad to see you. She returned with new eyes.

So did Cecil; but Italy had quickened Cecil, not to tolerance, but to irritation. He saw that the local society was narrow, but instead of saying, "Does this very much matter?" he rebelled, and tried to substitute for it the society he called broad. He did not realize that Lucy had consecrated her environment by the thousand little civilities that create a tenderness in time, and that though her eyes saw its defects her heart refused to despise it entirely. Nor did he realize a more important point—that if she was too great for this society she was too great for all society, and had reached the stage where personal intercourse would alone satisfy her. A rebel she was, but not of the kind he understood—a rebel who desired, not a wider dwelling-room, but equality beside the man she loved. For Italy was offering her the most priceless of all possessions—her own soul.

Playing bumble-puppy with Minnie Beebe, niece to the rector, and aged thirteen—an ancient and most honourable game, which consists in striking tennis-balls high into the air, so that they fall over the net and immoderately bounce; some hit Mrs Honeychurch; others are lost. The sentence is confused, but the better illustrates Lucy's state of mind, for she was trying to talk to Mr Beebe at the same time.

"Oh, it has been such a nuisance—first he, then they—no one knowing what they wanted, and everyone so tiresome."

"But they really are coming now," said Mr Beebe. "I wrote to Miss Teresa a few days ago—she was wondering how often the butcher called, and my reply of once a month must have impressed her favourably. They are coming. I heard from them this morning."

"I shall hate those Miss Alans!" Mrs Honeychurch cried. "Just because they're old and silly one's expected to say, 'How sweet!' I hate their 'if'-ing and 'but'-ing and 'and'-ing. And poor Lucy—serve her right—worn to a shadow."

Mr Beebe watched the shadow springing and shouting over the tennis court. Cecil was absent—one did not play bumble-puppy when he was there.

"Well, if they are coming—no, Minnie, not Saturn." Saturn was a tennis-ball whose skin was partially unsewn. When in motion his orb was encircled by a ring. "If they are coming, Sir Harry will let them move in before the twenty-ninth, and he will cross out the clause about whitewashing the ceilings, because it made them nervous, and put in the fair-wear-and-tear one.—That doesn't count. I told you not Saturn."

"Saturn's all right for bumble-puppy," cried Freddy, joining them. "Minnie, don't you listen to her."

"Saturn doesn't bounce."

"Saturn bounces enough."

"No, he doesn't."

"Well, he bounces better than the Beautiful White Devil."

"Hush, dear," said Mrs Honeychurch.

"But look at Lucy—complaining of Saturn, and all the time's got the Beautiful White Devil in her hand, ready to plug it in. That's right, Minnie, go for her—get her over the shins with the racquet—get her over the shins!"

Lucy fell; the Beautiful White Devil rolled from her hand.

Mr Beebe picked it up, and said: "The name of this ball is Vittoria Corombona, please." But his correction passed unheeded.

Freddy possessed to a high degree the power of lashing little girls to fury, and in half a minute he had transformed Minnie from a well-mannered child into a howling wilderness. Up in the house Cecil heard them, and, though he was full of entertaining news, he did not come down to impart it, in case he got hurt. He was not a coward, and bore necessary pain as well as any man. But he hated the physical violence of the young. How right he was! Sure enough it ended in a cry.

"I wish the Miss Alans could see this," observed Mr Beebe, just as Lucy, who was nursing the injured Minnie, was in turn lifted off her feet by her brother.

"Who are the Miss Alans?" Freddy panted.

"They have taken Cissie Villa."

"That wasn't the name—"

Here his foot slipped, and they all fell most agreeably onto the grass. An interval elapses.

"Wasn't what name?" asked Lucy, with her brother's head in her lap.

"Alan wasn't. The name of the people Sir Harry's let to."

"Nonsense, Freddy! You know nothing about it."

"Nonsense yourself! I've this minute seen him. He said to me: 'Ahem! Honeychurch' "—Freddy was an indifferent mimic—" 'Ahem! Ahem! I have at last procured really dee-sire-rebel tenants.' I said, 'Hooray, old boy!' and slapped him on the back."

"Exactly. The Miss Alans?"

"Rather not. More like Anderson."

"Oh, good gracious, there isn't going to be another muddle!" Mrs Honeychurch exclaimed. "Do you notice, Lucy, I'm always right? I *said* don't interfere with Cissie Villa. I'm always right. I'm quite uneasy at being always right so often."

"It's only another muddle of Freddy's. Freddy doesn't even know the name of the people he pretends have taken it instead."

"Yes, I do. I've got it. Emerson."

"What name?"

"Emerson. I'll bet you anything you like."

"What a weathercock Sir Harry is," said Lucy quietly. "I wish I had never bothered over it at all."

Then she lay on her back and gazed at the cloudless sky. Mr Beebe, whose opinion of her rose daily, whispered to his niece that *that* was the proper way to behave if any little thing went wrong.

Meanwhile the name of the new tenants had diverted Mrs Honeychurch from the contemplation of her own abilities.

"Emerson, Freddy? Do you know what Emersons they are?"

"I don't know whether they're any Emersons," retorted Freddy, who was democratic. Like his sister, and like most young people, he was naturally attracted by the idea of equality, and the undeniable fact that there are different kinds of Emersons annoyed him beyond due measure.

"I trust they are the right sort of person. All right, Lucy" —she was sitting up again—"I see you looking down your nose and thinking your mother's a snob. But there *is* a right sort and a wrong sort, and it's affectation to pretend there isn't."

"Emerson's a common enough name," Lucy remarked.

She was gazing sideways. Seated on a promontory herself, she could see the pine-clad promontories descending one beyond another into the Weald. The further one descended the garden, the more glorious was this lateral view.

"I was merely going to remark, Freddy, that I trusted they were no relations of Emerson the philosopher, a most trying man. Pray, does that satisfy you?"

"Oh yes," he grumbled. "And you will be satisfied, too, for they're friends of Cecil; so"—with elaborate irony— "you and the other county families will be able to call in perfect safety."

"*Cecil?*" exclaimed Lucy.

"Don't be rude, dear," said his mother placidly. "Lucy, don't screech. It's a new bad habit you're getting into."

"But has Cecil—"

"Friends of Cecil's," he repeated, " 'and so really dee-sire-rebel. Ahem! Honeychurch, I have just telegraphed to them.' "

She got up from the grass.

It was hard on Lucy. Mr Beebe sympathized with her very much. While she believed that her snub about the Miss Alans came from Sir Harry Otway, she had borne it like a good girl. She might well "screech" when she heard that it came partly from her lover. Mr Vyse was a tease—something worse than

a tease: he took a malicious pleasure in thwarting people.
The clergyman, knowing this, looked at Miss Honeychurch
with more than his usual kindness.

When she exclaimed, "But Cecil's Emersons—they can't
possibly be the same ones—there is that—" he did not consider that the exclamation was strange, but saw in it an
opportunity of diverting the conversation while she recovered
her composure. He diverted it as follows:

"The Emersons who were at Florence, do you mean? No,
I don't suppose it will prove to be them. It is probably a long
cry from them to friends of Mr Vyse's. Oh, Mrs Honeychurch,
the oddest people! The queerest people! For our part we
liked them, didn't we?" He appealed to Lucy. "There was a
great scene over some violets. They picked violets and filled
all the vases in the room of these very Miss Alans who have
failed to come to Cissie Villa. Poor little ladies! So shocked
and so pleased. It used to be one of Miss Catharine's great
stories. 'My dear sister loves flowers,' it began. They found
the whole room a mass of blue—vases and jugs—and the
story ends with 'So ungentlemanly and yet so beautiful. It is
all very difficult.' Yes, I always connect those Florentine
Emersons with violets."

"Fiasco's done you this time," remarked Freddy, not
seeing that his sister's face was very red. She could not recover herself. Mr Beebe saw it, and continued to divert the
conversation.

"These particular Emersons consisted of a father and a son
—the son a goodly, if not a good young man; not a fool, I
fancy, but very immature—pessimism, et cetera. Our special
joy was the father—such a sentimental darling, and people
declared he had murdered his wife."

In his normal state Mr Beebe would never have repeated
such gossip, but he was trying to shelter Lucy in her little
trouble. He repeated any rubbish that came into his head.

"Murdered his wife?" said Mrs Honeychurch. "Lucy,
don't desert us—go on playing bumble-puppy. Really, the
Pension Bertolini must have been the oddest place. That's the
second murderer I've heard of as being there. What ever

was Charlotte doing to stop? By the by, we really must ask Charlotte here some time."

Mr Beebe could recall no second murderer. He suggested that his hostess was mistaken. At the hint of opposition she warmed. She was perfectly sure that there had been a second tourist of whom the same story had been told. The name escaped her. What was the name? Oh, what was the name? She clasped her knees for the name. Something in Thackeray. She struck her matronly forehead.

Lucy asked her brother whether Cecil was in.

"Oh, don't go!" he cried, and tried to catch her by the ankles.

"I must go," she said gravely. "Don't be silly. You always overdo it when you play."

As she left them her mother's shout of "Harris!" shivered the tranquil air, and reminded her that she had told a lie and had never put it right. Such a senseless lie, too, yet it shattered her nerves, and made her connect these Emersons, friends of Cecil's, with a pair of nondescript tourists. Hitherto truth had come to her naturally. She saw that for the future she must be more vigilant, and be—absolutely truthful? Well, at all events, she must not tell lies. She hurried up the garden, still flushed with shame. A word from Cecil would soothe her, she was sure.

"Cecil!"

"Hullo!" he called, and leant out of the smoking-room window. He seemed in high spirits. "I was hoping you'd come. I heard you all bear-gardening, but there's better fun up here. I, even I, have won a great victory for the Comic Muse. George Meredith's right—the cause of Comedy and the cause of Truth are really the same; and I, even I, have found tenants for the distressful Cissie Villa. Don't be angry! Don't be angry! You'll forgive me when you hear it all."

He looked very attractive when his face was bright, and he dispelled her ridiculous forebodings at once.

"I have heard," she said. "Freddy has told us. Naughty Cecil! I suppose I must forgive you. Just think of all the trouble I took for nothing! Certainly the Miss Alans are a little tiresome, and I'd rather have nice friends of yours. But you oughtn't to tease one so."

"Friends of mine?" he laughed. "But, Lucy, the whole joke is to come! Come here." But she remained standing where she was. "Do you know where I met these desirable tenants? In the National Gallery, when I was up to see my mother last week."

"What an odd place to meet people!" she said nervously. "I don't quite understand."

"In the Umbrian Room. Absolute strangers. They were admiring Luca Signorelli—of course, quite stupidly. However, we got talking, and they refreshed me not a little. They had been to Italy."

"But, Cecil—"

He proceeded hilariously.

"In the course of conversation they said that they wanted a country cottage—the father to live there, the son to run down for weekends. I thought, 'What a chance of scoring off Sir Harry!' and I took their address and a London reference, found they weren't actual blackguards—it was great sport—and wrote to him, making out—"

"Cecil! No, it's not fair. I've probably met them before—"

He bore her down.

"Perfectly fair. Anything is fair that punishes a snob. That old man will do the neighbourhood a world of good. Sir Harry is too disgusting with his 'decayed gentlewomen'. I meant to read him a lesson some time. No, Lucy, the classes ought to mix, and before long you'll agree with me. There ought to be intermarriage—all sorts of things. I believe in democracy—"

"No, you don't," she snapped. "You don't know what the word means."

He stared at her, and felt again that she had failed to be Leonardesque. "No, you don't!" Her face was inartistic—that of a peevish virago.

"It isn't fair, Cecil. I blame you—I blame you very much indeed. You had no business to undo my work about the Miss Alans, and make me look ridiculous. You call it scoring off Sir Harry, but do you realize that it is all at my expense? I consider it most disloyal of you."

She left him.

"Temper!" he thought, raising his eyebrows.

No, it was worse than temper—snobbishness. As long as Lucy thought that his own smart friends were supplanting the Miss Alans, she had not minded. He perceived that these new tenants might be of value educationally. He would tolerate the father and draw out the son, who was silent. In the interests of the Comic Muse and of Truth, he would bring them to Windy Corner.

Chapter 11
In Mrs Vyse's
Well-Appointed Flat

The Comic Muse, though able to look after her own interests, did not disdain the assistance of Mr Vyse. His idea of bringing the Emersons to Windy Corner struck her as decidedly good, and she carried through the negotiations without a hitch. Sir Harry Otway signed the agreement, met Mr Emerson, and was duly disillusioned. The Miss Alans were duly offended, and wrote a dignified letter to Lucy, whom they held responsible for the failure. Mr Beebe planned pleasant moments for the newcomers, and told Mrs Honeychurch that Freddy must call on them as soon as they arrived. Indeed, so ample was the Muse's equipment that she permitted Mr Harris, never a very robust criminal, to droop his head, to be forgotten, and to die.

Lucy—to descend from bright heaven to earth, whereon there are shadows because there are hills—Lucy was at first plunged into despair, but settled after a little thought that it did not matter in the very least. Now that she was engaged, the Emersons would scarcely insult her, and were welcome to come into the neighbourhood. And Cecil was welcome to bring whom he would into the neighbourhood. Therefore Cecil was welcome to bring the Emersons into the neighbourhood. But, as I say, this took a little thinking, and—so illogical are girls—the event remained rather greater and rather more dreadful than it should have done. She was glad that a visit to Mrs Vyse now fell due; the tenants moved into Cissie Villa while she was safe in the London flat.

"Cecil—Cecil darling," she whispered the evening she arrived, and crept into his arms.

Cecil, too, became demonstrative. He saw that the needful fire had been kindled in Lucy. At last she longed for attention, as a woman should, and looked up to him because he was a man.

"So you do love me, little thing?" he murmured.

"Oh, Cecil, I do, I do! I don't know what I should do without you."

Several days passed. Then she had a letter from Miss Bartlett.

A coolness had sprung up between the two cousins, and they had not corresponded since they parted in August. The coolness dated from what Charlotte would call "the flight to Rome", and in Rome it had increased amazingly. For the companion who is merely uncongenial in the medieval world becomes exasperating in the classical. Charlotte, unselfish in the Forum, would have tried a sweeter temper than Lucy's, and once, in the Baths of Caracalla, they had doubted whether they could continue their tour. Lucy had said she would join the Vyses—Mrs Vyse was an acquaintance of her mother, so there was no impropriety in the plan—and Miss Bartlett had replied that she was quite used to being abandoned suddenly. Finally nothing happened; but the coolness remained, and, for Lucy, was even increased when she opened the letter and read as follows. It had been forwarded from Windy Corner.

Tunbridge Wells,
September.

Dearest Lucia,

I have news of you at last! Miss Lavish has been bicycling in your parts, but was not sure whether a call would be welcome. Puncturing her tyre near Summer Street, and it being mended while she sat very woebegone in that pretty churchyard, she saw, to her astonishment, a door open opposite and the younger Emerson man come out. He said his father had just taken the house. He *said* he did not know that you lived in the neighbourhood (?). He never suggested giving Eleanor a cup of tea. Dear Lucy, I am much worried, and I advise you to make a clean breast of his past behaviour to your mother, Freddy and Mr Vyse, who will forbid him to enter the house, etc. That was a great misfortune, and I dare say you have told them already. Mr Vyse is so sensitive. I remember how I used to get on his nerves at Rome.

I am very sorry about it all, and should not feel easy unless I warned you.

> Believe me,
> Your anxious and loving cousin,
> Charlotte.

Lucy was much annoyed, and replied as follows:

> Beauchamp Mansions, S.W.

Dear Charlotte,

Many thanks for your warning. When Mr Emerson forgot himself on the mountain, you made me promise not to tell mother, because you said she would blame you for not being always with me. I have kept that promise, and cannot possibly tell her now. I have said both to her and to Cecil that I met the Emersons at Florence, and that they are respectable people—which I *do* think—and the reason that he offered Miss Lavish no tea was probably that he had none himself. She should have tried at the Rectory. I cannot begin making a fuss at this stage. You must see that it would be too absurd. If the Emersons heard I had complained of them, they would think themselves of importance, which is exactly what they are not. I like the old father, and look forward to seeing him again. As for the son, I am sorry for *him* when we meet, rather than for myself. They are known to Cecil, who is very well, and spoke of you the other day. We expect to be married in January.

Miss Lavish cannot have told you much about me, for I am not at Windy Corner at all, but here. Please do not put "Private" outside your envelope again. No one opens my letters.

> Yours affectionately,
> L. M. Honeychurch.

Secrecy has this disadvantage: we lose the sense of proportion; we cannot tell whether our secret is important or not. Were Lucy and her cousin closeted with a great thing which would destroy Cecil's life if he discovered it, or with a little thing which he would laugh at? Miss Bartlett suggested the former. Perhaps she was right. It had become a great thing now. Left to herself, Lucy would have told her mother and her lover ingenuously, and it would have remained a little thing. "Emerson, not Harris": it was only that a few weeks ago. She tried to tell Cecil even now when they were laughing about some beautiful lady who had smitten his heart at school. But her body behaved so ridiculously that she stopped.

She and her secret stayed ten days longer in the deserted metropolis visiting the scenes they were to know so well later on. It did her no harm, Cecil thought, to learn the framework of society, while society itself was absent on the golf-links or the moors. The weather was cool, and it did her no harm. In spite of the season, Mrs Vyse managed to scrape together a dinner-party consisting entirely of the grandchildren of famous people. The food was poor, but the talk had a witty weariness that impressed the girl. One was tired of everything, it seemed. One launched into enthusiasms only to collapse gracefully, and pick oneself up amid sympathetic laughter. In this atmosphere the Pension Bertolini and Windy Corner appeared equally crude, and Lucy saw that her London career would estrange her a little from all that she had loved in the past.

The grandchildren asked her to play the piano. She played Schumann. "Now some Beethoven," called Cecil, when the querulous beauty of the music had died. She shook her head and played Schumann again. The melody rose, unprofitably magical. It broke; it was resumed broken, not marching once from the cradle to the grave. The sadness of the incomplete—the sadness that is often Life, but should never be Art—throbbed in its disjected phrases, and made the nerves of the audience throb. Not thus had she played on the little draped piano at the Bertolini, and "Too much Schumann" was not the remark that Mr Beebe had passed to himself when she returned.

When the guests were gone, and Lucy had gone to bed, Mrs Vyse paced up and down the drawing-room, discussing her little party with her son. Mrs Vyse was a nice woman, but her personality, like many another's, had been swamped by London, for it needs a strong head to live among many people. The too vast orb of her fate had crushed her; she had seen too many seasons, too many cities, too many men for her abilities, and even with Cecil she was mechanical, and behaved as if he was not one son, but, so to speak, a filial crowd.

"Make Lucy one of us," she said, looking round intelligently at the end of each sentence, and straining her lips apart until she spoke again. "Lucy is becoming wonderful—wonderful."

"Her music always was wonderful."

"Yes, but she is purging off the Honeychurch taint—most excellent Honeychurches, but you know what I mean. She is not always quoting servants, or asking one how the pudding is made."

"Italy has done it."

"Perhaps," she murmured, thinking of the museum that represented Italy to her. "It is just possible. Cecil, mind you marry her next January. She is one of us already."

"But her music!" he exclaimed. "The style of her! How she kept to Schumann when, like an idiot, I wanted Beethoven. Schumann was right for this evening. Schumann was the thing. Do you know, mother, I shall have our children educated just like Lucy. Bring them up among honest country folk for freshness, send them to Italy for subtlety, and then—not till then—let them come to London. I don't believe in these London educations—" He broke off, remembering that he had had one himself, and concluded, "At all events, not for women."

"Make her one of us," repeated Mrs Vyse, and processed to bed.

As she was dozing off, a cry—the cry of nightmare—rang from Lucy's room. Lucy could ring for the maid if she liked, but Mrs Vyse thought it kind to go herself. She found the girl sitting upright with her hand on her cheek.

"I am so sorry, Mrs Vyse—it is these dreams."

"Bad dreams?"

"Just dreams."

The elder lady smiled and kissed her, saying very distinctly: "You should have heard us talking about you, dear. He admires you more than ever. Dream of that."

Lucy returned the kiss, still covering one cheek with her hand. Mrs Vyse recessed to bed. Cecil, whom the cry had not awoke, snored. Darkness enveloped the flat.

Chapter 12
Twelfth Chapter

It was a Saturday afternoon, gay and brilliant after abundant rains, and the spirit of youth dwelt in it, though the season was now autumn. All that was gracious triumphed. As the motor-cars passed through Summer Street they raised only a little dust, and their stench was soon dispersed by the wind and replaced by the scent of the wet birches or of the pines. Mr Beebe, at leisure for life's amenities, leant over his rectory gate. Freddy leant by him, smoking a pendant pipe.

"Suppose we go and hinder those new people opposite for a little."

"M'm."

"They might amuse you."

Freddy, whom his fellow creatures never amused, suggested that the new people might be feeling a bit busy, and so on, since they had only just moved in.

"I suggested we should hinder them," said Mr Beebe. "They are worth it." Unlatching the gate, he sauntered over the triangular green to Cissie Villa. "Hullo!" he called, shouting in at the open door, through which much squalor was visible.

A grave voice replied, "Hullo!"

"I've brought someone to see you."

"I'll be down in a minute."

The passage was blocked by a wardrobe, which the removal men had failed to carry up the stairs. Mr Beebe edged round it with difficulty. The sitting-room itself was blocked with books.

"Are these people great readers?" Freddy whispered. "Are they that sort?"

"I fancy they know how to read—a rare accomplishment.

What have they got? Byron. Exactly. *A Shropshire Lad*. Never heard of it. *The Way of All Flesh*. Never heard of it. Gibbon. Hullo! Dear George reads German. Um—um—Schopenhauer, Nietzsche, and so we go on. Well, I suppose your generation knows its own business, Honeychurch."

"Mr Beebe, look at that," said Freddy in awestruck tones.

On the cornice of the wardrobe the hand of an amateur had painted this inscription: "Mistrust all enterprises that require new clothes."

"I know. Isn't it jolly? I like that. I'm certain that's the old man's doing."

"How very odd of him!"

"Surely you agree?"

But Freddy was his mother's son and felt that one ought not to go spoiling the furniture.

"Pictures!" the clergyman continued, scrambling about the room. "Giotto—they got that at Florence, I'll be bound."

"The same as Lucy's got."

"Oh, by the by, did Miss Honeychurch enjoy London?"

"She came back yesterday."

"I suppose she had a good time?"

"Yes, very," said Freddy, taking up a book. "She and Cecil are thicker than ever."

"That's good hearing."

"I wish I wasn't such a fool, Mr Beebe."

Mr Beebe ignored the remark.

"Lucy used to be nearly as stupid as I am, but it'll be very different now, mother thinks. She will read all kinds of books."

"So will you."

"Only medical books. Not books that you can talk about afterwards. Cecil is teaching Lucy Italian, and he says her playing is wonderful. There are all kinds of things in it that we have never noticed. Cecil says—"

"What on earth are those people doing upstairs? Emerson—we think we'll come another time."

George ran downstairs and pushed them into the room without speaking.

"Let me introduce Mr Honeychurch, a neighbour."

Then Freddy hurled one of the thunderbolts of youth. Perhaps he was shy, perhaps he was friendly, or perhaps he thought that George's face wanted washing. At all events, he greeted him with: "How d'ye do? Come and have a bathe."

"Oh, all right," said George, impassive.

Mr Beebe was highly entertained.

" 'How d'ye do? How d'ye do? Come and have a bathe,' " he chuckled. "That's the best conversational opening I've ever heard. But I'm afraid it will only act between men. Can you picture a lady who has been introduced to another lady by a third lady opening civilities with 'How do you do? Come and have a bathe'? And yet you will tell me that the sexes are equal."

"I tell you that they shall be," said Mr Emerson, who had been slowly descending the stairs. "Good afternoon, Mr Beebe. I tell you they shall be comrades, and George thinks the same."

"We are to raise ladies to our level?" the clergyman inquired.

"The Garden of Eden," pursued Mr Emerson, still descending, "which you place in the past, is really yet to come. We shall enter it when we no longer despise our bodies."

Mr Beebe disclaimed placing the Garden of Eden anywhere.

"In this—not in other things—we men are ahead. We despise the body less than women do. But not until we are comrades shall we enter the Garden."

"I say, what about this bathe?" murmured Freddy, appalled at the mass of philosophy that was approaching him.

"I believed in a return to Nature once. But how can we return to Nature when we have never been with her? Today, I believe that we must discover Nature. After many conquests we shall attain simplicity. It is our heritage."

"Let me introduce Mr Honeychurch, whose sister you will remember at Florence."

"How do you do? Very glad to see you, and that you are

taking George for a bathe. Very glad to hear that your sister is going to marry. Marriage is a duty. I am sure that she will be happy, for we know Mr Vyse, too. He has been most kind. He met us by chance in the National Gallery, and arranged everything about this delightful house. Though I hope I have not vexed Sir Harry Otway. I have met so few Liberal landowners, and I was anxious to compare his attitude towards the game laws with the Conservative attitude. Ah, this wind! You do well to bathe. Yours is a glorious country, Honeychurch!"

"Not a bit!" mumbled Freddy. "I must—that is to say, I have to—have the pleasure of calling on you later on, my mother says, I hope."

"*Call*, my lad? Who taught us that drawing-room twaddle? Call on your grandmother! Listen to the wind among the pines! Yours is a glorious country."

Mr Beebe came to the rescue.

"Mr Emerson, he will call, I shall call; you or your son will return our calls before ten days have elapsed. I trust that you have realized about the ten days' interval. It does not count that I helped you with the stair-eyes yesterday. It does not count that they are going to bathe this afternoon."

"Yes, go and bathe, George. Why do you dawdle talking? Bring them back to tea. Bring back some milk, cakes, honey. The change will do you good. George has been working very hard at his office. I can't believe he's well."

George bowed his head, dusty and sombre, exhaling the peculiar smell of one who has handled furniture.

"Do you really want this bathe?" Freddy asked him. "It is only a pond, don't you know. I dare say you are used to something much better."

"Yes—I have said 'Yes' already."

Mr Beebe felt bound to assist his young friend, and led the way out of the house and into the pine-woods. How glorious it was! For a little time the voice of old Mr Emerson pursued them, dispensing good wishes and philosophy. It ceased, and they only heard the fair wind blowing the bracken and the trees.

Mr Beebe, who could be silent, but who could not bear silence, was compelled to chatter, since the expedition looked like a failure, and neither of his companions would utter a word. He spoke of Florence. George attended gravely, assenting or dissenting with slight but determined gestures that were as inexplicable as the motions of the tree-tops above their heads.

"And what a coincidence that you should meet Mr Vyse! Did you realize that you would find all the Pension Bertolini down here?"

"I did not. Miss Lavish told me."

"When I was a young man I always meant to write a 'History of Coincidence'."

No enthusiasm.

"Though, as a matter of fact, coincidences are much rarer than we suppose. For example, it isn't pure coincidentality that you are here now, when one comes to reflect."

To his relief, George began to talk.

"It is. I have reflected. It is Fate. Everything is Fate. We are flung together by Fate, drawn apart by Fate—flung together, drawn apart. The twelve winds blow us—we settle nothing—"

"You have not reflected at all," rapped the clergyman. "Let me give you a useful tip, Emerson: attribute nothing to Fate. Don't say, 'I didn't do this,' for you did it, ten to one. Now I'll cross-question you. Where did you first meet Miss Honeychurch and myself?"

"Italy."

"And where did you meet Mr Vyse, who is going to marry Miss Honeychurch?"

"National Gallery."

"Looking at Italian art. There you are, and yet you talk of coincidence and Fate! You naturally seek out things Italian, and so do we and our friends. This narrows the field immeasurably, and we meet again in it."

"It is Fate that I am here," persisted George. "But you can call it Italy if it makes you less unhappy."

Mr Beebe slid away from such heavy treatment of the

subject. But he was infinitely tolerant of the young, and had no desire to snub George.

"And so for this and for other reasons my 'History of Coincidence' is still to write."

Silence.

Wishing to round off the episode, he added:

"We are all so glad that you have come."

Silence.

"Here we are!" called Freddy.

"Oh, good!" exclaimed Mr Beebe, mopping his brow.

"In there's the pond. I wish it was bigger," he added apologetically.

They climbed down a slippery bank of pine-needles. There lay the pond, set in its little alp of green—only a pond, but large enough to contain the human body, and pure enough to reflect the sky. On account of the rains, the waters had flooded the surrounding grass, which showed like a beautiful emerald path, tempting the feet towards the central pool.

"It's distinctly successful, as ponds go," said Mr Beebe. "No apologies are necessary for the pond."

George sat down where the ground was dry, and drearily unlaced his boots.

"Aren't those masses of willow-herb splendid? I love willow-herb in seed. What's the name of this aromatic plant?"

No one knew or seemed to care.

"These abrupt changes of vegetation—this little spongeous tract of water-plants, and on either side of it all the growths are tough or brittle—heather, bracken, hurts, pines. Very charming, very charming."

"Mr Beebe, aren't you bathing?" called Freddy, as he stripped himself.

Mr Beebe thought he was not.

"Water's wonderful!" cried Freddy, prancing in.

"Water's water," murmured George. Wetting his hair first—a sure sign of apathy—he followed Freddy into the divine, as indifferent as if he were a statue and the pond a pail of soapsuds. It was necessary to use his muscles. It was necessary to keep clean. Mr Beebe watched them, and watched the seeds of the willow-herb dance chorically above their heads.

"Apooshoo, apooshoo, apooshoo," went Freddy, swimming for two strokes in either direction, and then becoming involved in reeds or mud.

"Is it worth it?" asked the other, Michelangelesque on the flooded margin.

The bank broke away, and he fell into the pool before he had weighed the question properly.

"Hee—poof—I've swallowed a polly-wog. Mr Beebe, water's wonderful, water's simply ripping."

"Water's not so bad," said George, reappearing from his plunge, and sputtering at the sun.

"Water's wonderful. Mr Beebe, do."

"Apooshoo, kouf."

Mr Beebe, who was hot, and who always acquiesced where possible, looked around him. He could detect no parishioners except the pine trees, rising up steeply on all sides, and gesturing to each other against the blue. How glorious it was! The world of motor-cars and Rural Deans receded illimitably. Water, sky, evergreens, a wind—these things not even the seasons can touch, and surely they lie beyond the intrusion of man?

"I may as well wash too"; and soon his garments made a third little pile on the sward, and he too asserted the wonder of the water.

It was ordinary water, nor was there very much of it, and, as Freddy said, it reminded one of swimming in a salad. The three gentlemen rotated in the pool breast high, after the fashion of the nymphs in *Götterdämmerung*. But either because the rains had given a freshness, or because the sun was shedding a most glorious heat, or because two of the gentlemen were young in years and the third young in the spirit—for some reason or other a change came over them, and they forgot Italy and Botany and Fate. They began to play. Mr Beebe and Freddy splashed each other. A little deferentially, they splashed George. He was quiet; they feared they had offended him. Then all the forces of youth burst out. He smiled, flung himself at them, splashed them, ducked them, kicked them, muddied them, and drove them out of the pool.

"Race you round it, then," cried Freddy, and they raced in the sunshine, and George took a short cut and dirtied his shins, and had to bathe a second time. Then Mr Beebe consented to run—a memorable sight.

They ran to get dry, they bathed to get cool, they played at being Indians in the willow-herbs and in the bracken, they bathed to get clean. And all the time three little bundles lay discreetly on the sward, proclaiming:

"No. We are what matters. Without us shall no enterprise begin. To us shall all flesh turn in the end."

"A try! A try!" yelled Freddy, snatching up George's bundle and placing it beside an imaginary goalpost.

"Soccer rules," George retorted, scattering Freddy's bundle with a kick.

"Goal!"

"Goal!"

"Pass!"

"Take care my watch!" cried Mr Beebe.

Clothes flew in all directions.

"Take care my hat! No, that's enough, Freddy. Dress now. No, I say!"

But the two young men were delirious. Away they twinkled into the trees, Freddy with a clerical waistcoat under his arm, George with a wide-awake hat on his dripping hair.

"That'll do!" shouted Mr Beebe, remembering that after all he was in his own parish. Then his voice changed as if every pine tree was a Rural Dean. "Hi! Steady on! I see people coming, you fellows!"

Yells, and widening circles over the dappled earth.

"Hi! Hi! *Ladies!*"

Neither George nor Freddy was truly refined. Still, they did not hear Mr Beebe's last warning, or they would have avoided Mrs Honeychurch, Cecil and Lucy, who were walking down to call on old Mrs Butterworth. Freddy dropped the waistcoat at their feet, and dashed into some bracken. George whooped in their faces, turned, and scudded away down the path to the pond, still clad in Mr Beebe's hat.

"Gracious alive!" cried Mrs Honeychurch. "Who ever were those unfortunate people? Oh, dears, look away! And poor Mr Beebe, too! What ever has happened?"

"Come this way immediately," commanded Cecil, who always felt that he must lead women, though he knew not whither, and protect them, though he knew not against what. He led them now towards the bracken where Freddy sat concealed.

"Oh, poor Mr Beebe! Was that his waistcoat we left in the path? Cecil, Mr Beebe's waistcoat—"

"No business of ours," said Cecil, glancing at Lucy, who was all parasol and evidently "minded".

"I fancy Mr Beebe jumped back into the pond."

"This way, please, Mrs Honeychurch, this way."

They followed him up the bank, attempting the tense yet nonchalant expression that is suitable for ladies on such occasions.

"Well, *I* can't help it," said a voice close ahead, and Freddy reared a freckled face and a pair of snowy shoulders out of the fronds. "I can't be trodden on, can I?"

"Good gracious me, dear; so it's you! What miserable management! Why not have a comfortable bath at home, with hot and cold laid on?"

"Look here, mother: a fellow must wash, and a fellow's got to dry, and if another fellow—"

"Dear, no doubt you're right as usual, but you are in no position to argue. Come, Lucy." They turned. "Oh, look—don't look! Oh, poor Mr Beebe! How unfortunate again—"

For Mr Beebe was just crawling out of the pond, on whose surface garments of an intimate nature did float; while George, the world-weary George, shouted to Freddy that he had hooked a fish.

"And me, I've swallowed one," answered he of the

132

bracken. "I've swallowed a polly-wog. It wriggleth in my tummy. I shall die—Emerson, you beast, you've got on my bags."

"Hush, dears," said Mrs Honeychurch, who found it impossible to remain shocked. "And do be sure you dry yourselves thoroughly first. All these colds come of not drying thoroughly."

"Mother, do come away," said Lucy. "Oh, for goodness' sake, do come."

"Hullo!" cried George, so that again the ladies stopped.

He regarded himself as dressed. Barefoot, bare-chested, radiant and personable against the shadowy woods, he called:

"Hullo, Miss Honeychurch! Hullo!"

"Bow, Lucy; better bow. Who ever is it? I shall bow." Miss Honeychurch bowed.

That evening and all that night the water ran away. On the morrow the pool had shrunk to its old size and lost its glory. It had been a call to the blood and to the relaxed will, a passing benediction whose influence did not pass, a holiness, a spell, a momentary chalice for youth.

Chapter 13
How Miss Bartlett's Boiler
was so Tiresome

How often had Lucy rehearsed this bow, this interview! But she had always rehearsed them indoors, and with certain accessories, which surely we have a right to assume. Who could foretell that she and George would meet in the rout of a civilization, amidst an army of coats and collars and boots that lay wounded over the sunlit earth? She had imagined a young Mr Emerson, who might be shy or morbid or indifferent or furtively impudent. She was prepared for all of these. But she had never imagined one who would be happy and greet her with the shout of the morning star.

Indoors herself, partaking of tea with old Mrs Butterworth, she reflected that it is impossible to foretell the future with any degree of accuracy, that it is impossible to rehearse life. A fault in the scenery, a face in the audience, an irruption of the audience onto the stage, and all our carefully planned gestures mean nothing, or mean too much. "I will bow," she had thought. "I will not shake hands with him. That will be just the proper thing." She had bowed—but to whom? To gods, to heroes, to the nonsense of schoolgirls! She had bowed across the rubbish that cumbers the world.

So ran her thoughts, while her faculties were busy with Cecil. It was another of those dreadful engagement calls. Mrs Butterworth had wanted to see him, and he did not want to be seen. He did not want to hear about hydrangeas, why they change their colour at the seaside. He did not want to join the C.O.S. When cross he was always elaborate, and made long, clever answers where "Yes" or "No" would have done. Lucy soothed him and tinkered at the conversation in a way that promised well for their married peace. No one is perfect, and surely it is wiser to discover the imperfections before wedlock. Miss Bartlett, in deed, though not in word, had taught the girl that this our life contains nothing satisfactory. Lucy, though she disliked the teacher, regarded the teaching as profound, and applied it to her lover.

"Lucy," said her mother, when they got home, "is anything the matter with Cecil?"

The question was ominous: up till now Mrs Honeychurch had behaved with charity and restraint.

"No, I don't think so, mother; Cecil's all right."

"Perhaps he's tired."

Lucy compromised: perhaps Cecil was a little tired.

"Because otherwise"—she pulled out her bonnet-pins with gathering displeasure—"because otherwise I cannot account for him."

"I do think Mrs Butterworth is rather tiresome, if you mean that."

"Cecil has told you to think so. You were devoted to her as a little girl, and nothing will describe her goodness to you through the typhoid fever. No—it is just the same thing everywhere."

"Let me just put your bonnet away, may I?"

"Surely he could answer her civilly for one half-hour?"

"Cecil has a very high standard for people," faltered Lucy, seeing trouble ahead. "It's part of his ideals—it is really that that makes him sometimes seem—"

"Oh, rubbish! If high ideals make a young man rude, the sooner he gets rid of them the better," said Mrs Honeychurch, handing her the bonnet.

"Now mother! I've seen you cross with Mrs Butterworth yourself!"

"Not in that way. At times I could wring her neck. But not in that way. No. It is the same with Cecil all over."

"By the by—I never told you. I had a letter from Charlotte while I was away in London."

This attempt to divert the conversation was too puerile, and Mrs Honeychurch resented it.

"Since Cecil came back from London, nothing appears to please him. Whenever I speak he winces—I see him, Lucy; it is useless to contradict me. No doubt I am neither artistic nor literary nor intellectual nor musical, but I cannot help the drawing-room furniture: your father bought it and we must put up with it, will Cecil kindly remember."

"I—I see what you mean, and certainly Cecil oughtn't to. But he does not mean to be uncivil—he once explained—it is the *things* that upset him—he is easily upset by ugly things—he is not uncivil to *people*."

"Is it a thing or a person when Freddy sings?"

"You can't expect a really musical person to enjoy comic songs as we do."

"Then why didn't he leave the room? Why sit wriggling and sneering and spoiling everyone's pleasure?"

"We mustn't be unjust to people," faltered Lucy. Something had enfeebled her, and the case for Cecil, which she had mastered so perfectly in London, would not come forth in an effective form. The two civilizations had clashed—Cecil had hinted that they might—and she was dazzled and bewildered, as though the radiance that lies behind all civilization had blinded her eyes. Good taste and bad taste were only catchwords, garments of diverse cut; and music itself dissolved to a whisper through pine trees, where the song is not distinguishable from the comic song.

She remained in much embarrassment, while Mrs Honeychurch changed her frock for dinner; and every now and then she said a word, and made things no better. There was no concealing the fact—Cecil had meant to be supercilious, and he had succeeded. And Lucy—she knew not why—wished that the trouble could have come at any other time.

"Go and dress, dear; you'll be late."

"All right, mother—"

"Don't say 'All right' and stop. Go."

She obeyed, but loitered disconsolately at the landing window. It faced north, so there was little view, and no view of the sky. Now, as in the winter, the pine trees hung close to her eyes. One connected the landing window with depression. No definite problem menaced her, but she sighed to herself,

"Oh dear, what shall I do, what shall I do?" It seemed to her that everyone else was behaving very badly. And she ought not to have mentioned Miss Bartlett's letter. She must be more careful: her mother was rather inquisitive, and might have asked what it was about. Oh dear, what should she do?—and then Freddy came bounding upstairs, and joined the ranks of the ill-behaved.

"I say, those are topping people."

"My dear baby, how tiresome you've been! You had no business to take them bathing in the Sacred Lake; it's much too public. It was all right for you, but most awkward for everyone else. Do be more careful. You forget the place is growing half suburban."

"I say, is anything on tomorrow week?"

"Not that I know of."

"Then I want to ask the Emersons up to Sunday tennis."

"Oh, I wouldn't do that, Freddy, I wouldn't do that with all this muddle."

"What's wrong with the court? They won't mind a bump or two, and I've ordered new balls."

"I meant *it's* better not. I really mean it."

He seized her by the elbows and humorously danced her up and down the passage. She pretended not to mind, but she could have screamed with temper. Cecil glanced at them as he proceeded to his toilet and they impeded Mary with her brood of hot-water cans. Then Mrs Honeychurch opened her door and said: "Lucy, what a noise you're making! I have something to say to you. Did you say you had had a letter from Charlotte?" and Freddy ran away.

"Yes. I really can't stop. I must dress too."

"How's Charlotte?"

"All right."

"Lucy!"

The unfortunate girl returned.

"You've a bad habit of hurrying away in the middle of one's sentences. Did Charlotte mention her boiler?"

"Her *what*?"

"Don't you remember that her boiler was to be had out

in October, and her bath cistern cleaned out, and all kinds of terrible to-doing?"

"I can't remember all Charlotte's worries," said Lucy bitterly. "I shall have enough of my own, now that you are not pleased with Cecil."

Mrs Honeychurch might have flamed out. She did not. She said: "Come here, old lady—thank you for putting away my bonnet—kiss me." And, though nothing is perfect, Lucy felt for the moment that her mother and Windy Corner and the Weald in the declining sun were perfect.

So the grittiness went out of life. It generally did at Windy Corner. At the last minute, when the social machine was clogged hopelessly, one member or other of the family poured in a drop of oil. Cecil despised their methods—perhaps rightly. At all events, they were not his own.

Dinner was at half past seven. Freddy gabbled a grace, and they drew up their heavy chairs and fell to. Fortunately, the men were hungry. Nothing untoward occurred until the pudding. Then Freddy said:

"Lucy, what's Emerson like?"

"I saw him in Florence," said Lucy, hoping that this would pass for a reply.

"Is he the clever sort, or is he a decent chap?"

"Ask Cecil; it is Cecil who brought him here."

"He is the clever sort, like myself," said Cecil.

Freddy looked at him doubtfully.

"How well did you know them at the Bertolini?" asked Mrs Honeychurch.

"Oh, very slightly. I mean, Charlotte knew them even less than I did."

"Oh, that reminds me—you never told me what Charlotte said in her letter."

"One thing and another," said Lucy, wondering whether she would get through the meal without a lie. "Among other things, that an awful friend of hers had been bicycling through Summer Street, wondered if she'd come up and see us, and mercifully didn't."

"Lucy, I do call the way you talk unkind."

"She was a novelist," said Lucy craftily. The remark was a happy one, for nothing roused Mrs Honeychurch so much as literature in the hands of females. She would abandon every topic to inveigh against those women who (instead of minding their houses and their children) seek notoriety by print. Her attitude was: "If books must be written, let them be written by men"; and she developed it at great length, while Cecil yawned and Freddy played at "This year, next year, now, never" with his plum-stones, and Lucy artfully fed the flames of her mother's wrath. But soon the conflagration died down, and the ghosts began to gather in the darkness. There were too many ghosts about. The original ghost —that touch of lips on her cheek—had surely been laid long ago; it could be nothing to her that a man had kissed her on a mountain once. But it had begotten a spectral family— Mr Harris, Miss Bartlett's letter, Mr Beebe's memories of violets—and one or other of these was bound to haunt her before Cecil's very eyes. It was Miss Bartlett who returned now, and with appalling vividness.

"I have been thinking, Lucy, of that letter of Charlotte's. How is she?"

"I tore the thing up."

"Didn't she say how she was? How does she sound? Cheerful?"

"Oh yes, I suppose so—no—not very cheerful, I suppose."

"Then, depend upon it, it is the boiler. I know myself how water preys upon one's mind. I would rather anything else —even a misfortune with the Meat."

Cecil laid his hand over his eyes.

"So would I," asserted Freddy, backing his mother up— backing up the spirit of her remark rather than its substance.

"And I have been thinking," she added rather nervously, "surely we could squeeze Charlotte in here next week, and give her a nice holiday while the plumbers at Tunbridge Wells finish. I have not seen poor Charlotte for so long."

It was more than her nerves could stand. And yet she could not protest violently after her mother's goodness to her upstairs.

"Mother, no!" she pleaded. "It's impossible. We can't have Charlotte on the top of the other things; we're squeezed to death as it is. Freddy's got a friend coming Tuesday, there's Cecil, and you've promised to take in Minnie Beebe because of the diphtheria scare. It simply can't be done."

"Nonsense! It can."

"If Minnie sleeps in the bath. Not otherwise."

"Minnie can sleep with you."

"I won't have her."

"Then, if you're so selfish, Mr Floyd must share a room with Freddy."

"Miss Bartlett, Miss Bartlett, Miss Bartlett," moaned Cecil, again laying his hand over his eyes.

"It's impossible," repeated Lucy. "I don't want to make difficulties, but it really isn't fair on the maids to fill up the house so."

Alas!

"The truth is, dear, you don't like Charlotte."

"No, I don't. And no more does Cecil. She gets on our nerves. You haven't seen her lately, and don't realize how tiresome she can be, though so good. So please, mother, don't worry us this last summer; but spoil us by not asking her to come."

"Hear, hear!" said Cecil.

Mrs Honeychurch, with more gravity than usual, and with more feeling than she usually permitted herself, replied: "This isn't very kind of you two. You have each other and all these woods to walk in, so full of beautiful things; and poor Charlotte has only the water turned off and plumbers. You are young, dears, and however clever young people are, and however many books they read, they will never guess what it feels like to grow old."

Cecil crumbled his bread.

"I must say Cousin Charlotte was very kind to me that year I called on my bike," put in Freddy. "She thanked me for coming till I felt like such a fool, and fussed round no end to get an egg boiled for my tea just right."

"I know, dear. She is kind to everyone, and yet Lucy

makes this difficulty when we try to give her some little return."

But Lucy hardened her heart. It was no good being kind to Miss Bartlett. She had tried herself too often and too recently. One might lay up treasure in heaven by the attempt, but one enriched neither Miss Bartlett nor anyone else upon earth. She was reduced to saying: "I can't help it, mother. I don't like Charlotte. I admit it's horrid of me."

"From your own account, you told her as much."

"Well, she would leave Florence so stupidly. She flurried—"

The ghosts were returning; they filled Italy, they were even usurping the places she had known as a child. The Sacred Lake would never be the same again, and, on Sunday week, something would even happen to Windy Corner. How would she fight against ghosts? For a moment the visible world faded away, and memories and emotions alone seemed real.

"I suppose Miss Bartlett must come, since she boils eggs so well," said Cecil, who was in rather a happier frame of mind, thanks to the admirable cooking.

"I didn't mean the egg was *well* boiled," corrected Freddy, "because in point of fact she forgot to take it off, and as a matter of fact I don't care for eggs. I only meant how jolly kind she seemed."

Cecil frowned again. Oh, these Honeychurches! Eggs, boilers, hydrangeas, maids—of such were their lives compact. "May me and Lucy get down from our chairs?" he asked, with scarcely veiled insolence. "We don't want no dessert."

Chapter 14
How Lucy Faced the
External Situation Bravely

Of course Miss Bartlett accepted. And, equally of course, she felt sure that she would prove a nuisance, and begged to be given an inferior spare room—something with no view, anything. Her love to Lucy. And, equally of course, George Emerson could come to tennis on the Sunday week.

Lucy faced the situation bravely, though, like most of us, she only faced the situation that encompassed her. She never gazed inwards. If at times strange images rose from the depths, she put them down to nerves. When Cecil brought the Emersons to Summer Street, it had upset her nerves. Charlotte would burnish up past foolishness, and this might upset her nerves. She was nervous at night. When she talked to George—they met again almost immediately at the rectory—his voice moved her deeply, and she wished to remain near him. How dreadful if she really wished to remain near him! Of course, the wish was due to nerves, which love to play such perverse tricks upon us. Once she had suffered from "things that came out of nothing and meant she didn't know what". Now Cecil had explained psychology to her one wet afternoon, and all the troubles of youth in an unknown world could be dismissed.

It is obvious enough for the reader to conclude, "She loves young Emerson." A reader in Lucy's place would not find it obvious. Life is easy to chronicle, but bewildering to practise, and we welcome "nerves" or any other shibboleth that will cloak our personal desire. She loved Cecil; George made her nervous; will the reader explain to her that the phrases should have been reversed?

But the external situation—she will face that bravely.

The meeting at the rectory had passed off well enough.

Standing between Mr Beebe and Cecil, she had made a few temperate allusions to Italy, and George had replied. She was anxious to show that she was not shy, and was glad that he did not seem shy either.

"A nice fellow," said Mr Beebe afterwards. "He will work off his crudities in time. I rather mistrust young men who slip into life gracefully."

Lucy said: "He seems in better spirits. He laughs more."

"Yes," replied the clergyman. "He is waking up."

That was all. But, as the week wore on, more of her defences fell, and she entertained an image that had physical beauty.

In spite of the clearest directions, Miss Bartlett contrived to bungle her arrival. She was due at the South-Eastern station at Dorking, whither Mrs Honeychurch drove to meet her. She arrived at the London and Brighton station, and had to hire a cab up. No one was at home except Freddy and his friend, who had to stop their tennis and to entertain her for a solid hour. Cecil and Lucy turned up at four o'clock, and these, with little Minnie Beebe, made a somewhat lugubrious sextet upon the upper lawn for tea.

"I shall never forgive myself," said Miss Bartlett, who kept on rising from her seat, and had to be begged by the united company to remain. "I have upset everything. Bursting in on young people! But I insist on paying for my cab up. Grant me that, at any rate."

"Our visitors never do such a dreadful thing," said Lucy, while her brother, in whose memory the boiled egg had already grown unsubstantial, exclaimed in irritable tones: "Just what I've been trying to convince Cousin Charlotte of, Lucy, for the last half-hour."

"I do not feel myself an ordinary visitor," said Miss Bartlett, and looked at her frayed gloves.

"All right, if you'd really rather. Five shillings, and I gave a bob to the driver."

Miss Bartlett looked in her purse. Only sovereigns and pennies. Could anyone give her change? Freddy had half a quid and his friend had four half-crowns. Miss Bartlett accepted their moneys and then said: "But who am I to give the sovereign to?"

"Let's leave it all till mother comes back," suggested Lucy.

"No, dear; your mother may take quite a long drive now that she is not hampered with me. We all have our little foibles, and mine is the promptly settling of accounts."

Here Freddy's friend, Mr Floyd, made the one remark of his that need be quoted: he offered to toss Freddy for Miss Bartlett's quid. A solution seemed in sight, and even Cecil, who had been ostentatiously drinking his tea at the view, felt the eternal attraction of Chance, and turned round.

But this did not do, either.

"Please—please—I know I am a sad spoil-sport, but it would make me wretched. I should practically be robbing the one who lost."

"Freddy owes me fifteen shillings," interposed Cecil. "So it will work out right if you give the pound to me."

"Fifteen shillings," said Miss Bartlett dubiously. "How is that, Mr Vyse?"

"Because, don't you see, Freddy paid your cab. Give me the pound, and we shall avoid this deplorable gambling."

Miss Bartlett, who was poor at figures, became bewildered and rendered up the sovereign, amidst the suppressed gurgles of the other youths. For a moment Cecil was happy. He was playing at nonsense among his peers. Then he glanced at Lucy, in whose face petty anxieties had marred the smiles. In January he would rescue his Leonardo from this stupefying twaddle.

"But I don't see that!" exclaimed Minnie Beebe, who had narrowly watched the iniquitous transaction. "I don't see why Mr Vyse is to have the quid."

"Because of the fifteen shillings and the five," they said solemnly. "Fifteen shillings and five shillings make one pound, you see."

"But I don't see—"

They tried to stifle her with cake.

"No, thank you. I'm done. I don't see why—Freddy, don't poke me. Miss Honeychurch, your brother's hurting me. Ow! What about Mr Floyd's ten shillings? Ow! No, I don't see and I never shall see why Miss What's-her-name shouldn't pay that bob for the driver."

"I had forgotten the driver," said Miss Bartlett, reddening. "Thank you, dear, for reminding me. A shilling, was it? Can anyone give me change for half a crown?"

"I'll get it," said the young hostess, rising with decision. "Cecil, give me that sovereign. No—give me up that sovereign. I'll get Euphemia to change it, and we'll start the whole thing again from the beginning."

"Lucy—Lucy—what a nuisance I am!" protested Miss Bartlett, and followed her across the lawn. Lucy tripped ahead, simulating hilarity. When they were out of earshot, Miss Bartlett stopped her wails and said quite briskly: "Have you told him about him yet?"

"No, I haven't," replied Lucy, and then could have bitten her tongue for understanding so quickly what her cousin meant. "Let me see—a sovereign's worth of silver."

She escaped into the kitchen. Miss Bartlett's sudden transitions were too uncanny. It sometimes seemed as if she planned every word she spoke or caused to be spoken; as if all this worry about cabs and change had been a ruse to surprise the soul.

"No, I haven't told Cecil or anyone," she remarked, when she returned. "I promised you I shouldn't. Here is your money—all shillings, except two half-crowns. Would you count it? You can settle your debt nicely now."

Miss Bartlett was in the drawing-room, gazing at the photograph of St John ascending, who had been framed.

"How dreadful!" she murmured, "how more than dreadful, if Mr Vyse should come to hear of it from some other source."

"Oh no, Charlotte," said the girl, entering the battle, "George Emerson is all right, and what other source is there?"

Miss Bartlett considered. "For instance, the driver. I saw

him looking through the bushes at you. I remember he had a violet between his teeth."

Lucy shuddered a little. "We shall get the silly affair on our nerves if we aren't careful. How could a Florentine cab-driver ever get hold of Cecil?"

"We must think of every possibility."

"Oh, it's all right."

"Or perhaps old Mr Emerson knows. In fact, he is certain to know."

"I don't care if he does. I was grateful to you for your letter, but even if the news does get round, I think I can trust Cecil to laugh at it."

"To contradict it?"

"No, to laugh at it." But she knew in her heart that she could not trust him, for he desired her untouched.

"Very well, dear, you know best. Perhaps gentlemen are different to what they were when I was young. Ladies are certainly different."

"Now, Charlotte!" She struck at her playfully. "You kind, anxious thing! What *would* you have me do? First you say, 'Don't tell'; and then you say, 'Tell.' Which is it to be? Quick!"

Miss Bartlett sighed. "I am no match for you in conversation, dearest. I blush when I think how I interfered at Florence, and you so well able to look after yourself, and so much cleverer in all ways than I am. You will never forgive me."

"Shall we go out, then? They will smash all the china if we don't."

For the air rang with the shrieks of Minnie, who was being scalped with a teaspoon.

"Dear, one moment—we may not have this chance for a chat again. Have you seen the young one yet?"

"Yes, I have."

"What happened?"

"We met at the rectory."

"What line is he taking up?"

"No line. He talked about Italy, like any other person. It

is really all right. What advantage would he get from being a cad, to put it bluntly? I do wish I could make you see it my way. He really won't be any nuisance, Charlotte."

"Once a cad, always a cad. That is my poor opinion."

Lucy paused. "Cecil said one day—and I thought it so profound—that there are two kinds of cads—the conscious and the subsconcious." She paused again, to be sure of doing justice to Cecil's profundity. Through the window she saw Cecil himself, turning over the pages of a novel. It was a new one from Smith's library. Her mother must have returned from the station.

"Once a cad, always a cad," droned Miss Bartlett.

"What I mean by subconscious is that Mr Emerson lost his head. I fell into all those violets, and he was silly and surprised. I don't think we ought to blame him very much. It makes such a difference when you see a person with beautiful things behind him unexpectedly. It really does; it makes an enormous difference, and he lost his head; he doesn't admire me, or any of that nonsense, one straw. Freddy rather likes him, and has asked him up here on Sunday, so you can judge for yourself. He has improved: he doesn't always look as if he is going to burst into tears. He is a clerk in the General Manager's office at one of the big railways—not a porter!— and runs down to his father for week-ends. Papa was to do with journalism, but is rheumatic and has retired. There! Now for the garden." She took hold of her guest by the arm. "Suppose we don't talk about this silly Italian business any more. We want you to have a nice restful visit at Windy Corner, with no worriting."

Lucy thought this rather a good speech. The reader may have detected an unfortunate slip in it. Whether Miss Bartlett detected the slip one cannot say, for it is impossible to penetrate into the minds of elderly people. She might have spoken further, but they were interrupted by the entrance of her hostess. Explanations took place, and in the midst of them Lucy escaped, the images throbbing a little more vividly in her brain.

Chapter 15
The Disaster Within

The Sunday after Miss Bartlett's arrival was a glorious day, like most of the days of that year. In the Weald, autumn approached, breaking up the green monotony of summer, touching the parks with the gray bloom of mist, the beech trees with russet, the oak trees with gold. Up on the heights, battalions of black pines witnessed the change, themselves unchangeable. Either country was spanned by a cloudless sky, and in either arose the tinkle of church bells.

The garden of Windy Corner was deserted except for a red book, which lay sunning itself upon the gravel path. From the house came incoherent sounds, as of females preparing for worship. "The men say they won't go"—"Well, I don't blame them"—"Minnie says, need she go?"—"Tell her, no nonsense"—"Anne! Mary! Hook me behind!"—"Dearest Lucia, may I trespass upon you for a pin?" For Miss Bartlett had announced that she at all events was one for church.

The sun rose higher on its journey, guided, not by Phaethon, but by Apollo, competent, unswerving, divine. Its rays fell on the ladies whenever they advanced towards the bedroom windows; on Mr Beebe down at Summer Street as he smiled over a letter from Miss Catharine Alan; on George Emerson cleaning his father's boots; and lastly, to complete the catalogue of memorable things, on the red book mentioned above. The ladies move, Mr Beebe moves, George moves, and movement may engender shadow. But this book lies motionless, to be caressed all the morning by the sun and to raise its covers slightly, as though acknowledging the caress.

Presently Lucy steps out of the drawing-room window. Her new cerise dress has been a failure, and makes her look tawdry and wan. At her throat is a garnet brooch, on her finger a ring set with rubies—an engagement-ring. Her eyes are bent to the Weald. She frowns a little—not in anger, but as a brave child frowns when he is trying not to cry. In all that expanse no human eye is looking at her, and she may frown unrebuked and measure the spaces that yet survive between Apollo and the western hills.

"Lucy! Lucy! What's that book? Who's been taking a book out of the shelf and leaving it about to spoil?"

"It's only the library book that Cecil's been reading."

"But pick it up, and don't stand idling there like a flamingo."

Lucy picked up the book and glanced at the title listlessly: *Under a Loggia*. She no longer read novels herself, devoting all her spare time to solid literature in the hope of catching Cecil up. It was dreadful how little she knew, and even when she thought she knew a thing, like the Italian painters, she found she had forgotten it. Only this morning she had confused Francesco Francia with Piero della Francesca, and Cecil had said, "What! You aren't forgetting your Italy already?" And this too had lent anxiety to her eyes when she saluted the dear view and the dear garden in the foreground, and above them, scarce conceivable elsewhere, the dear sun.

"Lucy—have you a sixpence for Minnie and a shilling for yourself?"

She hastened in to her mother, who was rapidly working herself into a Sunday fluster.

"It's a special collection—I forget what for. I do beg, no vulgar clinking in the plate with halfpennies; see that Minnie has a nice bright sixpence. Where is the child? Minnie! That book's all warped. (Gracious, how plain you look!) Put it under the atlas to press. Minnie!"

"Oh, Mrs Honeychurch—" from the upper regions.

"Minnie, don't be late. Here comes the horse"—it was always the horse, never the carriage. "Where's Charlotte? Run up and hurry her. Why is she so long? She had nothing to do. She never brings anything but blouses. Poor Charlotte —how I do detest blouses! Minnie!"

Paganism is infectious—more infectious than diphtheria

or piety—and the Rector's niece was taken to church protesting. As usual, she didn't see why. Why shouldn't she sit in the sun with the young men? The young men, who had now appeared, mocked her with ungenerous words. Mrs Honeychurch defended orthodoxy, and in the midst of the confusion Miss Bartlett, dressed in the very height of the fashion, came strolling down the stairs.

"Dear Marian, I am very sorry, but I have no small change—nothing but sovereigns and half-crowns. Could anyone give me—"

"Yes, easily. Jump in. Gracious me, how smart you look. What a lovely frock! You put us all to shame."

"If I did not wear my best rags and tatters now, when should I wear them?" said Miss Bartlett reproachfully. She got into the victoria and placed herself with her back to the horse. The necessary uproar ensued, and then they drove off.

"Goodbye! Be good!" called out Cecil.

Lucy bit her lip, for the tone was sneering. On the subject of "church and so on" they had had rather an unsatisfactory conversation. He had said that people ought to overhaul themselves, and she did not want to overhaul herself; she did not know how it was done. Honest orthodoxy Cecil respected, but he always assumed that honesty is the result of a spiritual crisis; he could not imagine it as a natural birthright, that might grow heavenward like the flowers. All that he said on this subject pained her, though he exuded tolerance from every pore; somehow the Emersons were different.

She saw the Emersons after church. There was a line of carriages down the road, and the Honeychurch vehicle happened to be opposite Cissie Villa. To save time, they walked over the green to it, and found father and son smoking in the garden.

"Introduce me," said her mother. "Unless the young man considers that he knows me already."

He probably did; but Lucy ignored the Sacred Lake and introduced them formally. Old Mr Emerson claimed her with much warmth, and said how glad he was that she was going to be married. She said yes, she was glad too; and then, as Miss Bartlett and Minnie were lingering behind with Mr Beebe, she turned the conversation to a less disturbing topic, and asked him how he liked his new house.

"Very much," he replied, but there was a note of offence in his voice; she had never known him offended before. He added: "We find, though, that the Miss Alans were coming, and that we have turned them out. Women mind such a thing. I am very much upset about it."

"I believe that there was some misunderstanding," said Mrs Honeychurch uneasily.

"Our landlord was told that we should be a different type of person," said George, who seemed disposed to carry the matter further. "He thought we should be artistic. He is disappointed."

"And I wonder whether we ought to write to the Miss Alans and offer to give it up. What do you think?" He appealed to Lucy.

"Oh, stop now you have come," said Lucy lightly. She must avoid censuring Cecil. For it was on Cecil that the little episode turned, though his name was never mentioned.

"So George says. He says that the Miss Alans must go to the wall. Yet it does seem so unkind."

"There is only a certain amount of kindness in the world," said George, watching the sunlight flash on the panels of the passing carriages.

"Yes!" exclaimed Mrs Honeychurch. "That's exactly what I say. Why all this twiddling and twaddling over two Miss Alans?"

"There is a certain amount of kindness, just as there is a certain amount of light," he continued in measured tones. "We cast a shadow on something wherever we stand, and it is no good moving from place to place to save things; because the shadow always follows. Choose a place where you won't do harm—yes, choose a place where you won't do very much harm, and stand in it for all you are worth, facing the sunshine."

"Oh, Mr Emerson, I see you're clever!"

"Eh—?"

"I see you're going to be clever. I hope you didn't go behaving like that to poor Freddy."

George's eyes laughed, and Lucy suspected that he and her mother would get on rather well.

"No, I didn't," he said. "He behaved that way to me. It is his philosophy. Only he starts life with it; and I have tried the Note of Interrogation first."

"What *do* you mean? No, never mind what you mean. Don't explain. He looks forward to seeing you this afternoon. Do you play tennis? Do you mind tennis on Sunday—?"

"George mind tennis on Sunday! George, after his education, distinguish between Sunday—"

"Very well, George doesn't mind tennis on Sunday. No more do I. That's settled. Mr Emerson, if you could come with your son we should be so pleased."

He thanked her, but the walk sounded rather far: he could only potter about in these days.

She turned to George: "And then he wants to give up his house to the Miss Alans."

"I know," said George, and put his arm round his father's neck. The kindness that Mr Beebe and Lucy had always known to exist in him came out suddenly, like sunlight touching a vast landscape—a touch of the morning sun? She remembered that in all his perversities he had never spoken against affection.

Miss Bartlett approached.

"You know our cousin, Miss Bartlett," said Mrs Honeychurch pleasantly. "You met her with my daughter in Florence."

"Yes, indeed!" said the old man, and made as if he would come out of the garden to greet the lady. Miss Bartlett promptly got into the victoria. Thus entrenched, she emitted a formal bow. It was the Pension Bertolini again, the dining-table with the decanters of water and wine. It was the old, old battle of the room with the view.

George did not respond to the bow. Like any boy, he blushed and was ashamed; he knew that the chaperon remembered. He said: "I—I'll come up to tennis if I can manage it," and went into the house. Perhaps anything that he did would have pleased Lucy, but his awkwardness went straight to her heart: men were not gods after all, but as human and as clumsy as girls; even men might suffer from unexplained desires, and need help. To one of her upbringing, and of her destination, the weakness of men was a truth unfamiliar, but she had surmised it at Florence, when George threw her photographs into the river Arno.

"George, don't go," cried his father, who thought it a great treat for people if his son would talk to them. "George has been in such good spirits today, and I am sure he will end by coming up this afternoon."

Lucy caught her cousin's eye. Something in its mute appeal made her reckless. "Yes," she said, raising her voice, "I do hope he will." Then she went to the carriage and murmured, "The old man hasn't been told; I knew it was all right." Mrs Honeychurch followed her, and they drove away.

Satisfactory that Mr Emerson had not been told of the Florence escapade; yet Lucy's spirits should not have leapt up as if she had sighted the ramparts of heaven. Satisfactory; yet surely she greeted it with disproportionate joy. All the way home the horses' hoofs sang a tune to her: "He has not told, he has not told." Her brain expanded the melody: "He has not told his father—to whom he tells all things. It was not an exploit. He did not laugh at me when I had gone." She raised her hand to her cheek. "He does not love me. No. How terrible if he did! But he has not told. He will not tell."

She longed to shout the words: "It is all right. It's a secret between us two for ever. Cecil will never hear." She was even glad that Miss Bartlett had made her promise secrecy, that last dark evening at Florence, when they had knelt packing in his room. The secret, big or little, was guarded. Only three English people knew of it in the world.

Thus she interpreted her joy. She greeted Cecil with unusual radiance, because she felt so safe. As he helped her out of the carriage, she said:

"The Emersons have been so nice. George Emerson has improved enormously."

"Oh, how are my protégés?" asked Cecil, who took no real interest in them, and had long since forgotten his resolution to bring them to Windy Corner for educational purposes.

"Protégés!" she exclaimed with some warmth.

For the only relationship which Cecil conceived was feudal: that of protector and protected. He had no glimpse of the comradeship after which the girl's soul yearned.

"You shall see for yourself how your protégés are. George Emerson is coming up this afternoon. He is a most interesting man to talk to. Only don't—" She nearly said, "Don't protect him." But the bell was ringing for lunch, and, as often happened, Cecil had paid no great attention to her remarks. Charm, not argument, was to be her forte.

Lunch was a cheerful meal. Generally Lucy was depressed at meals. Someone had to be soothed—either Cecil or Miss Bartlett or a Being not visible to the mortal eye—a Being who whispered to her soul: "It will not last, this cheerfulness. In January you must go to London to entertain the grandchildren of celebrated men." But today she felt she had received a guarantee. Her mother would always sit there, her brother here. The sun, though it had moved a little since the morning, would never be hidden behind the western hills. After luncheon they asked her to play. She had seen Gluck's *Armide* that year, and played from memory the music of the enchanted garden—the music to which Renaud approaches, beneath the light of an eternal dawn, the music that never gains, never wanes, but ripples for ever like the tideless seas of fairyland. Such music is not for the piano, and her audience began to get restive, and Cecil, sharing the discontent, called out: "Now play us the other garden—the one in *Parsifal*."

She closed the instrument.

"Not very dutiful," said her mother's voice.

Fearing that she had offended Cecil, she turned quickly round. There George was. He had crept in without interrupting her.

"Oh, I had no idea!" she exclaimed, getting very red; and

then, without a word of greeting, she reopened the piano. Cecil should have the *Parsifal*, and anything else that he liked.

"Our performer has changed her mind," said Miss Bartlett, perhaps implying, "She will play the music to Mr Emerson." Lucy did not know what to do, nor even what she wanted to do. She played a few bars of the Flower Maidens' song very badly, and then she stopped.

"I vote tennis," said Freddy, disgusted at the scrappy entertainment.

"Yes, so do I." Once more she closed the unfortunate piano. "I vote you have a men's four."

"All right."

"Not for me, thank you," said Cecil. "I will not spoil the set." He never realized that it may be an act of kindness in a bad player to make up a fourth.

"Oh, come along, Cecil. I'm bad, Floyd's rotten, and so I dare say's Emerson."

George corrected him: "I am not bad."

One looked down one's nose at this. "Then certainly I won't play," said Cecil, while Miss Bartlett, under the impression that she was snubbing George, added: "I agree with you, Mr Vyse. You had much better not play. Much better not."

Minnie, rushing in where Cecil feared to tread, announced that she would play. "I shall miss every ball anyway, so what does it matter?" But Sunday intervened and stamped heavily upon the kind suggestion.

"Then it will have to be Lucy," said Mrs Honeychurch; "you must fall back on Lucy. There is no other way out of it. Lucy, go and change your frock."

Lucy's Sabbath was generally of this amphibious nature. She kept it without hypocrisy in the morning, and broke it without reluctance in the afternoon. As she changed her frock, she wondered whether Cecil was sneering at her; really she must overhaul herself and settle everything up before she married him.

Mr Floyd was her partner. She liked music, but how

much better tennis seemed. How much better to run about in comfortable clothes than to sit at the piano and feel girt under the arms. Once more music appeared to her the employment of a child. George served, and surprised her by his anxiety to win. She remembered how he had sighed among the tombs at Santa Croce because things wouldn't fit; how after the death of that obscure Italian he had leant over the parapet by the Arno and said to her: "I shall want to live, I tell you." He wanted to live now, to win at tennis, to stand for all he was worth in the sun—in the sun which had begun to decline and was shining in her eyes; and he did win.

Ah, how beautiful the Weald looked! The hills stood out above its radiance, as Fiesole stands above the Tuscan plain, and the South Downs, if one chose, were the mountains of Carrara. She might be forgetting her Italy, but she was noticing more things in her England. One could play a new game with the view, and try to find in its innumerable folds some town or village that would do for Florence. Ah, how beautiful the Weald looked!

But now Cecil claimed her. He chanced to be in a lucid critical mood, and would not sympathize with exaltation. He had been rather a nuisance all through the tennis, for the novel that he was reading was so bad that he was obliged to read it aloud to others. He would stroll round the precincts of the court and call out: "I say, listen to this, Lucy. Three split infinitives." "Dreadful!" said Lucy, and missed her stroke. When they had finished their set, he still went on reading; there was some murder scene, and really everyone must listen to it. Freddy and Mr Floyd were obliged to hunt for a lost ball in the laurels, but the other two acquiesced.

"The scene is laid in Florence."

"What fun, Cecil! Read away. Come, Mr Emerson, sit down after all your energy." She had "forgiven" George, as she put it, and she made a point of being pleasant to him.

He jumped over the net and sat down at her feet, asking: "You—and are you tired?"

"Of course I'm not!"

"Do you mind being beaten?"

She was going to answer "No" when it struck her that she did mind, so she answered "Yes". She added merrily: "I don't see *you're* such a splendid player, though. The light was behind you, and it was in my eyes."

"I never said I was."

"Why, you did!"

"You didn't attend."

"You said—oh, don't go in for accuracy at this house. We all exaggerate, and we get very angry with people who don't."

"The scene is laid in Florence," repeated Cecil, with an upward note.

Lucy recollected herself.

" 'Sunset. Leonora was speeding—' "

Lucy interrupted. "Leonora? Is Leonora the heroine? Who's the book by?"

"Joseph Emery Prank. 'Sunset. Leonora was speeding across the square. Pray the saints she might not arrive too late. Sunset—the sunset of Italy. Under Orcagna's Loggia— the Loggia de' Lanzi, as we sometimes call it now—' "

Lucy burst into laughter. " 'Joseph Emery Prank' indeed! Why, it's Miss Lavish! It's Miss Lavish's novel, and she's publishing it under somebody else's name."

"Who may Miss Lavish be?"

"Oh, a dreadful person—Mr Emerson, you remember Miss Lavish?" Excited by her pleasant afternoon, she clapped her hands.

George looked up. "Of course I do. I saw her the day I arrived at Summer Street. It was she who told me that you lived here."

"Weren't you pleased?" She meant—"to see Miss Lavish," but when he bent down to the grass without replying it struck her that she could mean something else. She watched his head, which was almost resting against her knee, and she thought that the ears were reddening. "No wonder the novel's bad," she added. "I never liked Miss Lavish. But I suppose one ought to read it as one's met her."

"All modern books are bad," said Cecil, who was annoyed

157

at her inattention, and vented his annoyance on literature. "Everyone writes for money in these days."

"Oh, Cecil—!"

"It is so. I will inflict Joseph Emery Prank on you no longer."

Cecil, this afternoon, seemed such a twittering sparrow. The ups and downs in his voice were noticeable, but they did not affect her. She had dwelt amongst melody and movement, and her nerves refused to answer to the clang of his. Leaving him to be annoyed, she gazed at the black head again. She did not want to stroke it, but she saw herself wanting to stroke it; the sensation was curious.

"How do you like this view of ours, Mr Emerson?"

"I never notice much difference in views."

"What do you mean?"

"Because they are all alike. Because all that matters in them is distance and air."

"H'm!" said Cecil, uncertain whether the remark was striking or not.

"My father"—he looked up at her (and he was a little flushed)—"says that there is only one perfect view—the view of the sky straight over our heads, and that all these views on earth are but bungled copies of it."

"I expect your father has been reading Dante," said Cecil, fingering the novel, which alone permitted him to lead the conversation.

"He told us another day that views are really crowds —crowds of trees and houses and hills—and are bound to resemble each other, like human crowds—and that the power they have over us is something supernatural, for the same reason."

Lucy's lips parted.

"For a crowd is more than the people who make it up. Something gets added to it—no one knows how—just as something has got added to those hills."

He pointed with his racquet to the South Downs.

"What a splendid idea!" she murmured. "I shall enjoy hearing your father talk again. I'm so sorry he's not so well."

"No, he isn't well."

"There's an absurd account of a view in this book," said Cecil.

"Also that men fall into two classes—those who forget views and those who remember them, even in small rooms."

"Mr Emerson, have you any brothers or sisters?"

"None. Why?"

"You spoke of 'us'."

"My mother, I was meaning."

Cecil closed the novel with a bang.

"Oh, Cecil—how you make me jump!"

"I will inflict Joseph Emery Prank on you no longer."

"I can just remember us all three going into the country for the day and seeing as far as Hindhead. It is the first thing that I remember."

Cecil got up: the man was ill-bred—he hadn't put on his coat after tennis—he didn't do. He would have strolled away if Lucy had not stopped him.

"Cecil, do read the thing about the view."

"Not while Mr Emerson is here to entertain us."

"No—read away. I think nothing's funnier than to hear silly things read out loud. If Mr Emerson thinks us frivolous, he can go."

This struck Cecil as subtle, and pleased him. It put their visitor in the position of a prig. Somewhat mollified, he sat down again.

"Mr Emerson, go and find tennis balls." She opened the book. Cecil must have his reading and anything else that he liked. But her attention wandered to George's mother, who—according to Mr Eager—had been murdered in the sight of God and—according to her son—had seen as far as Hindhead.

"Am I really to go?" asked George.

"No, of course not really," she answered.

"Chapter two," said Cecil, yawning. "Find me chapter two, if it isn't bothering you."

Chapter two was found, and she glanced at its opening sentences.

She thought she had gone mad.

"Here—hand me the book."

She heard her voice saying: "It isn't worth reading—it's too silly to read—I never saw such rubbish—it oughtn't to be allowed to be printed."

He took the book from her.

" 'Leonora,' " he read, " 'sat pensive and alone. Before her lay the rich champaign of Tuscany, dotted over with many a smiling village. The season was spring.' "

Miss Lavish knew, somehow, and had printed the past in draggled prose, for Cecil to read and for George to hear.

" 'A golden haze,' " he read. He read: " 'Afar off the towers of Florence, while the bank on which she sat was carpeted with violets. All unobserved, Antonio stole up behind her—' "

Lest Cecil should see her face she turned to George, and she saw his face.

He read: " 'There came from his lips no wordy protestation such as formal lovers use. No eloquence was his, nor did he suffer from the lack of it. He simply enfolded her in his manly arms.' "

There was a silence.

"This isn't the passage I wanted," he informed them. "There is another much funnier, further on." He turned over the leaves.

"Should we go in to tea?" said Lucy, whose voice remained steady.

She led the way up the garden, Cecil following her, George last. She thought a disaster was averted. But when they entered the shrubbery it came. The book, as if it had not worked mischief enough, had been forgotten, and Cecil must go back for it; and George, who loved passionately, must blunder against her in the narrow path.

"No—" she gasped, and, for the second time, was kissed by him.

As if no more was possible, he slipped back; Cecil rejoined her; they reached the upper lawn alone.

Chapter 16
Lying to George

But Lucy had developed since the spring. That is to say, she was now better able to stifle the emotions of which the conventions and the world disapprove. Though the danger was greater, she was not shaken by deep sobs. She said to Cecil, "I am not coming in to tea—tell mother—I must write some letters," and went up to her room. There she prepared for action. Love felt and returned, love which our bodies exact and our hearts have transfigured, love which is the most real thing that we shall ever meet, reappeared now as the world's enemy, and she must stifle it.

She sent for Miss Bartlett.

The contest lay not between love and duty. Perhaps there never is such a contest. It lay between the real and the pretended, and Lucy's first aim was to defeat herself. As her brain clouded over, as the memory of the views grew dim and the words of the book died away, she returned to her old shibboleth of nerves. She "conquered her breakdown". Tampering with the truth, she forgot that the truth had ever been. Remembering that she was engaged to Cecil, she compelled herself to confused remembrances of George: he was nothing to her; he never had been anything; he had behaved abominably; she had never encouraged him. The armour of falsehood is subtly wrought out of darkness, and hides a man not only from others, but from his own soul. In a few moments Lucy was equipped for battle.

"Something too awful has happened," she began, as soon as her cousin arrived. "Do you know anything about Miss Lavish's novel?"

Miss Bartlett looked surprised, and said that she had not read the book, nor known that it was published; Eleanor was a reticent woman at heart.

"There is a scene in it. The hero and heroine make love. Do you know about that?"

"Dear——?"

"Do you know about it, please?" she repeated. "They are on a hillside, and Florence is in the distance."

"My good Lucia, I am all at sea. I know nothing about it whatever."

"There are violets. I cannot believe it is a coincidence. Charlotte, Charlotte, how *could* you have told her? I have thought before speaking: it *must* be you."

"Told her what?" she asked, with growing agitation.

"About that dreadful afternoon in February."

Miss Bartlett was genuinely moved. "Oh, Lucy, dearest girl—she hasn't put that in her book?"

Lucy nodded.

"Not so that one could recognize it?"

"Yes."

"Then never—never—never more shall Eleanor Lavish be friend of mine."

"So you did tell?"

"I did just happen—when I had tea with her at Rome—in the course of conversation—"

"But, Charlotte—what about the promise you gave me when we were packing? Why did you tell Miss Lavish, when you wouldn't even let me tell mother?"

"I will never forgive Eleanor. She has betrayed my confidence."

"Why did you tell her, though? This is a most serious thing."

Why does anyone tell anything? The question is eternal, and it was not surprising that Miss Bartlett should only sigh faintly in response. She had done wrong—she admitted it; she only hoped that she had not done harm; she had told Eleanor in the strictest confidence.

Lucy stamped with irritation.

"Cecil happened to read out the passage aloud to me and to Mr Emerson; it upset Mr Emerson, and he insulted me again. Behind Cecil's back. Ugh! Is it possible that men are such brutes? Behind Cecil's back as we were walking up the garden."

Miss Bartlett burst into self-accusations and regrets.

"What is to be done now? Can you tell me?"

"Oh, Lucy—I shall never forgive myself, never to my dying day. Fancy if your prospects—"

"I know," said Lucy, wincing at the word. "I see now why you wanted me to tell Cecil, and what you meant by 'some other source'. You knew that you had told Miss Lavish, and that she was not reliable."

It was Miss Bartlett's turn to wince.

"However," said the girl, despising her cousin's shiftiness, "what's done's done. You have put me in a most awkward position. How am I to get out of it?"

Miss Bartlett could not think. The days of her energy were over. She was a visitor, not a chaperon, and a discredited visitor at that. She stood with clasped hands while the girl worked herself into the necessary rage.

"He must—that man must have such a setting down that he won't forget. And who's to give it him? I can't tell mother now—owing to you. Nor Cecil, Charlotte, owing to you. I am caught up every way. I think I shall go mad. I have no one to help me. That's why I've sent for you. What's wanted is a man with a whip."

Miss Bartlett agreed: one wanted a man with a whip.

"Yes—but it's no good agreeing. What's to be *done*? We women go maundering on. What *does* a girl do when she comes across a cad?"

"I always said he was a cad, dear. Give me credit for that, at all events. From the very first moment—when he said his father was having a bath."

"Oh, bother the credit and who's been right or wrong! We've both made a muddle of it. George Emerson is still down the garden there, and is he to be left unpunished, or isn't he? I want to know."

Miss Bartlett was absolutely helpless. Her own exposure had unnerved her, and thoughts were colliding painfully in her brain. She moved feebly to the window, and tried to detect the cad's white flannels among the laurels.

"You were ready enough at the Bertolini when you rushed me off to Rome. Can't you speak again to him now?"

"Willingly would I move heaven and earth—"

"I want something more definite," said Lucy contemptuously. "Will you speak to him? It is the least you can do, surely, considering it all happened because you broke your word."

"Never again shall Eleanor Lavish be friend of mine."

Really, Charlotte was outdoing herself.

"Yes or no, please; yes or no."

"It is the kind of thing that only a gentleman can settle."

George Emerson was coming up the garden with a tennis-ball in his hand.

"Very well," said Lucy, with an angry gesture. "No one will help me. I will speak to him myself." And immediately she realized that this was what her cousin had intended all along.

"Hullo, Emerson!" called Freddy from below. "Found the lost ball? Good man! Want any tea?" And there was an irruption from the house onto the terrace.

"Oh, Lucy, but that is brave of you! I admire you—"

They had gathered round George, who beckoned, she felt, over the rubbish, the sloppy thoughts, the furtive yearnings that were beginning to cumber her soul. Her anger faded at the sight of him. Ah! The Emersons were fine people in their way. She had to subdue a rush in her blood before saying:

"Freddy has taken him into the dining-room. The others are going down the garden. Come. Let us get this over quickly. Come. I want you in the room, of course."

"Lucy, do you mind doing it?"

"How can you ask such a ridiculous question?"

"Poor Lucy—" She stretched out her hand. "I seem to bring nothing but misfortune wherever I go." Lucy nodded. She remembered their last evening at Florence—the packing, the candle, the shadow of Miss Bartlett's toque on the door.

She was not to be trapped by pathos a second time. Eluding her cousin's caress, she led the way downstairs.

"Try the jam," Freddy was saying. "The jam's jolly good."

George, looking big and dishevelled, was pacing up and down the dining-room. As she entered he stopped, and said:

"No—nothing to eat."

"You go down to the others," said Lucy; "Charlotte and I will give Mr Emerson all he wants. Where's mother?"

"She's started on her Sunday writing. She's in the drawing-room."

"That's all right. You go away."

He went off singing.

Lucy sat down at the table. Miss Bartlett, who was thoroughly frightened, took up a book and pretended to read.

She would not be drawn into an elaborate speech. She just said: "I can't have it, Mr Emerson. I cannot even talk to you. Go out of this house, and never come into it again as long as I live here"—flushing as she spoke, and pointing to the door. "I hate a row. Go, please."

"What—"

"No discussion."

"But I can't—"

She shook her head. "Go, please. I do not want to call in Mr Vyse."

"You don't mean," he said, absolutely ignoring Miss Bartlett—"you don't mean that you are going to marry that man?"

The line was unexpected.

She shrugged her shoulders, as if his vulgarity wearied her. "You are merely ridiculous," she said quietly.

Then his words rose gravely over hers: "You cannot live with Vyse. He's only for an acquaintance. He is for society and cultivated talk. He should know no one intimately, least of all a woman."

It was a new light on Cecil's character.

"Have you ever talked to Vyse without feeling tired?"

"I can scarcely discuss—"

"No, but have you ever? He is the sort who are all right so long as they keep to things—books, pictures—but kill when they come to people. That's why I'll speak out through all this muddle even now. It's shocking enough to lose you in any case, but generally a man must deny himself joy, and I would have held back if your Cecil had been a different person. I would never have let myself go. But I saw him first in the National Gallery, when he winced because my father mispronounced the names of great painters. Then he brings us here, and we find it is to play some silly trick on a kind neighbour. That is the man all over—playing tricks on people, on the most sacred form of life that he can find. Next, I meet you together, and find him protecting and teaching you and your mother to be shocked, when it was for *you* to settle whether you were shocked or no. Cecil all over again. He daren't let a woman decide. He's the type who's kept Europe back for a thousand years. Every moment of his life he's forming you, telling you what's charming or amusing or ladylike, telling you what a man thinks womanly; and you, you of all women, listen to his voice instead of to your own. So it was at the rectory, when I met you both again; so it has been the whole of this afternoon. Therefore—not 'therefore I kissed you', because the book made me do that, and I wish to goodness I had more self-control. I'm not ashamed. I don't apologize. But it has frightened you, and you may not have noticed that I love you. Or would you have told me to go, and dealt with a tremendous thing so lightly? But therefore—therefore I settled to fight him."

Lucy thought of a very good remark.

"You say Mr Vyse wants me to listen to him, Mr Emerson. Pardon me for suggesting that you have caught the habit."

And he took the shoddy reproof and touched it into immortality. He said:

"Yes, I have," and sank down as if suddenly weary. "I'm the same kind of brute at bottom. This desire to govern a woman—it lies very deep, and men and women must fight it together before they shall enter the Garden. But I do love you—surely in a better way than he does." He thought. "Yes

—really in a better way. I want you to have your own thoughts even when I hold you in my arms." He stretched them towards her. "Lucy, be quick—there's no time for us to talk now—come to me as you came in the spring, and afterwards I will be gentle and explain. I have cared for you since that man died. I cannot live without you. 'No good,' I thought: 'she is marrying someone else'; but I meet you again when all the world is glorious water and sun. As you came through the wood I saw that nothing else mattered. I called. I wanted to live and have my chance of joy."

"And Mr Vyse?" said Lucy, who kept commendably calm. "Does he not matter? That I love Cecil and shall be his wife shortly? A detail of no importance, I suppose?"

But he stretched his arms over the table towards her.

"May I ask what you intend to gain by this exhibition?"

He said: "It is our last chance. I shall do all that I can." And, as if he had done all else, he turned to Miss Bartlett, who sat like some portent against the skies of evening. "You wouldn't stop us this second time if you understood," he said. "I have been into the dark, and I am going back into it, unless you will try to understand."

Her long, narrow head drove backwards and forwards, as though demolishing some invisible obstacle. She did not answer.

"It is being young," he said quietly, picking up his racquet from the floor and preparing to go. "It is being certain that Lucy cares for me really. It is that love and youth matter intellectually."

In silence the two women watched him. His last remark, they knew, was nonsense, but was he going after it or not? Would not he, the cad, the charlatan, attempt a more dramatic finish? No. He was apparently content. He left them, carefully closing the front door; and when they looked through the hall window they saw him go up the drive and begin to climb the slopes of withered fern behind the house. Their tongues were loosed, and they burst into stealthy rejoicings.

"Oh, Lucia—come back here—oh, what an awful man!"

Lucy had no reaction—at least, not yet. "Well, he amuses me," she said. "Either I'm mad, or else he is, and I'm inclined to think it's the latter. One more fuss through with you, Charlotte. Many thanks. I think, though, that this is the last. My admirer will hardly trouble me again."

And Miss Bartlett, too, essayed the roguish:

"Well, it isn't everyone who could boast such a conquest, dearest, is it? Oh, one oughtn't to laugh, really. It might have been very serious. But you were so sensible and brave—so unlike the girls of my day."

"Let's go down to them."

But, once in the open air, she paused. Some emotion—pity, terror, love, but the emotion was strong—seized her, and she was aware of autumn. Summer was ending, and the evening brought her odours of decay, the more pathetic because they were reminiscent of spring. That something or other mattered intellectually? A leaf, violently agitated, danced past her, while other leaves lay motionless. That the earth was hastening to re-enter darkness, and the shadows of those trees to creep over Windy Corner?

"Hullo, Lucy! There's still light enough for another set, if you two'll hurry."

"Mr Emerson has had to go."

"What a nuisance! That spoils the four. I say, Cecil, do play, do, there's a good chap. It's Floyd's last day. Do play tennis with us, just this once."

Cecil's voice came: "My dear Freddy, I am no athlete. As you well remarked this very morning, 'There are some chaps who are no good for anything but books'; I plead guilty to being such a chap, and will not inflict myself on you."

The scales fell from Lucy's eyes. How had she stood Cecil for a moment? He was absolutely intolerable, and the same evening she broke her engagement off.

Chapter 17
Lying to Cecil

He was bewildered. He had nothing to say. He was not even angry, but stood, with a glass of whiskey between his hands, trying to think what had led her to such a conclusion.

She had chosen the moment before bed, when, in accordance with their bourgeois habit, she always dispensed drinks to the men. Freddy and Mr Floyd were sure to retire with their glasses, while Cecil invariably lingered, sipping at his while she locked up the sideboard.

"I am very sorry about it," she said; "I have carefully thought things over. We are too different. I must ask you to release me, and try to forget that there ever was such a foolish girl."

It was a suitable speech, but she was more angry than sorry, and her voice showed it.

"Different—how—how—"

"I haven't had a really good education, for one thing," she continued, still on her knees by the sideboard. "My Italian trip came too late, and I am forgetting all that I learned there. I shall never be able to talk to your friends, or behave as a wife of yours should."

"I don't understand you. You aren't like yourself. You're tired, Lucy."

"Tired!" she retorted, kindling at once. "That is exactly like you. You always think women don't mean what they say."

"Well, you sound tired, as if something has worried you."

"What if I do? It doesn't prevent me from realizing the truth. I can't marry you, and you will thank me for saying so some day."

"You had that bad headache yesterday—all right"—for she had exclaimed indignantly—"I see it's much more than

169

headaches. But give me a moment's time." He closed his eyes. "You must excuse me if I say stupid things, but my brain has gone to pieces. Part of it lives three minutes back, when I was sure that you loved me, and the other part—I find it difficult—I am likely to say the wrong thing."

It struck her that he was not behaving so badly, and her irritation increased. She again desired a struggle, not a discussion. To bring on the crisis, she said:

"There are days when one sees clearly, and this is one of them. Things must come to a breaking-point some time, and it happens to be today. If you want to know, quite a little thing decided me to speak to you—when you wouldn't play tennis with Freddy."

"I never do play tennis," said Cecil, painfully bewildered; "I never could play. I don't understand a word you say."

"You can play well enough to make up a four. I thought it abominably selfish of you."

"No, I can't—well, never mind the tennis. Why couldn't you—couldn't you have warned me if you felt anything wrong? You talked of our wedding at lunch—at least, you let me talk."

"I knew you wouldn't understand," said Lucy quite crossly. "I might have known there would have been these dreadful explanations. Of course, it isn't the tennis—that was only the last straw to all I have been feeling for weeks. Surely it was better not to speak till I felt certain." She developed this position. "Often before, I have wondered if I was fitted for your wife—for instance, in London; and are you fitted to be my husband? I don't think so. You don't like Freddy, nor my mother. There was always a lot against our engagement, Cecil, but all our relations seemed pleased, and we met so often, and it was no good mentioning it until—well, until all things came to a point. They have today. I see clearly. I must speak. That's all."

"I cannot think you were right," said Cecil gently. "I cannot tell why, but though all that you say sounds true, I feel that you are not treating me fairly. It's all too horrible."

"What's the good of a scene?"

"No good. But surely I have a right to hear a little more."

He put down his glass and opened the window. From where she knelt, jangling her keys, she could see a slit of darkness, and, peering into it, as if it would tell him that "little more", his long, thoughtful face.

"Don't open the window; and you'd better draw the curtain, too; Freddy or anyone might be outside." He obeyed. "I really think we had better go to bed, if you don't mind. I shall only say things that will make me unhappy afterwards. As you say, it is all too horrible, and it is no good talking."

But to Cecil, now that he was about to lose her, she seemed each moment more desirable. He looked at her, instead of through her, for the first time since they were engaged. From a Leonardo she had become a living woman, with mysteries and forces of her own, with qualities that even eluded art. His brain recovered from the shock, and, in a burst of genuine devotion, he cried: "But I love you, and I did think you loved me!"

"I did not," she said. "I thought I did at first. I am sorry, and ought to have refused you this last time, too."

He began to walk up and down the room, and she grew more and more vexed at his dignified behaviour. She had counted on his being petty. It would have made things easier for her. By a cruel irony she was drawing out all that was finest in his disposition.

"You don't love me, evidently. I dare say you are right not to. But it would hurt a little less if I knew why."

"Because"—a phrase came to her, and she accepted it— "you're the sort who can't know anyone intimately."

A horrified look came into his eyes.

"I don't mean exactly that. But you will question me, though I beg you not to, and I must say something. It is that, more or less. When we were only acquaintances, you let me be myself, but now you're always protecting me." Her voice swelled. "I won't be protected. I will choose for myself what is ladylike and right. To shield me is an insult. Can't I be trusted to face the truth but I must get it second-hand

through you? A woman's place! You despise my mother—
I know you do—because she's conventional and bothers
over puddings; but, oh goodness!"—she rose to her feet—
"conventional, Cecil, you're that, for you may understand
beautiful things, but you don't know how to use them; and
you wrap yourself up in art and books and music, and would
try to wrap up me. I won't be stifled, not by the most glorious
music, for people are more glorious, and you hide them from
me. That's why I break off my engagement. You were all
right as long as you kept to things, but when you came to
people—" She stopped.

There was a pause. Then Cecil said with great emotion:
"It is true."

"True on the whole," she corrected, full of some vague
shame.

"True, every word. It is a revelation. It is—I."

"Anyhow, those are my reasons for not being your wife."

He repeated: " 'The sort that can know no one intimately.'
It is true. I fell to pieces the very first day we were engaged.
I behaved like a cad to Beebe and to your brother. You are
even greater than I thought." She withdrew a step. "I'm not
going to worry you. You are far too good to me. I shall never
forget your insight; and, dear, I only blame you for this: you
might have warned me in the early stages, before you felt you
wouldn't marry me, and so have given me a chance to
improve. I have never known you till this evening. I have
just used you as a peg for my silly notions of what a woman
should be. But this evening you are a different person: new
thoughts—even a new voice—"

"What do you mean by a new voice?" she asked, seized
with incontrollable anger.

"I mean that a new person seems speaking through you,"
said he.

Then she lost her balance. She cried: "If you think I am
in love with someone else, you are very much mistaken."

"Of course I don't think that. You are not that kind,
Lucy."

"Oh yes, you do think it. It's your old idea, the idea that has kept Europe back—I mean the idea that women are always thinking of men. If a girl breaks off her engagement, everyone says: 'Oh, she had someone else in her mind; she hopes to get someone else.' It's disgusting, brutal! As if a girl can't break it off for the sake of freedom."

He answered reverently: "I may have said that in the past. I shall never say it again. You have taught me better."

She began to redden, and pretended to examine the windows again.

"Of course, there is no question of 'someone else' in this, no 'jilting' or any such nauseous stupidity. I beg your pardon most humbly if my words suggested that there was. I only meant that there was a force in you that I hadn't known of up till now."

"All right, Cecil, that will do. Don't apologize to me. It was my mistake."

"It is a question between ideals, yours and mine—pure abstract ideals, and yours are the nobler. I was bound up in the old vicious notions, and all the time you were splendid and new." His voice broke. "I must actually thank you for what you have done—for showing me what I really am. Solemnly, I thank you for showing me a true woman. Will you shake hands?"

"Of course I will," said Lucy, twisting up her other hand in the curtains. "Good night, Cecil. Goodbye. That's all right. I'm sorry about it. Thank you very much for your gentleness."

"Let me light your candle, shall I?"

They went into the hall.

"Thank you. Good night again. God bless you, Lucy!"

"Goodbye, Cecil."

She watched him steal upstairs, while the shadows from the banisters passed over his face like the beat of wings. On the landing he paused, strong in his renunciation, and gave her a look of memorable beauty. For all his culture, Cecil was an ascetic at heart, and nothing in his love became him like the leaving of it.

She could never marry. In the tumult of her soul, that

stood firm. Cecil believed in her; she must some day believe in herself. She must be one of the women whom she had praised so eloquently, who care for liberty and not for men; she must forget that George loved her, that George had been thinking through her and gained her this honourable release, that George had gone away into—what was it?—the darkness.

She put out the lamp.

It did not do to think, nor, for the matter of that, to feel. She gave up trying to understand herself, and joined the vast armies of the benighted, who follow neither the heart nor the brain, and march to their destiny by catchwords. The armies are full of pleasant and pious folk. But they have yielded to the only enemy that matters—the enemy within. They have sinned against passion and truth, and vain will be their strife after virtue. As the years pass, they are censured. Their pleasantry and their piety show cracks, their wit becomes cynicism, their unselfishness hypocrisy; they feel and produce discomfort wherever they go. They have sinned against Eros and against Pallas Athene, and not by any heavenly intervention, but by the ordinary course of nature, those allied deities will be avenged.

Lucy entered this army when she pretended to George that she did not love him, and pretended to Cecil that she loved no one. The night received her, as it had received Miss Bartlett thirty years before.

Chapter 18
Lying to Mr Beebe,
Mrs Honeychurch,
Freddy and the Servants

Windy Corner lay, not on the summit of the ridge, but a few hundred feet down the southern slope, at the springing of one of the great buttresses that supported the hill. On either side of it was a shallow ravine, filled with ferns and pine trees, and down the ravine on the left ran the highway into the Weald.

Whenever Mr Beebe crossed the ridge and caught sight of these noble dispositions of the earth, and, poised in the middle of them, Windy Corner—he laughed. The situation was so glorious, the house so commonplace, not to say impertinent. The late Mr Honeychurch had affected the cube, because it gave him the most accommodation for his money, and the only addition made by his widow had been a small turret, shaped like a rhinoceros' horn, where she could sit in wet weather and watch the carts going up and down the road. So impertinent—and yet the house "did", for it was the home of people who loved their surroundings honestly. Other houses in the neighbourhood had been built by expensive architects, over others their inmates had fidgeted sedulously, yet all these suggested the accidental, the temporary; while Windy Corner seemed as inevitable as an ugliness of Nature's own creation. One might laugh at the house, but one never shuddered.

Mr Beebe was bicycling over this Monday afternoon with a little piece of gossip. He had heard from the Miss Alans. These admirable ladies, since they could not go to Cissie Villa, had changed their plans. They were going to Greece instead.

"Since Florence did my poor sister so much good," wrote Miss Catharine, "we do not see why we should not try Athens this winter. Of course, Athens is a plunge, and the doctor has ordered her special digestive bread; but, after all, we can take that with us, and it is only getting first into a steamer and then into a train. But is there an English Church?" And the letter went on to say: "I do not expect we shall go any further than Athens, but if you knew of a really comfortable pension at Constantinople, we should be so grateful."

Lucy would enjoy this letter, and the smile with which Mr Beebe greeted Windy Corner was partly for her. She would see the fun of it, and some of its beauty, for she must see some beauty. Though she was hopeless about pictures, and though she dressed so unevenly—oh, that cerise frock yesterday at church!—she must see some beauty in life, or she could not play the piano as she did. He had a theory that musicians are incredibly complex, and know far less than other artists what they want and what they are; that they puzzle themselves as well as their friends; that their psychology is a modern development, and has not yet been understood. This theory, had he known it, had possibly just been illustrated by facts. Ignorant of the events of yesterday, he was only riding over to get some tea, to see his niece, and to observe whether Miss Honeychurch saw anything beautiful in the desire of two old ladies to visit Athens.

A carriage was drawn up outside Windy Corner, and just as he caught sight of the house it started, bowled up the drive, and stopped abruptly when it reached the main road. Therefore it must be the horse, who always expected people to walk up the hill in case they tired him. The door opened obediently, and two men emerged, whom Mr Beebe recognized as Cecil and Freddy. They were an odd couple to go driving; but he saw a trunk beside the coachman's legs. Cecil, who wore a bowler, must be going away, while Freddy— a cap—was seeing him to the station. They walked rapidly, taking the short cuts, and reached the summit while the carriage was still pursuing the windings of the road.

They shook hands with the clergyman, but did not speak. "So you're off for a minute, Mr Vyse?" he asked.

Cecil said, "Yes," while Freddy edged away.

"I was coming to show you this delightful letter from those

friends of Miss Honeychurch's." He quoted from it. "Isn't it wonderful? Isn't it Romance? Most certainly they will go to Constantinople. They are taken in a snare that cannot fail. They will end by going round the world."

Cecil listened civilly, and said he was sure that Lucy would be amused and interested.

"Isn't Romance capricious! I never notice it in you young people; you do nothing but play lawn-tennis, and say that Romance is dead, while the Miss Alans are struggling with all the weapons of propriety against the terrible thing. 'A really comfortable pension at Constantinople!' So they call it out of decency, but in their hearts they want a pension with magic windows opening on the foam of perilous seas in fairylands forlorn! No ordinary view will content the Miss Alans. They want the Pension Keats."

"I'm awfully sorry to interrupt, Mr Beebe," said Freddy, "but have you any matches?"

"I have," said Cecil, and it did not escape Mr Beebe's notice that he spoke to the boy more kindly.

"You have never met these Miss Alans, have you, Mr Vyse?"

"Never."

"Then you don't see the wonder of this Greek visit. I haven't been to Greece myself, and don't mean to go, and I can't imagine any of my friends going. It is altogether too big for our little lot. Don't you think so? Italy is just about as much as we can manage. Italy is heroic, but Greece is godlike or devilish—I am not sure which, and in either case absolutely out of our suburban focus. All right, Freddy—I am not being clever, upon my word I am not—I took the idea from another fellow; and give me those matches when you've done with them." He lit a cigarette, and went on talking to the two young men. "I was saying, if our poor little Cockney lives must have a background, let it be Italian. Big enough in all conscience. The ceiling of the Sistine Chapel for me. There the contrast is just as much as I can realize. But not the Parthenon, not the frieze of Phidias at any price; and here comes the victoria."

"You're quite right," said Cecil. "Greece is not for our

little lot"; and he got in. Freddy followed, nodding to the clergyman, whom he trusted not to be pulling one's leg, really. And before they had gone a dozen yards he jumped out, and came running back for Vyse's matchbox, which had not been returned. As he took it, he said: "I am so glad you only talked about books. Cecil's hard hit. Lucy won't marry him. If you'd gone on about her, as you did about them, he might have broken down."

"But when—"

"Late last night. I must go."

"Perhaps they won't want me down there."

"No—go on. Goodbye."

"Thank goodness!" exclaimed Mr Beebe to himself, and struck the saddle of his bicycle approvingly. "It was the one foolish thing she ever did. Oh, what a glorious riddance!" And, after a little thought, he negotiated the slope into Windy Corner, light of heart. The house was again as it ought to be —cut off for ever from Cecil's pretentious world.

He would find Miss Minnie down the garden.

In the drawing-room Lucy was tinkling at a Mozart sonata. He hesitated a moment, but went down the garden as requested. There he found a mournful company. It was a blustering day, and the wind had taken and broken the dahlias. Mrs Honeychurch, who looked cross, was tying them up, while Miss Bartlett, unsuitably dressed, impeded her with offers of assistance. At a little distance stood Minnie and the "garden child", a minute importation, each holding either end of a long piece of bass.

"Oh, how do you do, Mr Beebe? Gracious, what a mess everything is! Look at my scarlet pompoms, and the wind blowing your skirts about, and the ground so hard that not a prop will stick in, and then the carriage having to go out, when I had counted on having Powell, who—give everyone their due—does tie up dahlias properly."

Evidently Mrs Honeychurch was shattered.

"How do you do?" said Miss Bartlett, with a meaning glance, as though conveying that more than dahlias had been broken off by the autumn gales.

"Here, Lennie, the bass," cried Mrs Honeychurch. The garden child, who did not know what bass was, stood rooted to the path with horror. Minnie slipped to her uncle and whispered that everyone was very disagreeable today, and that it was not her fault if dahlia-strings would tear longways instead of across.

"Come for a walk with me," he told her. "You have worried them as much as they can stand. Mrs Honeychurch, I only called in aimlessly. I shall take her up to tea at the Beehive Tavern, if I may."

"Oh, must you? Yes, do.—Not the scissors, thank you, Charlotte, when both my hands are full already—I'm perfectly certain that the orange cactus will go before I can get to it."

Mr Beebe, who was an adept at relieving situations, invited Miss Bartlett to accompany them to this mild festivity.

"Yes, Charlotte, I don't want you—do go; there's nothing to stop about for, either in the house or out of it."

Miss Bartlett said that her duty lay in the dahlia-bed, but, when she had exasperated everyone, except Minnie, by a refusal, she turned round and exasperated Minnie by an acceptance. As they walked up the garden, the orange cactus fell, and Mr Beebe's last vision was of the garden child clasping it like a lover, his dark head buried in a wealth of blossom.

"It is terrible, this havoc among the flowers," he remarked.

"It is always terrible when the promise of months is destroyed in a moment," enunciated Miss Bartlett.

"Perhaps we ought to send Miss Honeychurch down to her mother. Or will she come with us?"

"I think we had better leave Lucy to herself, and to her own pursuits."

"They're angry with Miss Honeychurch, because she was late for breakfast," whispered Minnie, "and Mr Floyd has gone, and Mr Vyse has gone, and Freddy won't play with me. In fact, Uncle Arthur, the house is not *at all* what it was yesterday."

"Don't be a prig," said her Uncle Arthur. "Go and put on your boots."

He stepped into the drawing-room, where Lucy was still attentively pursuing the sonatas of Mozart. She stopped when he entered.

"How do you do? Miss Bartlett and Minnie are coming with me to tea at the Beehive. Would you come too?"

"I don't think I will, thank you."

"No, I didn't suppose you would care to much."

Lucy turned to the piano and struck a few chords.

"How delicate those sonatas are!" said Mr Beebe, though, at the bottom of his heart, he thought them silly little things.

Lucy passed into Schumann.

"Miss Honeychurch!"

"Yes."

"I met them on the hill. Your brother told me."

"Oh, did he?" She sounded annoyed. Mr Beebe felt hurt, for he had thought that she would like him to be told.

"I needn't say that it will go no further."

"Mother, Charlotte, Cecil, Freddy, you," said Lucy, playing a note for each person who knew, and then playing a sixth note.

"If you'll let me say so, I am very glad, and I am certain that you have done the right thing."

"So I hoped other people would think, but they don't seem to."

"I could see that Miss Bartlett thought it unwise."

"So does mother. Mother minds dreadfully."

"I am very sorry for that," said Mr Beebe with feeling. Mrs Honeychurch, who hated all changes, did mind, but not nearly as much as her daughter pretended, and only for the minute. It was really a ruse of Lucy's to justify her despondency—a ruse of which she was not herself conscious, for she was marching in the armies of darkness.

"And Freddy minds."

"Still, Freddy never hit it off with Vyse much, did he? I gathered that he disliked the engagement, and felt it might separate him from you."

"Boys are so odd."

Minnie could be heard arguing with Miss Bartlett through the floor. Tea at the Beehive apparently involved a complete change of apparel. Mr Beebe saw that Lucy—very properly—did not wish to discuss her action, so after a sincere expression of sympathy he said: "I have had an absurd letter from Miss Alan. That was really what brought me over. I thought it might amuse you all."

"How delightful!" said Lucy, in a dull voice.

For the sake of something to do, he began to read her the letter. After a few words her eyes grew alert, and soon she interrupted him with—"Going abroad? When do they start?"

"Next week, I gather."

"Did Freddy say whether he was driving straight back?"

"No, he didn't."

"Because I do hope he won't go gossiping."

So she did want to talk about her broken engagement. Always complaisant, he put the letter away. But she at once exclaimed in a high voice: "Oh, do tell me more about the Miss Alans! How perfectly splendid of them to go abroad!"

"I want them to start from Venice, and go in a cargo steamer down the Illyrian coast!"

She laughed heartily. "Oh, delightful! I wish they'd take me."

"Has Italy filled you with the fever of travel? Perhaps George Emerson is right. He says that Italy is only an euphemism for Fate."

"Oh, not Italy, but Constantinople. I have always longed to go to Constantinople. Constantinople is practically Asia, isn't it?"

Mr Beebe reminded her that Constantinople was still unlikely, and that the Miss Alans only aimed at Athens, "with Delphi, perhaps, if the roads are safe". But this made no difference to her enthusiasm. She had always longed to go to Greece even more, it seemed. He saw, to his surprise, that she was apparently serious.

"I didn't realize that you and the Miss Alans were still such friends, after Cissie Villa."

"Oh, that's nothing; I assure you Cissie Villa's nothing to me; I would give anything to go with them."

"Would your mother spare you again so soon? You have scarcely been home three months."

"She *must* spare me!" cried Lucy, in growing excitement. "I simply *must* go away. I have to." She ran her fingers hysterically through her hair. "Don't you see that I *have* to go away? I didn't realize at the time— and of course I want to see Constantinople so particularly."

"You mean that since you have broken off your engagement you feel—"

"Yes, yes. I knew you would understand."

Mr Beebe did not quite understand. Why could not Miss Honeychurch repose in the bosom of her family? Cecil had evidently taken up the dignified line, and was not going to annoy her. Then it struck him that her family itself might be annoying. He hinted this to her, and she accepted the hint eagerly.

"Yes, of course; to go to Constantinople until they are used to the idea and everything has calmed down."

"I am afraid it has been a bothersome business," he said gently.

"No, not at all. Cecil was very kind indeed; only—I had better tell you the whole truth, since you have heard a little —it was that he is so masterful. I found that he wouldn't let me go my own way. He would improve me in places where I can't be improved. Cecil won't let a woman decide for herself—in fact, he daren't. What nonsense I do talk! But that is the kind of thing."

"It is what I gathered from my own observation of Mr Vyse; it is what I gather from all that I have known of you. I do sympathize and agree most profoundly. I agree so much that you must let me make one little criticism: is it worth while rushing off to Greece?"

"But I must go somewhere!" she cried. "I have been worrying all the morning, and here comes the very thing." She struck her knees with clenched fists, and repeated: "I must! And the time I shall have with mother, and all the money she spent on me last spring. You all think much too highly of me. I wish you weren't so kind." At this moment Miss Bartlett entered, and her nervousness increased. "I must get away, ever so far. I must know my own mind and where I want to go."

"Come along; tea, tea, tea," said Mr Beebe, and hustled his guests out of the front door. He hustled them so quickly that he forgot his hat. When he returned for it he heard, to his relief and surprise, the tinkling of a Mozart sonata.

"She is playing again," he said to Miss Bartlett.

"Lucy can always play," was the acid reply.

"One is very thankful that she has such a resource. She is evidently much worried, as, of course, she ought to be. I know all about it. The marriage was so near that it must have been a hard struggle before she could wind herself up to speak."

Miss Bartlett gave a kind of wriggle, and he prepared for a discussion. He had never fathomed Miss Bartlett. As he had put it to himself at Florence, "she might yet reveal depths of strangeness, if not of meaning." But she was so unsympathetic that she must be reliable. He assumed that much, and he had no hesitation in discussing Lucy with her. Minnie was fortunately collecting ferns.

She opened the discussion with: "We had much better let the matter drop."

"I wonder."

"It is of the highest importance that there should be no gossip in Summer Street. It would be *death* to gossip about Mr Vyse's dismissal at the present moment."

Mr Beebe raised his eyebrows. Death is a strong word— surely too strong. There was no question of tragedy. He said: "Of course, Miss Honeychurch will make the fact public in her own way, and when she chooses. Freddy only told me because he knew she would not mind."

"I know," said Miss Bartlett civilly. "Yet Freddy ought not to have told even you. One cannot be too careful."

"Quite so."

"I do implore absolute secrecy. A chance word to a chattering friend, and—"

"Exactly." He was used to these nervous old maids and to the exaggerated importance that they attach to words. A rector lives in a web of petty secrets, and confidences, and warnings, and the wiser he is the less he will regard them. He will change the subject, as did Mr Beebe, saying cheerfully: "Have you heard from any Bertolini people lately? I believe you keep up with Miss Lavish. It is odd how we of that pension, who seemed such a fortuitous collection, have been working into one another's lives. Two, three, four, six of us—no, eight; I had forgotten the Emersons—have kept more or less in touch. We must really give the Signora a testimonial."

And, Miss Bartlett not favouring the scheme, they walked up the hill in a silence which was only broken by the rector naming some fern. On the summit they paused. The sky had grown wilder since he stood there last hour, giving to the land a tragic greatness that is rare in Surrey. Gray clouds were charging across tissues of white, which stretched and shredded and tore slowly, until through their final layers there gleamed a hint of the disappearing blue. Summer was retreating. The wind roared, the trees groaned, yet the noise seemed insufficient for those vast operations in heaven. The weather was breaking up, breaking, broken, and it is a sense of the fit rather than of the supernatural that equips such crises with the salvos of angelic artillery. Mr Beebe's eyes rested on Windy Corner, where Lucy sat, practising Mozart. No smile came to his lips, and, changing the subject again, he said: "We shan't have rain, but we shall have darkness, so let us hurry on. The darkness last night was appalling."

They reached the Beehive Tavern at about five o'clock. That amiable hostelry possesses a veranda, in which the young and the unwise do dearly love to sit, while guests of more mature years seek a pleasant sanded room, and have tea at a table comfortably. Mr Beebe saw that Miss Bartlett would be cold if she sat out, and that Minnie would be dull if she sat in, so he proposed a division of forces. They would hand the child her food through the window. Thus he was incidentally enabled to discuss the fortunes of Lucy.

"I have been thinking, Miss Bartlett," he said, "and, unless you very much object, I would like to reopen that discussion." She bowed. "Nothing about the past. I know little and care less about that; I am absolutely certain that it is to your cousin's credit. She has acted loftily and rightly, and it is like her gentle modesty to say that we think too highly of her. But the future. Seriously, what do you think of this Greek plan?" He pulled out the letter again. "I don't know whether you overheard, but she wants to join the Miss Alans in their mad career. It's all—I can't explain —it's wrong."

Miss Bartlett read the letter in silence, laid it down, seemed to hesitate, and then read it again.

"I can't see the point of it myself."

To his astonishment, she replied: "There I cannot agree with you. In it I spy Lucy's salvation."

"Really. Now, why?"

"She wanted to leave Windy Corner."

"I know—but it seems so odd, so unlike her, so—I was going to say—selfish."

"It is natural, surely—after such painful scenes—that she should desire a change."

Here, apparently, was one of those points that the male intellect misses. Mr Beebe exclaimed: "So she says herself, and since another lady agrees with her, I must own that I am partially convinced. Perhaps she must have a change. I have no sisters or—and I don't understand these things. But why need she go as far as Greece?"

"You may well ask that," replied Miss Bartlett, who was evidently interested, and had almost dropped her evasive manner. "Why Greece? (What is it, Minnie dear—jam?) Why not Tunbridge Wells? Oh, Mr Beebe! I had a long and most unsatisfactory interview with dear Lucy this morning. I cannot help her. I will say no more. Perhaps I have already said too much. I am not to talk—a point on which she is almost bitter. I am not to talk. I wanted her to spend six months with me at Tunbridge Wells, and she refused."

Mr Beebe poked at a crumb with his knife.

185

"But my feelings are of no importance. I know too well that I get on Lucy's nerves. Our tour was a failure. She wanted to leave Florence, and when we got to Rome she did not want to be in Rome, and all the time I felt that I was spending her mother's money—"

"Let us keep to the future, though," interrupted Mr Beebe. "I want your advice."

"Very well," said Charlotte, with a choky abruptness that was new to him, though familiar to Lucy. "I for one will help her to go to Greece. Will you?"

Mr Beebe considered.

"It is absolutely necessary," she continued, lowering her veil and whispering through it with a passion, an intensity, that surprised him. "I know—I *know*." The darkness was coming on, and he felt that this odd woman really did know. "She must not stop here a moment, and we must keep quiet till she goes. I trust that the servants know nothing. Afterwards—but I may have said too much already. Only, Lucy and I are helpless against Mrs Honeychurch alone. If you help, we may succeed. Otherwise—"

"Otherwise—?"

"Otherwise," she repeated, as if the word held finality.

"Yes, I will help her," said the clergyman, setting his jaw firm. "Come, let us go back now, and settle the whole thing up."

Miss Bartlett burst into florid gratitude. The tavern sign— a beehive trimmed evenly with bees—creaked in the wind outside as she thanked him. Mr Beebe did not quite understand the situation; but then, he did not desire to understand it, nor to jump to the conclusion of "another man" that would have attracted a grosser mind. He only felt that Miss Bartlett knew of some vague influence from which the girl desired to be delivered, and which might well be clothed in the fleshly form. Its very vagueness spurred him into knight-errantry. His belief in celibacy, so reticent, so carefully concealed beneath his tolerance and culture, now came to the surface and expanded like some delicate flower. "They that marry do well, but they that refrain do better."

So ran his belief, and he never heard that an engagement was broken off but with a slight feeling of pleasure. In the case of Lucy, the feeling was intensified through dislike of Cecil; and he was willing to go further—to place her out of danger until she could confirm her resolution of virginity. The feeling was very subtle and quite undogmatic, and he never imparted it to any other of the characters in this entanglement. Yet it existed, and it alone explains his action subsequently, and his influence on the action of others. The compact that he made with Miss Bartlett in the tavern was to help not only Lucy, but religion also.

They hurried home through a world of black and gray. He conversed on indifferent topics: the Emersons' need of a housekeeper; servants; Italian servants; novels about Italy; novels with a purpose; could literature influence life? Windy Corner glimmered. In the garden, Mrs Honeychurch, now helped by Freddy, still wrestled with the lives of her flowers.

"It gets too dark," she said hopelessly. "This comes of putting off. We might have known the weather would break up soon; and now Lucy wants to go to Greece. I don't know what the world's coming to."

"Mrs Honeychurch," he said, "go to Greece she must. Come up to the house and let's talk it over. Do you, in the first place, mind her breaking with Vyse?"

"Mr Beebe, I'm thankful—simply thankful."

"So am I," said Freddy.

"Good. Now come up to the house."

They conferred in the dining-room for half an hour.

Lucy would never have carried the Greek scheme alone. It was expensive and dramatic—both qualities that her mother loathed. Nor would Charlotte have succeeded. The honours of the day rested with Mr Beebe. By his tact and common sense, and by his influence as a clergyman—for a clergyman who was not a fool influenced Mrs Honeychurch greatly—he bent her to their purpose.

"I don't see why Greece is necessary," she said; "but as you do, I suppose it is all right. It must be something I can't understand. Lucy! Let's tell her. Lucy!"

"She is playing the piano," Mr Beebe said. He opened the door, and heard the words of a song:

"Look not thou on beauty's charming—"

"I didn't know that Miss Honeychurch sang, too."

"Sit thou still when kings are arming,
        Taste not when the wine-cup glistens—"

"It's a song that Cecil gave her. How odd girls are!"

"What's that?" called Lucy, stopping short.

"All right, dear," said Mrs Honeychurch kindly. She went into the drawing-room, and Mr Beebe heard her kiss Lucy and say: "I am sorry I was so cross about Greece, but it came on the top of the dahlias."

Rather a hard voice said: "Thank you, mother; that doesn't matter a bit."

"And you are right, too—Greece will be all right; you can go if the Miss Alans will have you."

"Oh, splendid! Oh, thank you!"

Mr Beebe followed. Lucy still sat at the piano with her hands over the keys. She was glad, but he had expected greater gladness. Her mother bent over her. Freddy, to whom she had been singing, reclined on the floor with his head against her, and an unlit pipe between his lips. Oddly enough, the group was beautiful. Mr Beebe, who loved the art of the past, was reminded of a favourite theme, the *Santa Conversazione*, in which people who care for one another are painted chatting together about noble things—a theme neither sensual nor sensational, and therefore ignored by the art of today. Why should Lucy want either to marry or to travel when she had such friends at home?

"Taste not when the wine-cup glistens,
        Speak not when the people listens,"

she continued.

"Here's Mr Beebe."

"Mr Beebe knows my rude ways."

"It's a beautiful song and a wise one," said he. "Go on."

"It isn't very good," she said listlessly. "I forget why— harmony or something."

"I suspected it was unscholarly. It's so beautiful."

"The tune's right enough," said Freddy, "but the words are rotten. Why throw up the sponge?"

"How stupidly you talk!" said his sister. The *Santa Conversazione* was broken up. After all, there was no reason that Lucy should talk about Greece or thank him for per- suading her mother, so he said goodbye.

Freddy lit his bicycle-lamp for him in the porch, and, with his usual felicity of phrase, said: "This has been a day and a half."

"Stop thine ear against the singer—"

"Wait a minute; she is finishing."

"From the red gold keep thy finger;
    Vacant heart, and hand, and eye,
    Easy live and quiet die."

"I love weather like this," said Freddy.

Mr Beebe passed into it.

The two main facts were clear. She had behaved splendidly, and he had helped her. He could not expect to master the details of so big a change in a girl's life. If here and there he was dissatisfied or puzzled, he must acquiesce; she was choosing the better part.

"Vacant heart, and hand, and eye—"

Perhaps the song stated "the better part" rather too strongly. He half fancied that the soaring accompaniment— which he did not lose in the shout of the gale—really agreed with Freddy, and was gently criticizing the words that it adorned:

"Vacant heart, and hand, and eye,
    Easy live and quiet die."

However. For the fourth time Windy Corner lay poised below him—now as a beacon in the roaring tides of darkness.

Chapter 19
Lying to Mr Emerson

The Miss Alans were found in their beloved temperance hotel near Bloomsbury—a clean, airless establishment much patronized by provincial England. They always perched there before crossing the great seas, and for a week or two would fidget gently over clothes, guidebooks, mackintosh squares, digestive bread, and other continental necessaries. That there are shops abroad, even in Athens, never occurred to them, for they regarded travel as a species of warfare, only to be undertaken by those who have been fully armed at the Haymarket Stores. Miss Honeychurch, they trusted, would take care to equip herself duly. Quinine could now be obtained in tabloids; paper soap was a great help towards freshening up one's face in the train. Lucy promised, a little depressed.

"But, of course, you know all about these things, and you have Mr Vyse to help you. A gentleman is such a stand-by."

Mrs Honeychurch, who had come up to town with her daughter, began to drum nervously upon her card-case.

"We think it so good of Mr Vyse to spare you," Miss Catharine continued. "It is not every young man who would be so unselfish. But perhaps he will come out and join you later on."

"Or does his work keep him in London?" said Miss Teresa, the more acute and less kindly of the two sisters.

"However, we shall see him when he sees you off. I do so long to see him."

"No one will see Lucy off," interposed Mrs Honeychurch. "She doesn't like it."

"No, I hate seeings-off," said Lucy.

"Really? How funny! I should have thought that in this case—"

"Oh, Mrs Honeychurch, you aren't going? It is such a pleasure to have met you!"

They escaped, and Lucy said with relief: "That's all right. We just got through that time."

But her mother was annoyed. "I shall be told, dear, that I am unsympathetic. But I cannot see why you didn't tell your friends about Cecil and be done with it. There all the time we had to sit fencing, and almost telling lies, and be seen through, too, I dare say, which is most unpleasant."

Lucy had plenty to say in reply. She described the Miss Alans' character: they were such gossips, and, if one told them, the news would be everywhere in no time.

"But why shouldn't it be everywhere in no time?"

"Because I settled with Cecil not to announce it until I left England. I shall tell them then. It's much pleasanter. How wet it is! Let's turn in here."

"Here" was the British Museum. Mrs Honeychurch refused. If they must take shelter, let it be in a shop. Lucy felt contemptuous, for she was on the tack of caring for Greek sculpture, and had already borrowed a mythological dictionary from Mr Beebe to get up the names of the goddesses and gods.

"Oh, well, let it be a shop, then. Let's go to Mudie's. I'll buy a guidebook."

"You know, Lucy, you and Charlotte and Mr Beebe all tell me I'm so stupid, so I suppose I am, but I shall never understand this hole-and-corner work. You've got rid of Cecil—well and good, and I'm thankful he's gone, though I did feel angry for the minute. But why not announce it? Why this hushing up and tiptoeing?"

"It's only for a few days."

"But why at all?"

Lucy was silent. She was drifting away from her mother. It was quite easy to say, "Because George Emerson has been bothering me, and if he hears I've given up Cecil may begin again"—quite easy, and it had the incidental advantage of being true. But she could not say it. She disliked confidences, for they might lead to self-knowledge and to that king of terrors—Light. Ever since that last evening at Florence she had deemed it unwise to reveal her soul.

Mrs Honeychurch, too, was silent. She was thinking: "My daughter won't answer me; she would rather be with those inquisitive old maids than with Freddy and me. Any rag, tag and bobtail apparently does if she can leave her home." And, as in her case thoughts never remained unspoken long, she burst out with: "You're tired of Windy Corner."

This was perfectly true. Lucy had hoped to return to Windy Corner when she escaped from Cecil, but she discovered that her home existed no longer. It might exist for Freddy, who still lived and thought straight, but not for one who had deliberately warped the brain. She did not acknowledge that her brain was warped, for the brain itself must assist in that acknowledgement, and she was disordering the very instruments of life. She only felt: "I do not love George; I broke off my engagement because I did not love George; I must go to Greece because I do not love George; it is more important that I should look up gods in the dictionary than that I should help my mother; everyone else is behaving very badly." She only felt irritable and petulant, and anxious to do what she was not expected to do, and in this spirit she proceeded with the conversation.

"Oh, mother, what rubbish you talk! Of course I'm not tired of Windy Corner."

"Then why not say so at once, instead of considering half an hour first?"

She laughed faintly. "Half a *minute* would be nearer."

"Perhaps you would like to stay away from your home altogether?"

"Hush, mother! People will hear you"; for they had entered Mudie's. She bought Baedeker, and then continued: "Of course I want to live at home; but as we are talking about it, I may as well say that I shall want to be away in the future more than I have been. You see, I come into my money next year."

Tears came into her mother's eyes.

Driven by nameless bewilderment, by what is in older

people termed "eccentricity", Lucy determined to make this point clear. "I've seen the world so little—I felt so out of things in Italy. I have seen so little of life; one ought to come up to London more—not a cheap ticket like today, but to stop. I might even share a flat for a little with some other girl."

"And mess with typewriters and latchkeys," exploded Mrs Honeychurch. "And agitate and scream, and be carried off kicking by the police. And call it a Mission—when no one wants you! And call it Duty—when it means that you can't stand your own home! And call it Work—when thousands of men are starving with the competition as it is! And then to prepare yourself, find two doddering old ladies, and go abroad with them."

"I want more independence," said Lucy lamely; she knew that she wanted something, and independence is a useful cry; we can always say that we have not got it. She tried to remember her emotions in Florence: those had been sincere and passionate, and had suggested beauty rather than short skirts and latchkeys. But independence was certainly her cue.

"Very well. Take your independence and be gone. Rush up and down and round the world, and come back as thin as a lath with the bad food. Despise the house that your father built and the garden that he planted, and our dear view—and then share a flat with another girl."

Lucy screwed up her mouth and said: "Perhaps I spoke hastily."

"Oh, goodness!" her mother flashed. "How you do remind me of Charlotte Bartlett!"

"*Charlotte?*" flashed Lucy in her turn, pierced at last by a vivid pain.

"More every moment."

"I don't know what you mean, mother; Charlotte and I are not the very least alike."

"Well, I see the likeness. The same eternal worrying, the same taking back of words. You and Charlotte trying to divide two apples among three people last night might be sisters."

"What rubbish! And if you dislike Charlotte so, it's rather a pity you asked her to stop. I warned you about her;

I begged you, implored you not to, but of course I was not listened to."

"There you go."

"I beg your pardon?"

"Charlotte again, my dear; that's all; her very words."

Lucy clenched her teeth. "My point is that you oughtn't to have asked Charlotte to stop. I wish you would keep to the point." And the conversation dies off into a wrangle.

She and her mother shopped in silence, spoke little in the train, little again in the carriage, which met them at Dorking station. It had poured all day, and as they ascended through the deep Surrey lanes showers of water fell from the overhanging beech trees and rattled on the hood. Lucy complained that the hood was stuffy. Leaning forward, she looked out into the steaming dusk, and watched the carriage-lamp pass like a searchlight over mud and leaves, and reveal nothing beautiful. "The crush when Charlotte gets in will be abominable," she remarked. For they were to pick up Miss Bartlett at Summer Street, where she had been dropped as the carriage went down, to pay a call on Mr Beebe's old mother. "We shall have to sit three a side, because the trees drop, and yet it isn't raining. O for a little air!" Then she listened to the horse's hoofs—"He has not told—he has not told." That melody was blurred by the soft road. "*Can't* we have the hood down?" she demanded, and her mother, with sudden tenderness, said: "Very well, old lady, stop the horse." And the horse was stopped, and Lucy and Powell wrestled with the hood, and squirted water down Mrs Honeychurch's neck. But now that the hood was down she did see something that she would have missed—there were no lights in the windows of Cissie Villa, and round the garden gate she fancied she saw a padlock.

"Is that house to let again, Powell?" she called.

"Yes, miss," he replied.

"Have they gone?"

"It is too far out of town for the young gentleman, and his father's rheumatism has come on, so he can't stop on alone, so they are trying to let furnished," was the answer.

"They have gone, then?"

"Yes, miss, they have gone."

Lucy sank back. The carriage stopped at the rectory. She got out to call for Miss Bartlett. So the Emersons had gone, and all this bother about Greece had been unnecessary. Waste! That word seemed to sum up the whole of life. Wasted plans, wasted money, wasted love, and she had wounded her mother. Was it possible that she had muddled things away? Quite possible. Other people had. When the maid opened the door, she was unable to speak, and stared stupidly into the hall.

Miss Bartlett at once came forward, and after a long pre-amble asked a great favour: might she go to church? Mr Beebe and his mother had already gone, but she had refused to start until she obtained her hostess's full sanction, for it would mean keeping the horse waiting a good ten minutes more.

"Certainly," said the hostess wearily. "I forgot it was Friday. Let's all go. Powell can go round to the stables."

"Lucy dearest—"

"No church for me, thank you."

A sigh, and they departed. The church was invisible, but up in the darkness to the left there was a hint of colour. This was a stained window, through which some feeble light was shining, and when the door opened Lucy heard Mr Beebe's voice running through the litany to a minute congregation. Even their church, built upon the slope of the hill so artfully, with its beautiful raised transept and its spire of silvery shingle—even their church had lost its charm; and the thing one never talked about—religion—was fading like all the other things.

She followed the maid into the rectory.

Would she object to sitting in Mr Beebe's study? There was only that one fire.

She would not object.

Someone was there already, for Lucy heard the words: "A lady to wait, sir."

Old Mr Emerson was sitting by the fire, with his foot upon a gout-stool.

"Oh, Miss Honeychurch, that you should come!" he quavered; and Lucy saw an alteration in him since last Sunday.

Not a word would come to her lips. George she had faced, and could have faced again, but she had forgotten how to treat his father.

"Miss Honeychurch, dear, we are so sorry! George is so sorry! He thought he had a right to try. I cannot blame my boy, and yet I wish he had told me first. He ought not to have tried. I knew nothing about it at all."

If only she could remember how to behave!

He held up his hand. "But you must not scold him."

Lucy turned her back, and began to look at Mr Beebe's books.

"I taught him," he quavered, "to trust in love. I said: 'When love comes, that is reality.' I said: 'Passion does not blind. No. Passion is sanity, and the woman you love, she is the only person you will ever really understand.' " He sighed: "True, everlastingly true, though my day is over, and though there is the result. Poor boy! He is so sorry! He said he knew it was madness when you brought your cousin in; that whatever you felt you did not mean. Yet"—his voice gathered strength; he spoke out to make certain—"Miss Honeychurch, do you remember Italy?"

Lucy selected a book—a volume of Old Testament commentaries. Holding it up to her eyes, she said: "I have no wish to discuss Italy or any subject connected with your son."

"But you do remember it?"

"He has misbehaved himself from the first."

"I only was told that he loved you last Sunday. I never could judge behaviour. I—I—suppose he has."

Feeling a little steadier, she put the book back and turned round to him. His face was drooping and swollen, but his eyes, though they were sunken deep, gleamed with a child's courage.

"Why, he has behaved abominably," she said. "I am glad he is sorry. Do you know what he did?"

"Not 'abominably'," was the gentle correction. "He only tried when he should not have tried. You have all you want, Miss Honeychurch: you are going to marry the man you love. Do not go out of George's life saying he is abominable."

"No, of course," said Lucy, ashamed at the reference to Cecil. " 'Abominable' is much too strong. I am sorry I used it about your son. I think I will go to church, after all. My mother and my cousin have gone. I shall not be so very late—"

"Especially as he has gone under," he said quietly.

"What was that?"

"Gone under naturally." He beat his palms together in silence; his head fell on his chest.

"I don't understand."

"As his mother did."

"But, Mr Emerson—*Mr Emerson*—what are you talking about?"

"When I wouldn't have George baptized," said he.

Lucy was frightened.

"And she agreed that baptism was nothing, but he caught that fever when he was twelve, and she turned round. She thought it a judgement." He shuddered. "Oh, horrible, when we had given up that sort of thing and broken away from her parents. Oh, horrible—worst of all—worse than death, when you have made a little clearing in the wilderness, planted your little garden, let in your sunlight, and then the weeds creep in again! A judgement! And our boy had typhoid because no clergyman had dropped water on him in church! Is it possible, Miss Honeychurch? Shall we slip back into the darkness for ever?"

"I don't know," gasped Lucy. "I don't understand this sort of thing. I was not meant to understand it."

"But Mr Eager—he came when I was out, and acted according to his principles. I don't blame him or anyone . . . but by the time George was well she was ill. He made her think about sin, and she went under thinking about it."

It was thus that Mr Emerson had murdered his wife in the sight of God.

"Oh, how terrible!" said Lucy, forgetting her own affairs at last.

"He was not baptized," said the old man. "I did hold firm." And he looked with unwavering eyes at the rows of books, as if—at what cost!—he had won a victory over them. "My boy shall go back to the earth untouched."

She asked whether young Mr Emerson was ill.

"Oh—last Sunday." He started into the present. "George last Sunday—no, not ill; just gone under. He is never ill. But he is his mother's son. Her eyes were his, and she had that forehead that I think so beautiful, and he will not think it worth while to live. It was always touch and go. He will live; but he will not think it worth while to live. He will never think anything worth while. You remember that church at Florence?"

Lucy did remember, and how she had suggested that George should collect postage-stamps.

"After you left Florence—horrible. Then we take the house here, and he goes bathing with your brother, and became better. You saw him bathing?"

"I am so sorry, but it is no good discussing this affair. I am really deeply sorry about it."

"Then there came something about a novel. I didn't follow it all; I had to hear so much, and he minded telling me; he finds me too old. Ah, well, one must have failures. George comes down tomorrow, and takes me up to his London rooms. He can't bear to be about here, and I must be where he is."

"Mr Emerson," cried the girl, "don't leave—at least, not on my account. I am going to Greece. Don't leave your comfortable house."

It was the first time her voice had been kind, and he smiled. "How good everyone is! And look at Mr Beebe housing me—came over this morning and heard I was going! Here I am so comfortable with a fire."

"Yes, but you won't go back to London. It's absurd."

"I must be with George; I must make him care to live, and down here he can't. He says the thought of seeing you

198

and of hearing about you—I am not justifying him; I am only saying what has happened."

"Oh, Mr Emerson"—she took hold of his hand— "you mustn't. I've been bother enough to the world by now. I can't have you moving out of your house when you like it, and perhaps losing money through it—all on my account. You must stop! I am just going to Greece."

"All the way to Greece?"

Her manner altered.

"To Greece?"

"So you must stop. You won't talk about this business, I know. I can trust you both."

"Certainly you can. We either have you in our lives, or leave you to the life that you have chosen."

"I shouldn't want—"

"I suppose Mr Vyse is very angry with George? No, it was wrong of George to try. We have pushed our beliefs too far. I fancy that we deserve sorrow."

She looked at the books again—black, brown, and that acrid, theological blue. They surrounded the visitors on every side; they were piled on the tables, they pressed against the very ceiling. To Lucy—who could not see that Mr Emerson was profoundly religious, and differed from Mr Beebe chiefly by his acknowledgement of passion—it seemed dreadful that the old man should crawl into such a sanctum, when he was unhappy, and be dependent on the bounty of a clergyman.

More certain than ever that she was tired, he offered her his chair.

"No, please sit still. I think I will sit in the carriage."

"Miss Honeychurch, you do sound tired."

"Not a bit," said Lucy, with trembling lips.

"But you are, and there's a look of George about you. And what were you saying about going abroad?"

She was silent.

"Greece"—and she saw that he was thinking the word over—"Greece; but you were to be married this year, I thought."

"Not till January, it wasn't," said Lucy, clasping her hands. Would she tell an actual lie when it came to the point?

"I suppose that Mr Vyse is going with you. I hope—it isn't because George spoke that you are both going?"

"No."

"I hope that you will enjoy Greece with Mr Vyse."

"Thank you."

At that moment Mr Beebe came back from church. His cassock was covered with rain. "That's all right," he said kindly. "I counted on you two keeping each other company. It's pouring again. The entire congregation, which consists of your cousin, your mother and my mother, stands waiting in the church till the carriage fetches it. Did Powell go round?"

"I think so; I'll see."

"No—of course, I'll see. How are the Miss Alans?"

"Very well, thank you."

"Did you tell Mr Emerson about Greece?"

"I—I did."

"Don't you think it very plucky of her, Mr Emerson, to undertake the two Miss Alans? Now, Miss Honeychurch, go back—keep warm. I think three is such a courageous number to go travelling." And he hurried off to the stables.

"He is not going," she said hoarsely. "I made a slip. Mr Vyse does stop behind in England." Somehow it was impossible to cheat this old man. To George, to Cecil, she would have lied again; but he seemed so near the end of things, so dignified in his approach to the gulf, of which he gave one account, and the books that surrounded him another, so mild to the rough paths that he had traversed, that the true chivalry—not the worn-out chivalry of sex, but the true chivalry that all the young may show to all the old—awoke in her, and, at whatever risk, she told him that Cecil was not her companion to Greece. And she spoke so seriously that the risk became a certainty and he, lifting his eyes, said: "You are leaving him? You are leaving the man you love?"

"I—I had to."

"Why, Miss Honeychurch, why?"

Terror came over her, and she lied again. She made the long, convincing speech that she had made to Mr Beebe, and intended to make to the world when she announced that her engagement was no more. He heard her in silence, and then said: "My dear, I am worried about you. It seems to me"—dreamily; she was not alarmed—"that you are in a muddle."

She shook her head.

"Take an old man's word: there's nothing worse than a muddle in all the world. It is easy to face Death and Fate, and the things that sound so dreadful. It is on my muddles that I look back with horror—on the things that I might have avoided. We can help one another but little. I used to think I could teach young people the whole of life, but I know better now, and all my teaching of George has come down to this: beware of muddle. Do you remember in that church, when you pretended to be annoyed with me and weren't? Do you remember before, when you refused the room with the view? Those were muddles—little, but ominous—and I am fearing that you are in one now." She was silent. "Do trust me, Miss Honeychurch. Though life is very glorious, it is difficult." She was still silent. " 'Life,' wrote a friend of mine, 'is a public performance on the violin, in which you must learn the instrument as you go along.' I think he puts it well. Man has to pick up the use of his functions as he goes along—especially the function of Love." Then he burst out excitedly: "That's it; that's what I mean. You love George!" And after his long preamble the three words burst against Lucy like waves from the open sea.

"But you do," he went on, not waiting for contradiction. "You love the boy body and soul, plainly, directly, as he loves you, and no other word expresses it. You won't marry the other man for his sake."

"How dare you!" gasped Lucy, with the roaring of waters in her ears. "Oh, how like a man!—I mean, to suppose that a woman is always thinking about a man."

"But you are."

She summoned physical disgust.

"You're shocked, but I mean to shock you. It's the only hope at times. I can reach you no other way. You must marry, or your life will be wasted. You have gone too far to retreat. I have no time for the tenderness, and the comradeship, and the poetry, and the things that really matter, and *for which* you marry. I know that, with George, you will find them, and that you love him. Then be his wife. He is already part of you. Though you fly to Greece, and never see him again, or forget his very name, George will work in your thoughts till you die. It isn't possible to love and to part. You will wish that it was. You can transmute love, ignore it, muddle it, but you can never pull it out of you. I know by experience that the poets are right: love is eternal."

Lucy began to cry with anger, and, though her anger passed away soon, her tears remained.

"I only wish poets would say this, too: that love is of the body; not the body, but of the body. Ah! the misery that would be saved if we confessed that! Ah for a little directness to liberate the soul! Your soul, dear Lucy! I hate the word now, because of all the cant with which superstition has wrapped it round. But we have souls. I cannot say how they came nor whither they go, but we have them, and I see you ruining yours. I cannot bear it. It is again the darkness creeping in; it is hell." Then he checked himself. "What nonsense I have talked—how abstract and remote! And I have made you cry! Dear girl, forgive my prosiness; marry my boy. When I think what life is, and how seldom love is answered by love—marry him; it is one of the moments for which the world was made."

She could not understand him; the words were indeed remote. Yet as he spoke the darkness was withdrawn, veil after veil, and she saw to the bottom of her soul.

"Then, Lucy—"

"You've frightened me," she moaned. "Cecil—Mr Beebe —the ticket's bought—everything." She fell sobbing into the chair. "I'm caught in the tangle. I must suffer and grow old away from him. I cannot break the whole of life for his sake. They trusted me."

A carriage drew up at the front door.

"Give George my love—once only. Tell him, 'Muddle.' "
Then she arranged her veil, while the tears poured over her
cheeks inside.

"Lucy—"

"No—they are in the hall—oh, please not, Mr Emerson—
they trust me—"

"But why should they, when you have deceived them?"

Mr Beebe opened the door saying: "Here's my mother."

"You're not worthy of their trust."

"What's that?" said Mr Beebe sharply.

"I was saying, why should you trust her when she deceived you?"

"One minute, mother." He came in and shut the door.

"I don't follow you, Mr Emerson. To whom do you refer?
Trust whom?"

"I mean, she has pretended to you that she did not love
George. They have loved one another all along."

Mr Beebe looked at the sobbing girl. He was very quiet, and
his white face, with its ruddy whiskers, seemed suddenly in-
human. A long black column, he stood and awaited her reply.

"I shall never marry him," quavered Lucy.

A look of contempt came over him, and he said, "Why
not?"

"Mr Beebe—I have misled you—I have misled myself—"

"Oh, rubbish, Miss Honeychurch!"

"It is not rubbish!" said the old man hotly. "It's the part
of people that you don't understand."

Mr Beebe laid his hand on his shoulder pleasantly.

"Lucy! Lucy!" called voices from the carriage.

"Mr Beebe, could you help me?"

He looked amazed at the request, and said in a low, stern
voice: "I am more grieved than I can possibly express. It is
lamentable, lamentable—incredible."

"What's wrong with the boy?" fired up the other again.

"Nothing, Mr Emerson, except that he no longer interests
me. Marry George, Miss Honeychurch. He will do admirably."

He walked out and left them. They heard him guiding his mother upstairs.

"Lucy!" the voices called.

She turned to Mr Emerson in despair. But his face revived her. It was the face of a saint who understood.

"Now it is all dark. Now Beauty and Passion seem never to have existed. I know. But remember the mountains over Florence and the view. Ah, dear, if I were George, and gave you one kiss, it would make you brave. You have to go cold into a battle that needs warmth, out into the muddle that you have made yourself; and your mother and all your friends will despise you, oh my darling, and rightly, if it is ever right to despise. George still dark, all the tussle and the misery without a word from him. Am I justified?" Into his own eyes tears came. "Yes, for we fight for more than Love or Pleasure: there is Truth. Truth counts, Truth does count."

"You kiss me," said the girl. "You kiss me. I will try."

He gave her a sense of deities reconciled, a feeling that, in gaining the man she loved, she would gain something for the whole world. Throughout the squalor of her homeward drive—she spoke at once—his salutation remained. He had robbed the body of its taint, the world's taunts of their sting; he had shown her the holiness of direct desire. She "never exactly understood," she would say in after years, "how he managed to strengthen her. It was as if he had made her see the whole of everything at once."

Chapter 20
The End of
the Middle Ages

The Miss Alans did go to Greece, but they went by themselves. They alone of this little company will double Malea
and plough the waters of the Saronic gulf. They alone will
visit Athens and Delphi, and either shrine of intellectual
song—that upon the Acropolis, encircled by blue seas; that
under Parnassus, where the eagles build and the bronze
charioteer drives undismayed towards infinity. Trembling,
anxious, cumbered with much digestive bread, they did
proceed to Constantinople, they did go round the world.
The rest of us must be contented with a fair, but a less
arduous, goal. *Italiam petimus*: we return to the Pension
Bertolini.

George said it was his old room.

"No, it isn't," said Lucy; "because it is the room I had,
and I had your father's room. I forget why; Charlotte made
me, for some reason."

He knelt on the tiled floor, and laid his face in her lap.

"George, you baby, get up."

"Why shouldn't I be a baby?" murmured George.

Unable to answer this question, she put down his sock,
which she was trying to mend, and gazed out through the
window. It was evening and again the spring.

"Oh, bother Charlotte," she said thoughtfully. "What
can such people be made of?"

"Same stuff as parsons are made of."

"Nonsense!"

"Quite right. It is nonsense."

"Now you get up off the cold floor, or you'll be starting rheumatism next, and you stop laughing and being so
silly."

"Why shouldn't I laugh?" he asked, pinning her with

his elbows, and advancing his face to hers. "What's there to cry at? Kiss me here." He indicated the spot where a kiss would be welcome.

He was a boy, after all. When it came to the point, it was she who remembered the past, she into whose soul the iron had entered, she who knew whose this room had been last year. It endeared him to her strangely that he should be sometimes wrong.

"Any letters?" he asked.

"Just a line from Freddy."

"Now kiss me here; then here."

Then, threatened again with rheumatism, he strolled to the window, opened it (as the English will), and leant out. There was the parapet, there the river, there to the left the beginnings of the hills. The cab-driver, who at once saluted him with the hiss of a serpent, might be that very Phaethon who had set this happiness in motion twelve months ago. A passion of gratitude—all feelings grow to passions in the South—came over the husband, and he blessed the people and the things who had taken so much trouble about a young fool. He had helped himself, it is true, but how stupidly! All the fighting that mattered had been done by others—by Italy, by his father, by his wife.

"Lucy, you come and look at the cypresses; and the church, whatever its name is, still shows."

"San Miniato. I'll just finish your sock."

"Signorino, domani faremo un giro," called the cabman, with engaging certainty.

George told him that he was mistaken; they had no money to throw away on driving.

And the people who had not meant to help—the Miss Lavishes, the Cecils, the Miss Bartletts! Ever prone to magnify Fate, George counted up the forces that had swept him into this contentment.

"Anything good in Freddy's letter?"

"Not yet."

His own content was absolute, but hers held bitterness: the Honeychurches had not forgiven them; they were disgusted at her past hypocrisy; she had alienated Windy Corner, perhaps for ever.

"What does he say?"

"Silly boy! He thinks he's being dignified. He knew we should go off in the spring—he has known it for six months—that if mother wouldn't give her consent we should take the thing into our own hands. They had fair warning, and now he calls it an elopement. Ridiculous boy—"

"Signorino, domani faremo un giro—"

"But it will all come right in the end. He has to build us both up from the beginning again. I wish, though, that Cecil had not turned so cynical about women. He has, for the second time, quite altered. Why will men have theories about women? I haven't any about men. I wish, too, that Mr Beebe—"

"You may well wish that."

"He will never forgive us—I mean, he will never be interested in us again. I wish that he did not influence them so much at Windy Corner. I wish he hadn't—but if we act the truth, the people who really love us are sure to come back to us in the long run."

"Perhaps." Then he said more gently: "Well, I acted the truth—the only thing I did do—and you came back to me. So possibly you know." He turned back into the room. "Nonsense with that sock." He carried her to the window, so that she, too, saw all the view. They sank upon their knees invisible from the road, they hoped, and began to whisper one another's names. Ah! it was worth while; it was the great joy that they had expected, and countless little joys of which they had never dreamt. They were silent.

"Signorino, domani faremo—"

"Oh, bother that man!"

But Lucy remembered the vendor of photographs and said, "No, don't be rude to him." Then, with a catching of her breath, she murmured: "Mr Eager and Charlotte, dreadful frozen Charlotte! How cruel she would be to a man like that!"

"Look at the lights going over the bridge."

"But this room reminds me of Charlotte. How horrible to grow old in Charlotte's way! To think that evening at the rectory that she shouldn't have heard your father was in the house. For she would have stopped me going in, and he was the only person alive who could have made me see sense. You couldn't have made me. When I am very happy"—she kissed him—"I remember on how little it all hangs. If Charlotte had only known, she would have stopped me going in, and I should have gone to silly Greece, and become different for ever."

"But she did know," said George; "she did see my father, surely. He said so."

"Oh no, she didn't see him. She was upstairs with old Mrs Beebe, don't you remember, and then went straight to the church. She said so."

George was obstinate again. "My father," said he, "saw her, and I prefer his word. He was dozing by the study fire, and he opened his eyes, and there was Miss Bartlett. A few minutes before you came in. She was turning to go as he woke up. He didn't speak to her."

Then they spoke of other things—the desultory talk of those who have been fighting to reach one another, and whose reward is to rest quietly in each other's arms. It was long ere they returned to Miss Bartlett, but when they did her behaviour seemed more interesting. George, who disliked any darkness, said: "It's clear that she knew. Then, why did she risk the meeting? She knew he was there, and yet she went to church."

They tried to piece the thing together.

As they talked, an incredible solution came into Lucy's mind. She rejected it, and said: "How like Charlotte to undo her work by a feeble muddle at the last moment." But something in the dying evening, in the roar of the river, in their very embrace, warned them that her words fell short of life, and George whispered: "Or did she mean it?"

"Mean what?"

"Signorino, domani faremo un giro—"

Lucy bent forward and said with gentleness: "Lascia, prego, lascia. Siamo sposati."

"Scusi tanto, signora," he replied, in tones as gentle, and whipped up his horse.

"Buona sera—e grazie."

"Niente."

The cabman drove away singing.

"Mean what, George?"

He whispered: "Is it this? Is this possible? I'll put a marvel to you. That your cousin has always hoped. That from the very first moment we met, she hoped, far down in her mind, that we should be like this—of course, very far down. That she fought us on the surface, and yet she hoped. I can't explain her any other way. Can you? Look how she kept me alive in you all the summer; how she gave you no peace; how month after month she became more eccentric and unreliable. The sight of us haunted her—or she couldn't have described us as she did to her friend. There are details—it burned. I read the book afterwards. She is not frozen, Lucy, she is not withered up all through. She tore us apart twice, but in the rectory that evening she was given one more chance to make us happy. We can never make friends with her or thank her. But I do believe that, far down in her heart, far below all speech and behaviour, she is glad."

"It is impossible," murmured Lucy, and then, remembering the experiences of her own heart, she said: "No—it is just possible."

Youth enwrapped them; the song of Phaethon announced passion requited, love attained. But they were conscious of a love more mysterious than this. The song died away; they heard the river, bearing down the snows of winter into the Mediterranean.

209